THE
FAMILY JEWELS

OTHER BOOKS BY VINCENT GRAZIANO

Die Laughing

THE
FAMILY JEWELS

A Novel

VINCENT GRAZIANO

To Nicholas

Vinnie G

GGP

GGP Publishing, Inc.

This is a work of fiction. Any similarities to persons or events are purely coincidental.
The characters are composites. Their traits and flaws are exaggerations meant for dramatic
or comic effect. References to events, establishments, organizations, or locales are
intended only to provide a sense of authenticity, and are used fictitiously.

Designed by Jessica Shatan Heslin/Studio Shatan, Inc.

Library of Congress Cataloging-in-Publication Data has been applied for.

ISBN 978-0-692-93683-2

For
Emma, Mia & Vincent

ACKNOWLEDGMENTS

It has been nearly ten years since I wrote *Die Laughing*. Prolific, aren't I? At this rate there should be another book coming out in 2027. I would like to thank the people who believed in this book and were so helpful in getting it published. First and foremost, I would like to thank Generosa Gina Protano, my editor at GGP Publishing, Inc., who I am sure is sorry she ever met me. She put in much time and effort along with her team. Special thanks go also to Andrea M. Molitor for hearing my voice in the prose; and to Jessica Shatan Heslin, of Studio Shatan, Inc., for designing and typesetting the book. There were others as well who read early versions of the manuscript and *still* encouraged me. Lastly, many thanks to Flora and Mary C. and Mike Valentino.

THE
FAMILY JEWELS

PROLOGUE

*F*ather Bryce Gleason's head popped off his arms with a jolt. He had fallen asleep slumped over his desk, his head coming to rest on pages of an accounting ledger. Horn-rimmed glasses shifted off his head. He did not recall dozing off; numbers made him weary, especially when they didn't add up. His fingers flipped through the pages, then closed the book with a thud. He rubbed his eyes, and the room came into focus. Torchères cast a dim light across a framed canvas portrait of Pope Benedict VXI in an appropriately surreal way.

The Reverend Gleason stretched his arms, hearing tiny cracks from bones in his neck and shoulder. It was an uncomfortable sleep. He expected nothing less from sitting in a wooden swivel chair. He was awakened by a car door slamming, distant voices; but as he became fully awake, there was quiet. He guessed at the time. It must be early morning. Light from street lamps leaked through the blinds.

Then he heard it again; now it was a shuffling of movement and muffled voices coming from the pavement outside his window. He needed to get back to sleep. A glass of milk might help. He slipped his feet into the black loafers beneath the desk and was drawn again to the activity outside the church office's window. He went to the window and drew the blind ever so slightly. The fog of sleep still misted his eyes.

The street lamps cast an eerie halo glow, reflecting a damp gloss off the concrete sidewalks. He saw a car parked outside in front of his window. It looked familiar. His mentor, Monsignor Burns, had a similar car, a white 2008 Lincoln Continental. *Maybe he's back.* He looked closer. The vehicle was backed up onto the sidewalk. He saw three men struggling to remove a bundle from the trunk under the watchful eye of a fourth man who directed them with gestures. The men were sizable, and would be a credit to any defensive line. He watched as the man directing reached into his pocket and pulled out a cell phone. Gleason jumped out of his socks as the phone on his desk rang, at the same time as the clock struck three. He reached back for the phone, never turning from the window. No doubt the late-night phone call would summon him to some unforeseen tragedy, a deathbed request for last rites or to the scene of an accident. It was in the job description.

He cleared his throat before answering. "Hello," he said, "this is Father Gleason."

"Where's Monsignor Burns?" a voice asked.

Gleason wiped the veil of sleep from his eyes. "Monsignor? He's not here at the moment. He's on . . . sabbatical." The lie didn't sit well with him, but it was the official line from the brass at St. Patrick's.

The monsignor's unexpected departure had put a damper on an otherwise sweet assignment. Being sent to a church in the heart of Little Italy, bordering New York's Lower East Side, was a real treat, especially for an Irishman. In fact, Gleason noted that Burns had carte blanche in this Old World Italian neighborhood. A rare sign of approval. "I'm an honorary wop," the monsignor would say, out of the earshot of those who'd take offense. "They love me, these people. I'm like one of them."

"Sabbatical?" the voice repeated. "That's a good one. I guess you can say that." He heard a laugh, as the voice continued, "As a matter of fact, it is gonna be a long sabbatical."

Gleason felt the hair on his neck and arms stand at attention. More watchful now, using his fingers to separate the blinds, he muttered, "What? Who is this? How can I help you?"

A chill came over him; his hands were shaking. He realized he was talking to the man on the sidewalk, the man giving instructions. He shielded himself from view, turning only to reach for his glasses. It was clear now. He watched the man motion the others into the car as he rested against the trunk, still speaking into the phone.

"Well, I'll tell you how you can help. You can learn a lesson from the good monsignor. Don't put your nose where it don't belong, or you'll wind up like him. How did you put it? 'On sabbatical.'"

"What do you mean?"

"Check the front steps of the church. You have a package."

Click. He watched the man put the phone into his pocket, then survey the street until his eyes came to gaze for the briefest moment at the very window where he stood. Gleason saw him, clear as day, and recoiled from the window. He heard the car engine rev and forced himself to peek out, only to see the car disappear into the night.

The next sound was the phone falling from his hand. He scratched his head trying to determine if he was even awake, perhaps trapped in some dream or out-of-body experience. He shuffled along the hardwood floors into the hall of the rectory and down darkened steps.

"Christ!" he yelled as he bumped into the credenza.

The floors squeaked beneath him, doors needed oiling as well; and the echo of his steps resounded through the lofty spires of the Church of the Most Precious Blood. Votive candles cast ominous shadows of the Roman Catholic Church's hierarchy, cloned in stone and marble across the expanse of the mini-cathedral. Under the still eyes of Peter, Paul, and Mary he made his way toward the front doors of the church. He fumbled with interior locks and pulled on the Gothic doors. A gust of cold air howled into the cathedral and sent a chill to his bones. He rubbed goose bumps from his arms as he looked up and down the street. Nothing seemed askance.

He turned to close the doors and saw something out of the corner of his eye. It was a large bundle in the grotto at the foot of the statue of San Gennaro. He walked closer to it, one hesitant step after another. It was substantial. He knelt down beside it. He felt the covering. It was a thick plastic pouch, wet, cold. There was a zipper running the length of it. Dare he? His chills had turned to sweat now, and his body trembled. He steadied the hand reaching for the tab of the zipper and pulled it down.

"Oh my God," he blurted, "oh my God." He fell to his knees and made the sign of the cross. He ran back into the church, picking up speed as he approached the phone in the rectory office. Dialing a private line to the Cardinal's personal secretary at St. Patrick's Cathedral on Fifth Avenue, he shouted, though trying to control himself,

"I need to speak to the Cardinal immediately! The Cardinal, I need to speak to him!"

A voice said, "I'm sorry, but you must call back in the morning. I'll not wake His Eminence."

"No, now!" he insisted. "Tell him it's about Monsignor Burns. Tell him . . . he's returned."

Then he dialed 911.

Within an hour a cadre of New York's Finest and a host of crime-scene investigators had encircled the Church of the Most Precious Blood. Police barricades lined the perimeter and yellow crime-scene tape encircled the grotto. A contingent from the Office of the Chief Medical Examiner photographed the scene; and Louis Fong, chief medical examiner, knelt alongside the pouch and pulled the zipper delicately with rubber-gloved hands.

"Some say the world will end in fire, some say in ice," he said.

"Robert Frost?"

The medical examiner heard a voice from behind him. He looked up to see Santo Olivetti, cigar in hand. "What brings the chief detective of the Organized Crime Task Force out in the middle of the night?" Fong asked.

"I couldn't sleep," Olivetti said. "What can you tell me?"

"He's dead," Fong said.

"You're a genius."

Fong turned back toward the corpse. "Nothing," Fong said. "Nothing yet."

Olivetti stared at the corpse, the colorless face, the damp sheen glistening off his skin, the eyes and mouth open, a small red dot on his forehead.

"He almost seems surprised," Olivetti noted.

"Wherever he was kept, it couldn't have been far from here. He was refrigerated. His body is still cold."

"Time of death?"

Fong did not look up. "Hard to say right now, if ever. Time of death will be hard to determine, as there's no way to know how long he was kept on ice. Without a core temperature reading from the liver or the presence or lapse of rigor mortis, it's tough."

"That's interesting. How about the cause of death?"

"Well, this bullet in his forehead is a clue. Up close and personal."

"Not an accident."

Looking up, a smirk on his face, Fong said, "Now who's the genius?"

"I guess it would be too much to ask if he had any ID on him. A wallet, maybe?"

"Ah, my dear detective, you do want this to be too easy. Sorry, though, I can't help you; nothing on his person, no wallet. He seems to be wearing a black cassock with red buttons. I don't think this was a robbery, though."

"Why's that?"

Fong lifted up the corpse's hand. A ring was visible. "This man was a monsignor. A Prince of the Church."

Olivetti took a deep breath. "Our missing monsignor! Fast-track this, Fong. Do it for me."

"Of course," he said.

The detective tossed his cigar onto the steps and stepped on it.

"You should give those things up," he said.

"Only smoke them at crime scenes like this," Olivetti said. "It covers the smell of rotten eggs."

"Ah, yes." Fong nodded. "Putrefaction takes some getting used to. He's not that bad yet, though."

Olivetti looked up at the church doors to see a man wrapped in a blanket. He was being questioned by another detective.

"Is that the man who found him?"

"Yes," Fong acknowledged. "A fellow priest. Pretty shaken up."

The man's eyes were transfixed on the human form wrapped in a plastic pouch, tossed unceremoniously at the base of the statue of San Gennaro.

He walked up to him knowing he shared the same gut feeling as the priest. Neither would have to wait for the official identification or manner of death. It was Monsignor Burns, and he had been murdered.

Monsignor Matthew Burns, among other duties, was pastor emeritus of Most Precious Blood and former administrator of the now-defunct St. Vincent's Hospital in New York City. That position put Burns on Olivetti's radar as he investigated the alleged mob influence that ran the venerable institution into bankruptcy. He met and interviewed the monsignor on various occasions. It would seem now that his investigation had gone cold. He grinned at his pun.

As Olivetti got close to putting the pieces together to build his RICO case against organized-crime families, Monsignor Matthew Burns, a dupe or player or both, disappeared from the face of the earth, leaving his superiors at St. Patrick's on Fifth Avenue and the

Organized Crime Task Force dumbfounded. The high-profile disappearance held the headlines, became the story du jour until the press moved on to the next headline that captivated the twenty-four-hour news cycle. The story of the missing monsignor took a backseat. But the press was back on it beginning with the early edition of the *Post*: GODFELLA SLEEPS WITH THE SAINTS.

In the rectory Gleason took a seat in a faded Queen Anne chair. The blanket covered him, but Olivetti could see he was still shaking. He walked over to an armoire and opened a door, then another, then a third until he found what he was looking for. There were bottles of liquor—Martell, Louie tre'. *Top-shelf booze,* Olivetti thought, *expensive taste.* He reached for the Louie and two shot glasses.

"Never met a priest yet who didn't have a stash, but this is special." He poured and handed one to Gleason. "Drink it," he said. "It'll help calm you, Father. Father . . . ?"

"Gleason, Gleason. I don't drink." He took the glass and sipped it, then tossed it down in one swallow. He had a boyish mop of unruly red hair and light eyebrows that disappeared into a ruddy complexion.

Olivetti continued to look around the office. "So, what can you tell me, Father?"

Gleason shrugged. "Not much, really. I thought I was dreaming; car doors slamming, muffled voices. I fell asleep at my desk, but heard noise from the sidewalk outside the window. I thought about getting some milk, and something made me stop at the window. I saw some men . . ."

"How many men?"

"I don't know, three, four."

"Three *or* four?" Olivetti asked. "Think."

Gleason rubbed his forehead. "It was dark. I was half asleep."

"Think," Olivetti said again.

"Four, I think there were four. I remember three were huddled around the trunk of the car."

"What kind of car?"

"Oh, that's easy. It was a Lincoln Continental. I know because Monsignor . . . has the same model." His voice faded. "As a matter of fact, for a moment I thought he had returned."

"Kind of an expensive car. For a priest, I mean. Don't you think?"

"Oh, well, you see, he won that car at the church fund-raiser. It was first prize in the raffle. Believe me, no one was more surprised than he was when he pulled his own winning ticket. I'll never forget the look on his face."

"I'm sure," Olivetti said, looking for signs of epiphany. Gleason fumbled with his glass. Olivetti poured another for him. "Go on."

"Well, just about then the clock chimed and the phone rang. My heart nearly jumped out of my chest. It was bizarre. I answered the phone, and eventually realized I was talking to the other man, the fourth man. He was standing on the sidewalk, kind of directing the other three who pulled the bundle from the trunk. I heard him talking to them through the phone. 'Hurry,' he said, 'let's go! Over there, by the statue,' then into the phone to me."

"You got a good look at him?"

Gleason thought for a moment. "I guess so, I guess I did, I can't remember."

"Then what?"

"He asked where monsignor was, and I gave him the standard answer from the diocese."

"What answer was that?"

"'Sabbatical!' I said, and he laughed, really loud. Then he continued; and at some point he turned, and he was facing me."

"So you did see him, see him clearly?"

"I-I saw him."

"Did he see you?"

"I-I don't think so. I don't think so. He looked my way, but I was in the dark. I was behind the blinds. No, I don't think so."

"So you'd be able to identify him?"

"I guess so. I don't know."

"Well, which is it? Can you or can't you?"

Gleason put his head down. "I guess I could. I guess I could."

Olivetti sat behind the desk. "What is your position with the diocese, Father?" Olivetti asked, changing direction.

"Oh, well," he said. "Just a parish priest. I was assigned here a year ago. Previously, I was the accountant; and I was stationed here to get a better grasp of the finances. It was too much for Monsignor Burns, what with his other duties and all. I was helping to update the books, you know, bring them up to date with Excel spreadsheets instead of those pencil entries in those old accounting ledgers. That was monsignor's way of doing things."

Olivetti flipped through the pages of the ledger. "And what else did he do?"

"Oh, he had a full plate. Monsignor Burns was administrator of St. Vincent's Hospital." He coughed, reached for the bottle, and poured another drink. "This is so unlike me. I don't drink."

"You were saying?"

"Yes, yes. St. Vincent's; until that unfortunate turn of events," he continued, "he was also head of a committee assigned the task of identifying church property that might be sold. Economics of the day is making that necessary. Some schools or churches that are in the red were to be sold."

"What else can you tell me about Monsignor Burns?"

"Well, he was larger than life, that's for sure. When he walked into a room, he lit it up. He was a presence."

"Nothing suspicious?"

"Burns? Not a chance." He paused and spoke slowly. "He was a saint; a saint, I tell you."

"Sounds like you're trying to convince yourself, Father." *There's a thin line between saint and sinner*, he thought. "I'll send for you later this morning. We'll have you look at some mug shots. In the meantime, I wouldn't tell anyone what you saw. Anyone," he reiterated. "It might not be healthy for you."

On the steps of the church a plainclothes detective relayed the news to Olivetti. "We found the car under the Brooklyn Bridge, torched to a crisp."

PART

I

CHAPTER 1

More than two thousand miles away, and a month earlier, Tommy
Rossini feigned paying attention to the moving lips of three men
across the table. Their voices faded into his consciousness. He already knew his answer to their request would be a simple no. This
meeting was a perfunctory courtesy before the anvil came down on
them. *Novices*, he thought! A deal is a deal, a balloon payment is a
balloon payment. But he thought it was only right to go through
the motions, accept their invitation to lunch at Morton's, enjoy a
steak, then tell them no. It was difficult for him to act as if he were
even considering their request. He played with the bezel of his Rolex,
which showed the time in gold in all time zones. It was a gift from
himself to himself.

"So you see, Mr. Rossini," one of the men said, "if you would consider extending the terms, a slight modification, it would give us the opportunity to restructure once the economy rebounds."

White noise to Rossini. He was staring at the flat-screen hanging behind the bar, watching the images playing across it. *Probably feds*, he thought. He'd recognize those goons anywhere. They were in the middle of a perp walk, no doubt designed to embarrass the hell out of their collar, an elderly well-dressed man. The images intrigued him. The droning voices at his table did not.

The man on the screen had his head low on his chest, his hands behind his back, as two of the feds held his arms, guiding him to a waiting car. Paparazzi clicked away with abandon and reporters shoved microphones into his face.

"Mr. Rossini, Mr. Rossini." He focused again. "As we said, if you give us this accommodation, we can fulfill our commitment when the economy rebounds."

Right, he thought, *when the economy rebounds. Which may be never if this yo-yo Obama gets reelected. I'll bet a hundred to one these yahoos voted for him in the first place. Well, you have him to thank for your problems.*

Tommy took the napkin off his lap, folded it, and placed it on the table. "I thank you for lunch," he said. "I cannot accommodate your request. Now, if you will excuse me, I have another appointment."

Without giving them a chance to beg, he placed his massive palms down on the table and raised his considerable frame. He felt their eyes stare at his hands. They were always attention-getters, one normal in size and shape, but the right hand, knuckles swollen and slightly grotesque, the disfigurement worthy of the Elephant Man. "You can expect the foreclosure papers within the next few days.

Again, thank you for lunch. It was a pleasure doing business with you."

He turned his back to the gentlemen at the table, trying to imagine the stunned looks, the words left half unsaid on their tongues, the last-ditch-effort gestures to get him back to the table, the plea for him to reconsider. He had seen it before, and it bored him. Business is business. He looked at his watch again. He had enough time to make the next appointment across the park. It was a last-minute call from his accountant, who had made an odd request for an unscheduled meeting.

In his peripheral vision, images from the television behind the bar again caught his attention.

An hour later, following specific instructions, Rossini made his way to a bench across from Town Hall. Tommy Rossini believed in omens. A bird's droppings on his shoulder was a portentous one. He wiped the fowl's calling card away and regretted wearing his distressed suede jacket, madder still at his accountant for choosing this park for a meeting.

"It'll only take a minute," Sol had assured him. "But it's important."

It was an unusual place for a business meeting; that much was clear. A park bench in Scottsdale was an unlikely venue, but his accountant was eccentric. So he chalked it up to quirkiness.

As he sat, a late-October breeze revealed itself, teasing blades of grass with a chill breath and propelling sagebrush along an earthen street. The skyline was visible beyond the square. *If you can call* that *a skyline*, he thought. He was from a real city, the Big Apple. Every other skyline was relative. The scene in the square played out before him, in the colors of an O'Keefe painting. He studied the people, pedestrians and cyclists, hustling from one end to the other. He allowed himself a moment to enjoy the tranquil harmony, sights, and sounds. He had ambivalence toward the skateboarders and cyclists. *Caba fresco*, clear heads, he thought. *Don't they work, doesn't anybody work? Maybe I'm jealous,* he thought, *maybe I'd like to be able to get up in the morning and go bike riding aimlessly with not a care in the world.* But then he thought again. *Not really, they're probably broke,* he concluded. Keeping with his philosophy, there are two types of people, takers and bakers. Those who produce and those who take. That was not for him, he was a doer, a producer.

He stretched his legs and tried to relax, cradling his right hand in his left, massaging the aching palm. It was the result of an unattended injury when he was young. *This is a nice place, a peaceful place to be,* he thought, and not once had he regretted the move from New York, skyline and all. Years earlier he had traded his sharkskin pants for khakis and leather Gucci loafers for snakeskin cowboy boots. They fit him just fine now. As he thought about it, there was not much he missed about New York with the exception of his mother . . . and a hot dog. And oh yes . . . perhaps the only woman he had ever loved. But he was not the type to dwell.

As he surveyed the park it came to him. *That's what's missing,* he thought. There was not one hot dog stand in this town square park. Now his mouth watered for one, cooked like only they can in New York, boiled in New York dirty water, smothered with sauerkraut cooked in New York dirty water, and covered with onions simmering in New York dirty water. Maybe, he thought, I'll import a few of those quaint Sabrett umbrella-covered wagons to this town. Show them what they've been missing; I'll put an apron on my brother Jake and make him sell them. Ha, he laughed out loud. That's funny. Jake would find a way to muck it up. Of that he was sure. He'll blame it on the water. It needed New York's water. That was the key ingredient.

Tommy was always thinking. He always knew how to earn, but investing was another matter, best left to professionals. Professionals like his accountant and business adviser, Sol, who had called him to this unusual meeting place. It was a far cry from the boardroom in Sol's office, the oval mahogany conference table, leather chairs, and plush carpeting. Or better yet, having a martini lunch at Morton's. As he shifted in his seat, a splinter on the park bench caught his pants leg.

He didn't recognize the man who sat next to him, a bit too close for his taste. Tommy slid across the bench, but the splinter held on to his pants leg.

"Jesus," he said, as he examined the tear. His eyes shot like a dagger toward the man. *A dozen benches around the square and this shmuck decides to sit in my lap,* he thought. *I ought to make him pay for the repair.* On closer inspection, he realized that would be impossible. The man was dressed in ragged clothes. On a scale from derelict to hobo, he was more hobo. A newspaper covered most of his face, his eyes peeking out above the fold. He spoke.

"Were you followed?" the man asked. His voice was muffled.

Tommy looked over. "Excuse me?" he said. He reached and brought the paper away from the man's face.

He took a closer look at the man, noticing a tattered leather bomber jacket with the fur collar turned up, a hat with the brim turned down, sunglasses, and a variety-store mustache with faulty adhesive.

"It's me, Tommy," the man said.

Tommy recognized something familiar in the man's voice. "Sol?"

"Shush," Sol pleaded. "Not so loud." He looked around the park.

"Sol, is that you? Since when do you have a mustache? What the f . . ."

"Tommy, please. I can explain. I think I can explain." He pressed the mustache to his lip.

"Explain what?" Tommy asked.

"It's kind of a long story, and I don't know where to begin. I really don't know where to begin, it's a long story. I don't . . ."

"Sol, what the hell is going on? What's wrong?"

"I've been indicted. The feds have a warrant on me. They're in my office now, ripping it apart; my home, too."

This got Tommy's attention. "Indicted? Indicted for what? What do you mean, 'too'?"

"Tommy, I don't have time to explain." He continued, but only certain words stuck out—words like "money laundering," "Ponzi schemes," and "subprime."

"You'll read about it, probably tomorrow. In the meantime, I just wanted to tell you in person. I'm leaving the country. I'm making aliyah. It's my only chance. I didn't mean for this particular outcome."

"Tell me what in person?"

"You're broke, Tommy. I'm sorry. You lost everything. You're broke. It was all an illusion, a house of cards, a house of cards. I just wanted to give you a heads-up. I'm sorry."

Tommy felt his heart pumping and sweat beginning to form on his brow. His insides began to shake. A hammer to the head could not have been more numbing. He sat with his mouth open, about to ask questions, but before he had a chance to question Sol, he disappeared down a sloping path.

Tommy shook his head to clear it, but the questions wouldn't stop. Did he hear what he heard? Was that man Sol, his trusted friend and adviser? What was he sorry for? Was this all in his imagination? Could the fruits of twenty years' hard work be lost? He rose to follow the man as the splinter completed the tear.

Dazed, Rossini reached for his cell phone. His hands were shaking, and he fumbled with it, dropping it at the very edge of a puddle. As he bent to retrieve it, a cyclist bumped him, knocking him to the ground, into a tree. The bark scratched his face. He had crawled the few feet to the phone when another cyclist sped through a puddle, dousing him with a cascade of dirty water. He was soaked and covered with muddy soil. He ran his hand across his chin and examined his blood-stained palm. As he stared at his open hand, an elderly man walking a shih tzu paused, looked at him, and dropped two quarters into his hand. He growled at the kind gesture and dialed his office.

"Beatrice."

"Mr. Rossini, I'm so glad you called." He could barely hear her. "Speak up," he said.

"There are gentlemen here from the District Attorney's Office. They won't leave. They are going through your office. They had a warrant."

"The DA?" he repeated. "I'll be right there."

He walked across the park toward his car, just in time to see it being hoisted onto a flat-bed truck. "Hey!" he shouted. "What the hell are you doing to my car? It's brand new, that's my car."

The Lexus LS430 was secured by metal cable to the truck. Tommy argued, "Where are the signs? This isn't a tow-away zone."

The tow truck driver continued inking papers attached to a clipboard. He looked at Tommy from head to toe. "You're Thomas Rossini?" he asked.

"Of course I am."

"Guess you have hit bottom," the man said. "I hope you were good to the people on the way up."

"What the hell are you talking about? Why are you towing my car? Where are the signs?"

"It's not a tow-away zone. The car is being repossessed for non-payment." He ripped off a piece of paper and handed it to Rossini, who felt like he had been hit with another hammer.

"But that's my baby," he said. The tow truck disappeared, carrying with it the validation of his success; a sleek black-on-black, four-door show stopper, showroom-new, with 290 horses under the hood, dual exhaust, and GPS. "It parks itself . . ." were the only words he could muster as he waved good-bye.

This is The Twilight Zone, he thought. It must be.

On foot he hurried the few blocks toward his office, stopping to catch his breath and to dial Sol, only to hear the obligatory "I'm sorry, your call cannot be completed" line of Verizon bullshit he always heard when the connection was bad. *They suck, these cell phones,* he thought. *They all suck.*

He plotted a course of action as he walked. He would call Sol from his office and tell him about the nut impersonating him in the park. Then he would call his attorney, Goldfarb, and have these goons kicked out of his office. As he walked into his outer office, his secretary stood agape in front of him.

"Are you all right, Mr. Rossini? You've been assaulted. Are you hurt?"

"No, no, I'm fine," he said. "Do you have a Band-Aid?"

She took one from her desk and handed it to him as she prattled on. He opened the Band-Aid with his teeth and good hand and applied it to his cut. He noticed Beatrice was jittery, blocking his forward progress. Her hair was pinned far back on her head. Her eyebrows twitched, wrinkling the skin of her forehead. Her lips moved, mouthing something in a clear attempt to communicate.

In a throaty whisper, she said, "There are men from the District Attorney's Office . . ." Seamlessly, her pitch resumed its normal level as his office door opened, "And these gentlemen have been waiting for you as well, Mr. Rossini," she added.

"You're Tommy Rossini?" one asked.

"He's been assaulted," she suggested.

"Yes," he answered; then, "No. I mean, yes, I'm Tommy Rossini; and no, I haven't been assaulted." He looked down at himself. With his pants torn, dirty, and wet from puddles and perspiration, and a trace of blood on his hand and chin, he would have to agree that he was far from the Tommy Rossini that only months ago was featured in the *Scottsdale Independent* as "Business Man of the Year."

The investigators did not seem impressed as they walked back into his office. Two men had made themselves comfortable in his office as others went through file cabinets. Another sat in Tommy's swivel chair at his desk.

"What the fuck? You have no right!" he screamed.

They handed him a copy of a search warrant. "Yes, we do," one said. "It's all in here." The man tapped his finger on the warrant. Tommy walked over to the palladium window in his office, pretending to read the warrant as they went about violating his space. They opened drawers and cabinets; they took out books and ledgers.

"I don't know what this is all about," he protested.

"Then you'll have nothing to worry about," one answered.

His secretary came in. "Your brother is on the line. He's called three times."

"Not now, Bea. Tell him I'll get back to him."

"I did, Mr. Rossini, but he's insisting. Says it's an emergency."

"Just tell him later."

Tommy watched as boxes were carried out of his office, then one of the men handed him a slip of paper.

"This is a receipt for all we've taken. We'll be in touch."

Tommy walked behind his desk and steadied himself. He took a deep breath and surveyed his office. *They're not the neatest people,* he thought. He knew he had to talk to Sol.

"Bea, get Sol on the phone. Don't give up, keep trying."

"All right, Mr. Rossini, I'm very sorry," Beatrice tiptoed into the office. "But your brother has called again. He says it's an emergency."

"An emergency? Which brother?" he asked. It was a rhetorical question. He knew which one. He had two brothers. The oldest had everything and needed everything; the youngest had nothing and needed nothing. This had to be Jake, the needy one. An emergency, to him, could mean he lost his laundry ticket and was unable to get his custom-made white-on-white voile shirts from the Chinaman. For a moment he thought about having his secretary tell him he was not there.

"I'll take it here," he said, against his better judgment. "And Bea," he said, "remember that vacation you wanted?" She nodded. "Best to start it. Call Goldfarb first. Get him in here." He picked up the phone.

"How much, Jake?"

"Tommy, hey, Tommy, how are you?"

"Great, Jake, just friggin' great."

"How's the weather out there?"

"Terrible," Tommy said. "Rain and more rain, followed by sleet, snow, and ice." The erroneous weather report was purposeful, in case Jake was thinking of coming west with another harebrained scheme that needed financial backing; his backing.

"Hey, that's too bad. It's beautiful here. The snowbirds are coming down. Our season will be in full swing. I can't wait for the TPC golf tournament."

"That's great, Jake. Now, what can I do for you?"

Silence. Tommy knew what the silences meant.

"Tommy, I'm in trouble."

"You're in trouble?" For a moment he wanted to tell his older brother what real trouble was. *Why bother,* he decided. He knew his brother enough to know he wouldn't care to know that his world had come crashing down. He knew his problem would fall on un-sympathetic ears. Tommy sat at his desk and awaited the story. He wondered if it would be a new tale of woe or a different take on an old tale of woe.

"Jake. I'm sorry, but make it quick. I have a few problems of my own, and . . ."

"This is serious, Tommy. I'm losing the nightclub, creditors up the ass, but I could deal with all that. I got some irons in the fire, some big deals ready to click. I've got some interested investors who can't wait to back me."

"Good for you, Jake. So take care and keep in touch."

"No, no, Tommy, wait. You don't understand. I'm not in good health. Sugar is out of control. I need medicine."

"Really?" He leaned forward on the desk, running his hand through his brow. "I give you credit, Jake. This is a new one."

"It is not a joke, Tommy."

"Don't you have medical insurance?"

"No, no more. I lost it when I lost the restaurant."

Jake knew nothing about the restaurant business but convinced himself he did. He fancied himself a modern-day Jilly, Sinatra's sidekick. Jake, too, was a larger-than-life man about town—a raconteur whose company was sought by all the beautiful people. Jake operated in an alternate universe where he was Jilly.

Jake had, no doubt, his own personality—generosity and business acumen would lead to bigger and better things. He gave up a wife of twenty-five years and more important, her father; *capo di tutti i capi,* his ace in the hole; the very man who made all things possible, known affectionately on the street as Fat Pauly Fazzula. With all Jake had, he convinced himself he was unhappy. He would show his ex-father-in-law how to make real money.

But before he became an ex-father-in-law, he was the muscle behind Jake. Land deals or Boar's Head routes, from livery services to restaurants, no deal was too big, no scheme too small. It helped that it was on someone else's dime and clout; namely, that of his father-in-law, Don Pauly Fazzula's, a man with whom he had now fallen into disfavor. Divorces can do that, Tommy warned him.

"Oh, you're losing the restaurant I told you was a bad idea?" Tommy asked. No answer. Tommy continued, "Or the restaurant before that one; or the one before that? Now that I think of it, didn't I tell you not to open any restaurant? You knew nothing about the business. You've closed more restaurants than the Board of Health. You were a foot doctor. You should have stayed a foot doctor."

Jake's fall was fast. At each business venture Jake gave away more drinks than he sold and chalked it up to promotion. It did insure he had a large following. Jake was a regional celebrity in South Beach. Hangers-on followed him from one failed restaurant to another, for a meal, a bottle of wine, champagne, tickets to a show, or a golf tournament. They clapped when he grabbed the microphone off the lounge singer. They egged him on to sing a few Sinatra ballads, energizing him, surrounding him with adulation to the point he believed they loved him. And he would love them back; *Drinks on the house, no check to table six.* They followed him until he had nothing to give. And with that life—the late nights, the free-flowing booze, and fast women—there was bound to be a bump in the road. It wasn't a good mix. When one of those fast women became Jake's biggest fan, there was only one direction in which to go; down. On his downward spiral there was no room for an entourage; so the adulation of the crowds disappeared, looking for greener pastures.

"The tiki tapas wine bar was a gold mine, Tommy," Jake insisted. "It's still the only one on Collins Avenue."

"Yeah, tiki this," he said grabbing his crotch. "And, anyway, you didn't have the brains not to piss off your father-in-law."

"You know there was more to it than that."

"No, no I don't. You were on top of the world as long as you stayed married to that Rosemary Clooney look-alike."

"I was unhappy," Jake explained.

"Hey, *stunata*, everybody's unhappy. Who said you got to be happy. We're talking marriage here. You were living large with her. Your ship came in when you married her. All you had to do was keep your tugboat docked." It was a metaphor not even he fully understood.

"Tommy . . ."

"Don't 'Tommy' me. Call Looney, maybe he'll help you out this time."

"Come on, Tommy. Looney still has his communion money. You know that."

"Now, listen, Jake. You've been living extravagantly, never saved a dime, you've pissed away more money than can be imagined. You're on the balls of your ass now. I don't know how you're living. You gave up a good thing for some whim. You gave up your security blanket for some piece of ass. I warned you. If I find out Mom is sending you money, I'm going to be pissed. Pack up whatever you have left and go home. You can stay with Mom until you get back on your feet, and you can take care of her at the same time. She could use some help. You can catch up on old times, like the last twenty-five years when you were nowhere to be found."

"I can't go back to New York. It would mean I'm a failure."

"Newsflash, asshole, you ARE a failure. Look it up in the dictionary—*failure*, one who has failed. You don't have a choice now. You made your bed, now lie in it."

"Tommy, please. I've got to take care of this problem."

"I'll tell you what, Jake. Give me the name of the doctor or of the drugstore, and I'll send money directly to them."

"You don't trust me? You think I'd make this up?"

"Duh! . . ." Tommy said.

"Thanks, Tommy, thanks."

"Pack up your wagon, Jake. Pack your silk suits and custom shirts; your fitted shoes and pine-scented shoe trees; your floral soaps, herbal conditioners, and skin softener creams—do that and go home."

Click.

Jake remained with the receiver in his hand. A waitress peeked into his office.

"Jake, there are four couples at table five. They think they know you from New York. They'd like to say hello."

He scratched his head and lit a cigarette. "Tell them I'll be over in a minute." She turned to leave. "Wait," he said, "send them a round of drinks on me."

CHAPTER 2

After hanging up the phone, Tommy felt guilty—not a lot, a little. *I've got my own problems,* he thought; and Jake's needs were a full-time job. Jake always needed tough love, and Tommy was the only one to dispense it. He consoled himself. *It's not like I didn't warn him,* he thought. Don't marry that woman. She's a wiseguy's daughter, run the other way. But Jake didn't listen. He married her. His meal ticket, a spoiled prima donna who would have wound up in a nunnery if not for his brother. The Don blessed the union with one proviso, "Til death do you part." Old-time Mustache Petes take those words seriously when it comes to their daughters. Now Jake was stuck with her. You don't leave a wiseguy's daughter. It's not healthy. A special mission to Miami became necessary.

It came about when Tommy received a call from his brother

Looney telling him that Jake was contemplating a divorce. That was just a year ago, as he recalled. A phone call from Looney was a rare event, something to do with long-distance charges and his general lack of anything new or interesting to say. Tommy had to think for a minute when he heard Looney's frantic voice on the phone.

"Hey, hey, slow down, who is this?"

"It's me, Phil." Then he conceded, "Looney."

That rang a bell. "Looney, what's up? Has Mom died? Is she okay?" He heard him hyperventilating. "Slow down, breathe, breathe."

"Mom is fine. It's Jake. He wants to know if he can hide out with me until things settle down."

"Hide out? What things?"

"I don't know. He's thinking of leaving his wife. Is he crazy? That guy will kill him. What's Jake going to do without that guy behind him? He wants to come here. I have no room here. I'm worried. I don't want to get involved with all this."

Tommy imagined Looney's face as he weathered this crisis. The bushy, curled eyebrows of a mad scientist, contorting like those of Groucho Marx on speed. Tommy had his father's looks—classic, olive-skinned—and Jake was fair like his mother. Looney looked like no one. It was a fact they were never shy to remind him of, suggesting to their younger brother that he had been adopted. Tommy guessed that Looney was breaking out in a rash at the thought of a houseguest, especially one in disfavor with a mobster. It was much too much drama for a guy who signaled when changing lanes.

For all his bluster he understood that Looney had a point. Jake was about to make a big mistake.

"I already tried talking to him. It's no use. He's stubborn."

"Tommy, you got to try again."

Tommy agreed. Jake had to come to his senses. He had personal motives as well. He did not want to be on the wrong side of Don Pauly Fazzula either. Fazzula had long reach and a longer memory. That prompted his humanitarian mission to Jake's Williams Island Club home off Miami's coast. Tommy was pausing in the driveway to admire the fire-engine-red Corvette when Jake appeared in the doorway.

"You actually drive this?"

"You bet, it's a chick magnet. They cling to me."

Tommy adjusted his Maui Jims. "Maybe," he suggested, "they want to stay in the shade."

Jake was wearing a full-length white terry cloth robe and matching fluffy slippers. They hugged. Jake walked him through the house; overstated elegance, just how Tommy pictured it.

"You're getting fat," Tommy said. "You look like a cloud in that thing."

"You're still the same," Jake said with a smirk.

Tommy looked around. "Is Bernadette home?" he whispered.

"No, she's shopping, then going for a pedicure."

Tommy cringed at the thought. "Good, I could do without seeing her."

He followed his brother through a great room, out sliding glass doors that led to the lanai. He sat next to his brother alongside the massive inground swimming pool with a golf course view and a hint of ocean waves caressing the shore just beyond the fairway. It was impressive.

"Bianca will get us a drink. What will you have?"

A middle-aged domestic was standing behind him.

"Vodka and tonic," Tommy said.

"Two," Jake chimed in.

Tommy took in the scenery. This was a valuable piece of property. "You've come a long way, Jake. You slept your way to the top."

"It's not all gold that glitters. You don't know what I put up with." Bianca brought the drinks. "Nuts, Bianca, where are the nuts?" Jake complained.

"Sorry, Mr. Rossini." She walked back toward the house.

"You can't find good illegals anymore." He sat in a lounge chair and let his robe fall open to bask naked in the sun. "So, what brings you here, Tommy boy?"

Tommy sat back in a cushioned chaise lounge and wiped his brow.

"Hey, *capodosta*, I hear you're thinking of leaving all this. Thinking you can make it on your own. I'm here to tell you to think again."

"I'll be all right. The guy holds me back. His thinking is too Old World."

"Holds you back? You mean like when he financed your purchase of the medical building on Queens Boulevard, or when he financed your purchase of the private livery company, or a dozen other harebrained ideas you've had?"

"He thinks small. If I had his cash and connections, I'd . . ."

"But you don't have his cash or connections. So stop the bullshit. Without this puppeteer pulling your strings you'd be removing calluses from old ladies at Mother Cabrini Nursing Home. This is Fat Pauly Beans's kid we're talking about. And how bad could it be? Look at all this; you can't give all this up."

"Toys," Jake said. "These are just toys. There are more important things in life."

"Sure there are. Like your yacht, like your jewelry, like your fancy clothes and your Corvette. How do you even fit in that thing? Probably need the Jaws of Life to get you out of it. Believe me, Jake. I know you. You can't live without those toys and without that *pezzanovante* backing you up."

"Just toys," Jake said again.

"So now you're a philosopher. 'Just toys, hey?' What? This Sabrina chick you're banging is not a toy? You're fooling yourself." He sipped on his vodka and tonic and leaned in closer. "Listen, Jake, you know this guy better than most. He won't let you get away with disrespecting him. It will set a bad precedent. If he allows you to throw dirt in his face, his crew will think he's getting old. It's like a wolf family. If the head wolf shows signs of weakness, his days as head wolf are numbered."

"There are more important things," Jake said.

"What? Don't tell me you're talking about this Sabrina dame. You're giving all this up for a pot-smoking astrologer?"

"She reads the charts," Jake said. "She helped me lose weight. She told me I eat because my moon is in the house of Aries."

"You eat because your moon is in the House of Pancakes."

"You're very funny."

"I'm not trying to be funny. I am serious. This will be the mistake of your life. You will regret this."

Jake motioned to calm his brother. "You don't understand. The guy and me are tight. He'll understand. It won't affect my relationship with him. I've become his *consigliere*. He's got two women on the side, too. He'll understand."

"I can't believe what you're saying. He can have two women on the side. He makes the rules. You think you got this figured out, but you're not figuring right. I'm here to ask you to think again, to come to your senses."

Jake was determined. He didn't go for the wolf analogy. A few days after the visit, Tommy heard Jake had packed his belongings and moved out. He thought he was smart enough to make a go of it, even without the Don's help. *Stupid bastard,* Tommy thought. He blamed Sabrina for some of it, explaining to Looney, "She caught Jake during 'man-o-pause.'"

"What's that?" Looney asked.

"It's a condition that afflicts men in their fifties requiring fast cars and faster broads, which, ironically, tend to make the condition worse. Time and common sense are the only cure. Unfortunately," he explained, "common sense decreases as age increases, making the cure elusive."

"I still don't understand," Looney said.

"That doesn't surprise me."

"What now?" Looney asked.

Tommy heard the tremor in his voice. "I don't know," he said. "He's a wacko."

"I know. Couldn't you talk sense into him?"

"Never could. He can have everything. The Don wouldn't care if he had twelve broads on the side as long as he goes home at night. What a setup. But I guess he's bored after twenty-five years with her. The Garden of Eden is not enough. He has to bite the apple."

"Does this apple have a name?"

"Sabrina."

CHAPTER 3

Tommy first met Sabrina when Jake flew out to Vegas on a business trip about three years earlier. He knew she was trouble at first sight. She landed an hour after the plane did. She looked flighty, spaced out, and illegally young. He could swear she made a play for him. Why not? He was the better-looking brother, he admitted. He had an inkling then that Jake was headed down a dangerous path. Tommy knew she had a spell on Jake, and that spelled trouble.

As he thought about his brother now, Tommy recalled his mother's words "There's no fool like an old fool." When he was young, he heard her whisper those words over and over at his father's grave. He didn't understand their significance back then. He did now.

As Sabrina indulged herself in a seaweed wrap at the spa, Tommy and Jake sipped piña coladas by the poolside at the Tropicana in 110-

degree heat. Even then he warned, "Jake, stay married, please. Don't do anything stupid. They're all the same, anyway. Sure, she's young and beautiful and certainly has less of a mustache than Bernadette; but when you turn them upside down, they're all the same. Besides, how do you keep up with her? She's half your age."

"Younger, even," he said, smiling.

"You must be popping Viagra like M&M'S. When it runs out, she'll be gone anyway. She's looking for a sugar daddy, and the only thing you have is diabetes."

"You don't understand, I'm in love. The sex is fantastic."

"Jake, listen to yourself. Wise up. Reintroduce yourself to your right hand. You're not thinking right. She's a whim. She's using you. What for, I don't know."

"No, not Sabrina. She's different."

Famous last words. "And what about me?" Tommy reasoned. "Pauly might take it out on me."

"Nah! . . ."

"Nah . . . ? Don't be so sure. I introduced you to her, kind of. I'll never forget that day. I was yelling at three *jamoke* laborers on a job site when I turn to see Pauly's henchman Johnny Pump standing right behind me, saying, 'Pauly wants to see you, *yesterday!*' I remember thinking, '*Christ, what did I do wrong; or worse yet, who does he want me to go pay a visit to?*' I go over to the café, and he's sitting in his famous barber chair."

"Do you want to eat something?"

"No," I say.

"Drink?"

"No, thank you, Pauly."

"Okay," he says. Then he looks and asks, "Are you related to some-one named Jake Rossini? More specifically, a *Doctor* Jake Rossini?"

"'Jake?' I says. 'Jake's my brother.' Now I'm thinking, *Christ, what the hell did* he *do? Am I gonna have to go smack my own brother or whack him? Oh Christ!* 'Is everything okay?'"

"You got a brother who's a doctor?"

He sounded surprised; like that someone had brains in my family.

"Well, not really a doctor-doctor. He's a podiatrist."

"Well, ain't that a doctor?" he asked.

"I guess, but not like a regular doctor. More like a foot doctor," I said again.

"Right, well, he took care of my daughter. Seems she had some warts, and anyway, she likes him. I want . . . you should arrange with him to take my daughter out on a date; and if she likes him, we'll plan the wedding."

"I nearly choked. I says, 'Mr. Fazzula, I think my brother is seeing someone.' I mean, what else could I say? This guy had it all figured out."

"It can't be serious," the Don suggested. "Tell him to come by Sat-urday night." He handed me a piece of paper. "These are the directions. They'll be going to the Rainbow Room, so make sure he wears a nice suit and a tie. I assume he has one. If not, tell him to go to Harry Kaplan Clothing & Haberdashers on Canal Street. Put it on my ac-count. I want . . . he shouldn't look like a *shmo*. I'll take care of the rest."

Jake took the story from there. "So, it is your entire fault," Jake rec-ollected. "I was going out with that Jewish girl from Long Island. I was her first lover."

"Did she tell you that?"

"Yes."

"You must have looked familiar," Tommy said. "You were never a good judge of these things. That broad let so many guys through they started wearing E-ZPass."

Jake ignored him. "I found out a few years ago she became a lesbian."

"You must have been a great lover," Tommy said.

"Did I tell you how funny you are?"

They clinked glasses and sipped.

"I remember," Jake said, "the day you told me I was taking out this Fazzula girl. I should have known things would turn out bad. I remembered her. She had the ugliest feet. That pinky toe was non-existent and fused with the fourth toe. It even gave me the chills, and I've seen everything. That should have been a warning. You know, you can tell a lot about a person by their feet. The Chinese believe that feet are a window to the soul. Those ugly toes should have been a warning. She had no pinky toe, and, as it turns out, no soul."

"So, you dated her. You could have figured some way to get rid of her. Why did you have to marry her? You should have made sure she didn't want to see you again."

Jake laughed. "Come on, you know she had to fall in love with me. To know me is to love me. I think I was the first man to see her bare feet. What a sight. Anyway, the rest is history. Can't blame her—my charm, my blue bedroom eyes, my curly red hair!"

"Right, a regular Don John."

"I had the feeling she would fall in love with me right then and there. I am so damn irresistible! She actually blushed when I had her remove her size-nine shoes—wide, by the way. She must have lived a sheltered life. I was the first guy to ever touch her feet, or any other part of her body for that matter. This was as intimate as it got. She wanted me when she left my office; after all, I had violated her, sort of. Whenever she wanted something, she only had to ask her father. She did."

"Yeah, in retrospect you should have picked your nose or passed gas or something."

"What can I tell you? But I didn't fall in love with her. I fell in love with the glitz. Who wouldn't? When I drove up to that fortress home in Todt Hill. Man, this was livin' Staten *Italian* style."

"You were impressed."

"I was more than impressed."

"Your ticket out, that's what you figured."

"I guess so," Jake noted. "But I tell you, Tommy, who could blame me? I never knew people lived like this. It was like something out of the movies. The home was unreal, a circular gravel drive-way that led to a mansion complete with a portico and wraparound porch. I ring the bell and hear door chimes echoing, then these humongous inlaid glass doors opened. There was a tremendous ro-tunda, a crystal chandelier that must have hung fifty feet. There were Lladros and Capodimonte statues as big as me, and French provincial furniture and rugs as plush as anything I had ever stepped on. I kept hearing mom's voice in my head telling me to take off my shoes. It was museum-like, original oil paintings on the walls—from Tuscan villas and Roman emperors to Impressionist portraits."

"Probably fell off a truck, the spoils of some heist," Tommy said.

"I was escorted into the dining room and saw him. Don Fazzula sat at the head of a long table with vases of fresh flowers and flatware that reflected the light from candelabras. Tommy, I tell ya, he looked like something off a Hollywood set. He was tanned, slick-haired—a primed, pinky-ring-wearing middle-aged man with deep black eyes and waxed eyebrows on a pampered face. He was built like a Sherman tank camouflaged by a paisley silk smoking jacket that fit his torso like a glove. There were a dozen men sitting around him. They seemed strangely out of place in this cultured setting. *Hmmm*, I remember thinking, *what doesn't belong?* They all turned their heads and stared at me, like I was an intruder. The Don did not get up to greet me. Instead, with cutlery, he points around the table.

"Dis is Louie, Ally Boy, Nunzi, Frankie, Chillie, Ballsy."

"The names were coming too fast. I remember thinking of Disney's movie with Sleepy and Dopey and whoever. I hoped there wouldn't be a test later.

"I'm shaking in my shoes as the Don explained to his friends, 'This is Doctor Rossini. He's dating Bernadette.' Even I was surprised to hear that. I sensed pride in the Don's voice, especially when he emphasized the word *Doctor.*

"I understood quickly that for the Don, having Bernadette marrying a doctor—or anyone, for that matter—was a sign that the 'family' was advancing.

"So, when he introduces me, *Doctor* Rossini, as Bernadette's date, I hear random coughing, gulping, and choking at the table. 'A fig went down the wrong way,' one of the goons explained as another hulk pounded his back. One thing I knew, at that moment I knew I was in love. I could get used to this."

"I'm sure," Tommy said as he sipped his drink.

"Then I saw her."

"Speak of the devil," Tommy added.

"This Bernadette broad, and I do mean broad, appears at the top of the circular stairway. There were two women with her, a total of about nine hundred pounds on the landing, as best I could guesstimate. They came down the stairs, single file. The introductions were blurry, mother and aunt. They all had one face, one body type, and similar feet, I figured."

"You kids enjoy the show," the Don ordered. "I hope you like Vic Damone. Best pipes in the business. I am sending my personal driver with you. Johnny Pump will drive you and bring you home."

"I jumped as I sensed this presence behind me. I turn and see a short man with stubby arms and a bulldog face and wool cap pulled over his head. He looked like a hydrant with arms and given his nickname, I figure I wasn't the only one who thought so."

"The rest is history," Tommy said.

"Yep, history. I admit, I was impressed, if not with my new girlfriend, with the trappings."

PART
II

CHAPTER 4

Jake and Bernadette were married soon after, and Jake rode her all the way to the top. His podiatry practice was small potatoes. With the help of the Don, he bought his medical practice, and with the help of the Don, he lost it along with the building in a Medicare scam that netted the Don a few millions. He assured Jake that his share was safely invested. Only because of the Don's lawyers and connections did he skate with a suspended license. A small price to pay for the gravy train it produced.

Jake didn't mind losing the practice. Feet were something of the past. He figured with his brains, harebrained ideas, and the Don's money and influence, the sky was the limit. Sleeping with Bernadette, especially when her feet touched his under the blankets, was a small price to pay. He was somebody now. Not only Bernadette Fazzula's husband, more important, he was Don Fazzula's son-in-law. Allegiance to Don Fazzula was a full-time commitment; one hundred ten percent loyalty. It was always, "yes, Don" never "no, Don." If not for the astrologist that eventually stole his heart away, there would have been another decade of kissing the Don's considerable ass.

After twenty-five years, Jake was closer to the Don than to Bernadette. The Don was a secretive man who trusted no one, which made it all the more surprising that he took Jake into his confidence. In the time Jake had been married to his daughter, Don Pauly became close to his son-in-law; as close as he was to anyone. He felt secure with him. Jake believed he could divorce Bernadette and still remain a confidant to the Don. *Business is business,* he thought. *The guy will understand.* He was wrong.

"Stay married, Jake," Tommy advised again. "You're going through a stage, like a change-of-life thing. You're nothing without this guy backing you."

"I don't need him," he insisted. "He's old-school; small thinker."

Jake went through his change of life. Sabrina was the answer to his crisis—or the cause. After marrying the Don's daughter, Jake was rounding third base and thought he had hit a home run. Now, after the divorce, he couldn't buy a bleacher ticket. A string of bad investments and business ventures followed. Thanks to the Don, doors closed. His connections dried up. Associates made their choices. Best not to cross the Don. Tommy often wondered if the Don would pull a vanishing act on his brother, then thought better of it.

He understood Don Fazzula too well. Killing Jake would be too easy. Tommy was sure Fazzula had another plan, one more in keeping with his sociopathic personality. Witnessing Jake lose everything would be more interesting than swatting him like a fly. Jake was the Don's pet project now. Watching Jake's demise would be even more fun than killing him. He wanted to see Jake suffer, broke, beaten. Then he'd kill him. It would be a teachable moment for his crew as well.

The Don's crew, the largest in New York, knew how close he was with his son-in-law. When Jake went off the deep end, the Don felt personally violated. This was a giant, public slap in the face. Jake took the Don's trust, his money, his daughter's virginity, warts and all, and thumbed his nose at him. If left to stand, it would show weakness. Jake would have to pay. By doing so, Don Fazzula would be setting an example for everyone in his crew. The pack leader is alive and well, and feeds on red meat.

The memories of those conversations in Vegas and Williams Island were vivid. Tommy rocked back and forth in his chair satisfied with the thought that he had tried his best to warn his brother. *Che sarà sarà!* Now he had to deal with his own problems.

"Mr. Rossini, Mr. Rossini." Tommy came back to the reality around him. "Will there be anything else before I close up?"

Tommy sat behind his desk and tried to put the pieces together.

He looked at his watch—2:00 p.m.; 5:00 p.m. New York time. "No, Bea! But get my mother on the phone before you leave."

It took a moment. "Pick up, Mr. Rossini." He did, and heard his mother's voice.

"Who is it?" she asked.

"Ma, it's Tommy."

"Who is it?" she asked again.

"Ma, it's me, Tommy, your son."

"My son? He's not home. He's in Jersey."

"No, Ma. I'm Tommy. I'm in Scottsdale."

"Scottsdale? Scottsdale, New Jersey?"

Tommy ran his fingers through his hair and took a deep cleansing breath. "Ma, is anyone there with you?"

"Who wants to know?"

"Me." His voice grew louder. "Tommy; it's Tommy."

He heard the phone drop and talking in the background.

"Hey, see who this is. I think it's a crank call. If he tries to sell you something, like insurance, hang up on him. I already have insurance."

A woman's voice came over the phone. "Hello, who is this?"

"Hi. I'm Tommy, Maddie's son."

"Oh, hello! I'm Dory from Visiting Nurses. I was just taking some blood from her. She talks about you all the time. I see your pictures all over the apartment. Your mom wrote all your names on the photographs. You're the tall, thin one with all the black hair."

Must have been an old picture, he thought.

"You're from New Jersey, right? Bayonne, I think?"

Don't fight it. "Right. Hey, what's going on there? What's wrong with her?"

"Oh, she's all right. A little forgetful and a bit of the tremors, some aches and a little hard of hearing, that's all."

"But I bought her hearing aids."

"Oh, yes, but she only wears them for an hour or so in the morning. She wants to save the battery so it will last longer."

His mother's frugal financial planning was familiar to him. It was a necessity when raising three sons without a father.

"Your brother stopped by a few minutes ago. He couldn't stay long. He was afraid of traffic back to Staten Island." He heard Dory explain, "Maddie, this is your son Thomas."

"I don't have a son Thomas."

That feels good to hear, Tommy thought.

"She's confused," Dory explained. "Sometimes her medicine doesn't kick in like it should. Maddie, do you want to talk to your son?"

"Which one?"

"Thomas."

"Sure, where is he? Let him in."

"No sweetheart, he's calling on the phone." She handed the phone to Maddie.

"Hello, hello, who is this?"

"It's Tommy," he said again.

In a moment of clarity, she said, "Oh, my dear son Tommy. How are you? I miss you. What do you want? Do you need anything?"

"Just to say hello to you is all. Are you okay?"

"Me, I'm fine. But this *mulignane* here won't stop poking and prodding me."

"Ma, be nice. Don't call her that. She's trying to help you."

"Help me. She's taking blood out of me by the gallon. I don't have much of it left."

Change the subject. "Ma, did Looney stop by?"

"Who? Looney?" she asked. "Yes, he came, he saw, he left. How's the weather there?"

"Gloomy," he said, thinking she'd feel better if they were both in gloomy weather.

"What do you expect in New Jersey? Jersey is crap."

"Okay, okay, Ma. I just wanted to say hello."

Dory took the phone. "Tommy, what's a *mulignane*?" she asked.

"Uh . . . a delicious vegetable."

Tommy ended the conversation and rubbed his temples. After talking to his mother he wasn't sure who he was or where he was, Jersey or Arizona. He had a migraine. That much he knew.

Dory returned the phone to its cradle and noticed Maddie's eyes staring off into the distance. "What's wrong, Maddie?"

Maddie turned her gaze out the window. She lifted her arthritic arm and pointed. "Nothing," she said. "I thought I saw my mother across the street." Her hand fell to her lap, coming to rest on the Bible, her head lowered. "My uncle, too. They were probably headed to church."

"Of course, dear one," Dory said.

"I should go, too, but I'm tired," Maddie said. With that she sat back in her chair and opened the book. "I'll have them up after mass. We'll have a big lunch and laugh about old times."

"Sounds good, dear one," Dory said.

"I've got to get to the cemetery soon. Haven't visited for a while."

CHAPTER 5

*I*n Manhattan, Father Bryce Gleason walked along Elizabeth Street into the 5th Precinct. "I have an appointment with Officer Olivetti."

The desk sergeant didn't stop shuffling papers. He peeked above his reading glasses and pointed to a bench. "Lieutenant Olivetti," he corrected him. "Cool your heels there," he said pointing.

Gleason was unfamiliar with the lobby of a police station. With a tourist's wide eyes he stared at the mass of humanity being dragged and otherwise escorted without ceremony.

Olivetti tapped him on the shoulder. He looked tired and disheveled, with a five o'clock shadow. Gleason figured he had worked all night.

He followed him to a room where stacks of books were piled on a table.

"Do you want me to look through all those?" Gleason asked.

"No," Olivetti said. "I think I can narrow your choices down considerably."

Gleason sat behind the desk. "Father, tell me more about Burns's duty with the diocese. You mentioned he was the real estate guy, the guy who made the call on what stays and what goes."

Gleason unbuttoned his coat. "Well, yes. That was one of his duties. He took a close look at individual parishes, studied their books, their attendance numbers, put it in context with the surrounding area, and made decisions about what needed to be closed and what should be kept."

"Guess a guy could make some enemies in a position like that, or some friends for that matter."

"Well, I never thought of it like that, but sure. I guess a decision to close a church doesn't sit well with the community. Do you think it has something to do with . . . ?"

"What were some of his other duties?"

"Well, as I said, he was the administrator of St. Vincent's Hospital; and Lord knows, they had been having a hard time of late."

"In what sense?"

"Well, I can't speak firsthand, but the charity went bankrupt. The hospital is closed. It had been a long time in coming. The neighborhood has changed so much, from what I am told. There are some things to which I am not privy."

Olivetti nodded. He sat down across from the priest and opened a book of photographs. "Do you see the man you saw last night; the man on the phone?"

Gleason pulled his chair closer to the table and leaned in. He ran his fingers across each photograph, moving left to right, row to row. It didn't take long. "This is him. Yes, this is the man."

"You're sure?"

Gleason studied the photograph once again. "Yes, this is the man."

Olivetti looked at the photograph, confirming what he already knew. "Father, for your protection I'm going to detain you as a material witness."

Gleason rose. "You can't do that."

"It's for your own good."

"I can't, I have much to do, much responsibility."

"You don't understand. You could be in danger."

"No one knows what I saw or did not see. I can't be detained. It's impossible."

Olivetti closed the book. "You are not to speak with anyone about this. You understand why?"

"I guess so."

"No, don't 'guess so.' You are the eyewitness to a murder. Don't advertise it."

Gleason nodded. "Can I go?"

Olivetti motioned him to the door.

"Is there anything else you are not telling me, Father?"

Gleason didn't answer.

Olivetti continued, "Last night you said you were up late working on church finances. Is that usual for you?" Gleason fidgeted. "Father?" Olivetti probed.

"Well," he said, "not really. Truth be told, I have found some troubling discrepancies in our books, and I was trying to reconcile the accounts."

"Discrepancies? You mean like there is money missing?"

Gleason nodded.

"Like how much?" Olivetti asked.

Gleason looked at him. "Like all of it," he said. "The church's endowment is gone."

When Gleason left, Olivetti sat back at the table, opened the book, and stared at the photo. Finally, he thought. *Red-handed, I've got him red-handed.* He traced his fingers over the photo of Don Pauly Fazzula.

Santo Olivetti was not happy the day he was first assigned to look into the goings-on at St. Vincent's Hospital. "It's not my field," he argued. "Get a forensic accountant." He was an organized-crime expert and knew nothing about hospitals. He took the assignment reluctantly and soon after realized the two might not be mutually exclusive. He knew that where there was money to be made in New York, organized crime would not be far behind.

As Olivetti drove up to St. Vincent's Hospital, he second-guessed his decision to let Father Gleason leave. If his own investigation into the fraud at Saint Vincent's had made Monsignor Burns a target in some way, perhaps there was a bull's-eye on Gleason, too. He put two detectives on him. "Like white on rice," he said. "Don't let him out of your sight. I want to know anyone who gets close to him."

He pulled his car along a hydrant on Twelfth Street and stood on the sidewalk. St. Vincent's Hospital was an impressive array of buildings spanning an entire city block in the midst of Greenwich Village. It was founded in 1849 by the Sisters of Charity, under the auspices of the Roman Catholic Diocese of Brooklyn.

The hospital had served the people well for more than 160 years. There now was an eerie feel to it after being vacated for filing for bankruptcy a few months earlier, Olivetti noted. He stood in the lobby and looked down the expanse of hallways, imagining the ghosts of patients and doctors who had filled them just months ago. He remembered being here on 9/11 when the hospital became the primary triage for the victims on the day the Towers fell. And now it was empty, thousands of jobs lost, an oasis for lower Manhattan gone—a result of the crime, corruption, greed, and now murder, pillars upon which all Mafia fortunes are built.

He walked into the administrator's office, where a team of forensic accountants from One Police Plaza had set up a makeshift office. They had been working for months, trying to unravel the hospital's books.

"What do you have for me?" he asked.

A young accountant scribbled some notes, then moved back from his computer. "Textbook," he said. "Textbook." He pointed to the Excel spreadsheets on the computer. "This place was a piggy bank, it was bilked of millions, multimillions, maybe a billion over the years."

"How?" Olivetti asked as he followed the cursor moving across the screen.

"The old-fashioned way: union infiltration, rigged billing, theft, bogus donations to bogus charities. You name it."

"How long?"

"Oh, I'd say at least ten years, at least ten. It was pretty easy, actually, considering they had help."

"What do you mean?"

"They had help on the inside, had to."

"What was the end game? Why drain it? What good would that do, to drain it? Why not keep it going, keep the gravy train going?"

"Ah," the young man said, "that's the best part, the cherry on the sundae." He pointed to another stack of papers. "By law, this property can never be sold. Unless . . . "

"Well, unless what?"

"If, and only if, the charity that runs the hospital goes bankrupt, can the property be sold. They were in contract to do just that. Sell the entire complex, for a song, no less."

Olivetti was not surprised by the trail. "How long was Burns the administrator?"

"Ten years," the accountant said.

"Who bid on the buildings?"

"A New York company, Green Apple Development. Probably a shell."

"*Ya think?*"

PART
III

CHAPTER 6

Back in Scottsdale, Tommy paced the floor of his office. Images on the fifty-inch flat-screen caught his eye. He picked up the remote and increased the volume. Neil Cavuto was reporting a breaking news story.

"Yesterday, federal agents swooped in and confiscated all the records of Bernard Madoff. There is speculation that the Ponzi scheme he orchestrated to the tune of fifty billion dollars will have serious repercussions throughout the economy, ensnaring many innocent investors as well."

Tommy's head fell to his chest, and he collapsed back into a chair.

Tommy Rossini had once witnessed an avalanche on a ski trip to Vail. At that time, he was safely perched on the sundeck of a chateau, sipping eggnog laced with cognac. He was surrounded by friends and their acquaintances. He was happy to share. The avalanche itself was stunning, a paradox of nature—awesome, majestic, and deadly. He remembered thinking, *I'm glad I'm not under that*. And now he was, as an avalanche of bankers, creditors, and brokers came down on him.

Tommy had a poker face. He kept balancing all the balls in the air unwilling to admit defeat, but he knew adjustments were ahead. He held off telling Vanna, his own trophy. Love is lovelier the second time around. They were closing in on ten years together, and he knew her as well as he knew anyone. She didn't react well to change, and bankruptcy was a change of sorts. Big change to her was leasing a Lexus instead of a Mercedes. A student loan might be in store for her daughter, who, until now, was on his dime. His life-altering news would be difficult to swallow, but he was sure she would stick with him; for better or for worse and all that stuff. He put off telling her, but the time had come. She met him for dinner at Mastro's. It was her suggestion, her favorite restaurant based on her criteria: $$$$$. He did not want to tip his hand on the phone, explaining why a different choice, like McDonald's, might be advisable; so he agreed.

Ordinarily, he was comfortable in the dimly lit atmosphere of the steak house. Mahogany walls, tuxedoed waiters, top-shelf liquors—they all reeked of money. Tommy was sitting at his usual table sipping a ginger ale when he saw his wife enter. She was late. She did nothing all day, but she was always late. Vanna was a head-turner. She was decked out in a full-length chinchilla coat. Earrings stretched her lobes to her shoulders. Her auburn hair—long, natural, flowing, glowing—and her makeup, airbrushed, accentuated her classic high cheekbones. Full, sensuous lips that needed annual, then biannual, injections of fillers plumped her smile in perpetuity. Still, she was a looker. A tight body hid under a torrent of shopping bags filled with neatly wrapped boxes. Her shopping trips always involved picking up a few necessities, but more often pure luxuries.

Tommy stared at her, doing mental calculations. He didn't like the totals he was coming up with. His stomach made an audible groan as it churned. The restaurant manager commandeered waiters to relieve her of her burdens and take her coat.

"Don't put this with the others," she said as she deftly swooped the chinchilla from her shoulders as effortlessly as Zorro might his cape. A ginger toss of her head propelled her hair backward, capturing it as if in slow motion—a move even Catherine Deneuve would envy.

"As usual, Madame. I'll make sure."

Only then did she relent, her fingers lingering on the furry sleeve. Beneath the fur was the result of hours working with a personal trainer. He'll have to go, Tommy thought. He wasn't sad about that. The thought of that stud working her inner thigh muscles never thrilled him, anyway. A St. John knit accentuated every curve. She flowed to the table, under the gaze of every male patron, and bent to give him a peck on the cheek.

"I've had a day from hell," she said. "My car was stolen. I came out of Neiman's, and it was gone. Be a doll and report it. I had to take a taxi here." Her face contorted, displaying her displeasure. "First I had to return that sweater you didn't like, and the salesgirl had an attitude you wouldn't believe. I don't know why you didn't like it. It was one hundred percent cashmere, very expensive. Anyway, she finally took it back, and

I saw this lovely two-piece suit I just had to have. Anyway, I bought a few things I needed for when we go to Hawaii; and you know, you'll need a few things as well. And after all that, she can't get authorization from Amex . . . a terminal problem, no doubt. Thank God I had cash on me."

"Vanna, I sent you to return the sweater and get the money back. You returned it, and spent the money and more money."

"And your point is?" she said.

This wasn't going to be easy.

The waiter came with menus. "Good evening, Mr. and Mrs. Rossini. It is good of you to dine with us again." He attempted to hand her a menu. She brushed him off.

"I know what I'm having. The shrimp cocktail as an appetizer, and how large are the lobster tails?" she asked.

"Four ounces, Madame," he said.

"Hmm, I'd better take two. I'm famished. And wine? Tommy, have you ordered the wine?"

"No, I . . ."

"I've an idea," she said, cutting him short, "I feel like celebrating. Let's have champagne, a bottle of Cristal," she said.

Tommy heard the groans of his stomach again. The ginger ale wasn't helping.

"And for you, Mr. Rossini? Will it be your usual porterhouse?"

He loosened the collar on his shirt. "No, no! I think I'll do something different tonight." He reached for the menu and studied it. "I'll pass on the appetizer," he said. "And maybe just a large salad. Is that possible?"

"Certainly," the waiter said. "A blue cheese iceberg wedge appetizer, and for your main course?"

"Well, I thought I would just have the salad as the main course. Is that doable?"

"Doable?" he asked.

By his intonation Tommy didn't know if he was questioning his order or the grammatical accuracy of turning a verb into an adjective. "A salad for your entrée, Mr. Rossini?"

Tommy sensed a problem. He had broken some culinary rule. He heard it in the waiter's voice.

"Yes, yes, is that possible?"

"Possible? Why, of course, I *suppose* we can do that for you, sir."

"Well, thank you," Tommy said.

"Would you like anything on the salad, sir?"

Yes, moron. I'd like a porterhouse on the salad, he thought. "Of course he does," Vanna volunteered. "What do you suggest?" she asked.

"Perhaps chicken or steak," the waiter offered.

Chicken has to be cheaper, he thought. "Chicken; chicken works for me."

"Very well, Mr. Rossini."

The waiter left, and Tommy saw him whisper in the manager's ear. An animated discussion ensued, complete with dramatic hand gestures.

"Since when do you eat chicken salad?" Vanna asked.

"It's not chicken salad, it's a salad with chicken on top."

"Whatevvvver," she said.

"Vanna," he said, "we've got to talk."

"Do you like this?" she said. She reached her hand across the table wiggling her freshly manicured nails.

"Very nice," he said. "Nice color."

"Not the nails, silly, the ring. I just had to have it, and you won't believe the price they let it go at."

His eyes bulged out of his head.

"Vanna, did you need another . . . ?"

"It's my birthstone," she said.

"Di-di-diamond?" He finished his question.

"Yes, silly, diamond is for April. My birthstone is diamond. You know that."

Lucky me, he thought. *What month is coal?*

"You had to buy me a birthday present, didn't you?"

"April is six months away."

"Excuse me, Mr. Rossini."

Tommy looked up and saw the manager standing at the table. "Is everything satisfactory?"

"Sure, Mauro, everything is fine."

"Mr. Rossini, I just want to make sure. My waiter is a bit of a, how do you say, numskull. Did you order chicken salad?"

As the manager spoke, Tommy felt the stare of nearby diners. He sensed the whole dining room was involved now.

"No, no! I ordered the salad with chicken," Tommy spoke softly, trying to set an example for Mauro.

"Fine, sir! I'm just checking because we know how much you love the porterhouse here at Mastro's, and I just want to make sure we have done nothing wrong."

"No, Mauro, everything is . . ."

"I told him, Mauro," Vanna interjected. "I told him, why are you ordering chicken salad in a steak house when you love steak? It doesn't make any sense to me either." She flicked her finger, trying to reflect the light from the candle into the diamond baguettes.

Tommy was sweating. "I'm just not very hungry tonight, Mauro. That's all."

"Very well, sir, chicken salad it is!" he said emphatically.

Tommy felt flushed.

"I told you," Vanna said.

"It's not chicken salad; it's a salad with chicken," Tommy explained.

"Whatevvvver."

The pop of the champagne bottle coincided with his gastric distress. The waiter poured it into cut-crystal flutes.

He watched her eat the shrimp cocktail, six huge shrimp as he counted. She did not offer him any. *Maybe because I said I wasn't hungry*, he thought. Her lobster tails looked more like six ounces than four. They were grilled to perfection, and she ate them with expertise.

"How's your chicken salad?" she asked.

"Fine."

"You're quiet tonight. Are you okay?"

Praise the Lord, she noticed.

"Well, not really," he said. "That's what I needed to talk to you about."

"Well, how could you be all right? You're eating like a bird. You should have had a steak. You need protein."

"Enough of the friggin' steak already."

"What's with you?" she asked. "You don't seem to be yourself."

"Vanna." His mouth was dry. "Vanna, darling."

"Excuse me, have you left room for dessert?" the waiter asked. "Should you choose the soufflé, it will take time to prepare."

Pushy bastard, Tommy thought. "Not for me."

Vanna wiped her lips. "Just coffee," she said.

Thank God, he thought, *she didn't order the soufflé.* He handed the waiter his credit card. "Just the check as well, when you are ready."

He tried again. "Vanna, I must talk to you."

"Okay, talk. Is it about Hawaii?"

"No, not about Hawaii. Well, that's not true. It is about Hawaii, in a way." In a way like there is no more Hawaii.

"I can't wait to get there. I like it here, but only because I know we can get away from the wretched cold we're in for."

"Vanna, I need to talk to you. I'm trying to tell you something that is very important to both of us."

"Well, go ahead then."

"I, I just don't know where to begin, or how to explain. I don't know how to tell you . . . I'm not sure I understand it myself."

The waiter came to the table and whispered, "Mr. Rossini, there seems to be a problem."

She looked up from studying the intricate ways light refracted off her ring.

"Your card has been denied," he said. "I'm sure it is a mistake of some kind."

Well, that's as good a way as any to broach the subject, Tommy thought. He wanted to hide under the table, but it would have been cramped. Vanna was already there.

~ ❧ ~

Slowly at first, then faster and faster, the extent of the financial debacle revealed itself. The unraveling was like Chinese water torture. Creditors repossessed all his valuables and auctioned them off for pennies on the dollar. The ranch now had a lien on it. The centerpiece of his great room took the first hit with the sale of the baby grand player piano. He watched as men in coveralls rolled it out the door, taking a thousand memories with it. He recalled the countless parties where his friends and their friends gravitated to the baby grand. He wondered, where were they now? No phone calls were returned.

Vanna was the last asset to go. She blamed him for not being more careful with the family finances. She didn't buy into his better or worse, richer or poorer pleadings. Things were better when they were richer. He sat in the center of the empty ranch. There was glass all around him with stunning vistas, a place he had called home. He saw men erecting a sign on the front yard; the word FORECLOSED was in red.

He walked over to the window and looked down over the cliff. *It's over*, he thought. *The work of twenty-five years, the rewards for hard work, the perks, the people, the good life, all gone because of some shmuck. Who was the shmuck?* he thought. He stared at the pearl-handled pistol in his palm. It was a fleeting thought, nothing more than that. That's not the answer, he decided. Time to go home.

PART
IV

CHAPTER 7

*L*ater on the very day his brother had hung up on him, Jake Rossini was falling in and out of consciousness, in a diabetic coma in the ICU of Aventura Hospital. He had no way of knowing gangrene had already eaten his toes and the infection was spreading. In his medicated state, he thought he saw his ex-wife huddled with doctors near his bed. He was almost happy; she had forgiven him. Love conquered all; and in the end, she came to his side. *Not surprising,* he thought. *I'm irresistible. Thank God,* he remembered thinking, *she will take me back. Her choices, after all, are limited. Her father will have to forgive me. Of course he will. I was the only suitor who was stupid enough to take her off his hands. There had to be some points for that. Rest, rest,* he told himself. *You will be back on your yacht before you can say "vendetta."*

Snippets of the medical explanation the doctors were providing circulated in his brain. The foot must go, they explained, in order to stop the infection. There was talk about circulation or a lack of circulation and talk of time being of the essence. He didn't understand, but knew he was in good hands. She would save him.

In an outer room his wife was deferring to a higher authority for medical decisions. Fat Don Pauly Beans Fazzula, affectionately known as Fat Pauly Beans to those few who loved him, was the de facto healthcare proxy.

Don Fazzula sat in the private waiting room outside the ICU hoping to be of some help with his daughter's medical decisions. He sat critiquing a rerun episode of *The Sopranos* playing on television, disappointed in some of the language and other stylistic details. He brushed the brim of the Borsalino fedora he held as he awaited word of his son-in-law's condition.

Medical terminology, or big words of any kind, were not Bernadette's strong suit. She was happy that her father had accompanied her. He was always there when she needed him. Always there to help with the big decisions, like whom to marry, where to marry, where to invest the wedding boost, where to live, to have or not have children, where to spend her holidays.

"If they don't amputate his foot," she explained to her father, "the infection will spread up his leg."

Don Fazzula digested the information. "You know, Bernadette, these doctors think they're God. Really, what do they know? I think you should wait."

As the infection moved up the leg, her reports became dire.

"The doctors said, 'Amputation is unavoidable.' If it is done now, it can be amputated below the knee, and it will be easier for him to learn to walk."

Don Fazzula fingered the brim of his hat again. "I think we should wait," he said. Then he said, "You know, God is in charge here. We can hope for a miracle."

Bernadette thought it odd to hear her father mention God without *damn it* following, but she agreed. Her father was never wrong. It was two days later that she reported the infection was above the knee and God must have other things on his mind.

"Above the knee?" he asked.

She nodded, teary-eyed.

"Stop crying," he said. "You know I'm a sucker for tears." Then, in the best medical terminology he could muster, he said, "Okay, tell them to chop it off. It's a start, anyway."

He put on his hat and walked out, satisfied that he had done all he could; to that point.

"I'll catch up with you later. I've got to stop at the admissions office to take care of a little matter."

"Thank you, Daddy."

CHAPTER 8

After two days, Jake Rossini opened his eyes, post-op, in the ICU. The room was dark. He was disoriented. He had a major-league headache. Daylight was just beginning to peek through drawn window blinds. He adjusted his eyes to get his bearings. An oxygen tube snaked from his face, lines in his arms disappeared into the fold of antiseptic white sheets, and machines at the bedside emitted methodic beeps to the rhythm of blinking red and green lights. He tried to remember the last vivid thought he'd had. It came to him. He was at his wine bar and bistro, the Blue Note, singing a Sinatra tune, "Summer Wind." Somewhere in the middle of "*Black painted kites, those days and nights,*" he went flying off the stage. The lights went out. When was that? He had no idea. Time was a blur. He felt his face, scruffy, a few days' growth, he figured; hard to tell. A quintessential metrosexual, he looked at his fingers and was overcome with horror. *Oh my God,* he thought. *My nails haven't been manicured. How long have I been in here?*

I've got to get out of here, he thought. He had no strength to move. Groggy and disoriented, he tried to swing his legs off the bed. *That felt funny,* he thought. He moved his right hand to his stomach, then across his hip and thigh, then to . . . nothing; nothing. His screams could be heard echoing down the linoleum hallways of Aventura Hospital. "No, no! My leg, my leg!"

Out of the shadow a figure approached his bed. Jake felt a hand covering his mouth, muffling his screams. It was cold, the skin soft, with a suggestion of moisturizer.

"There, there," a voice said, "it's gonna be all right."

In a drug-induced stupor he saw the figure at his bedside. He recognized his father-in-law, Don Pauly Fazzula, *his fedora tilted down on his brow, to cover horns,* Jake thought. Fazzula caressed the tube of the morphine drip, tenderly sliding his fingers up and down the clear plastic, as if admiring a string of pearls.

Jake realized who had made the medical decision.

"Why didn't you let me die?" Jake asked. "Why didn't you let me die?"

Fazzula sat back in a chair and crossed his legs. "You know, Jake, when I was a boy on a farm in Sicily, I met a farmer who had a pig with three legs. I asked him why he didn't kill the pig and put it out of its misery. He became quite indignant. 'Young man,' he said, 'when there was a fire in our home one night, it was this pig that banged his snout on the door to awaken me; and that saved our family. When my boy was stuck under the tractor in the fields, it was this pig that came and squealed until I followed it and found my boy. No . . . a pig like this,' the farmer said, 'you don't eat all at once.'"

Fazzula rose again, stroking the intravenous line between his meaty fingers. "Everything you lean on, I'm gonna take away," he said. He pinched the tube as Jake started to yell, then he released it, and turned to leave as a contingent of nurses invaded Jake's room, shouting orders to each other. One swabbed alcohol on Jake's arm while another prepared a sedative to calm him.

"*Dormi bene,*" Fazzula said as he walked out the door.

CHAPTER 9

The hamlet of Richmond in Staten Island, one of the five boroughs of New York City, is a neighborhood of row houses dedicated to blue-collar workers who during the day run the trains, police the streets, collect the garbage, and extinguish fires in Manhattan; and who at night leave the asphalt madhouse for quieter pastures on the other side of the Verrazano Bridge. On his side of a two-family town-home, Phil, aka Looney Rossini, studied the thermostat. He lowered it to sixty degrees and listened to make sure the furnace shut down. Then he buttoned his sweater and sat in his La-Z-Boy recliner. *Global warming my ass,* he thought. He covered himself with an afghan and looked for the remote. Not on his left side or right, not between his legs. He pushed his hand under the seat cushion, right and left. Then he saw it, on the end table in front of him. Damn it!

"Penny, Penny," he yelled. "Penny!"

He heard her from deep in the basement. "What?"

Damn it. "Where are you?" He knew. "Can you get me the remote?"

"Get off your fat ass and get it yourself!" she yelled from the laundry room.

He extended his foot, thinking he might be able to knock it off and then help it along the floor until he could reach it—anything not to leave the chair where he'd just gotten comfortable. It didn't work. He extended his leg toward the end table. The table was just out of reach. He contorted his body to get an extra-inch extension, and suddenly he was in the grip of both a charley horse and a cramp in his side. He writhed in pain, trying to stretch his leg against the muscle contraction. That made it worse as two more cramps gripped his back. He fell to the floor, squirming and stretching this way and that until he felt both muscles relax. *I'm such a moron,* he admitted to himself. *Good thing no one saw me.*

Back in his chair, he adjusted the blanket on his lap. After a few adjustments he reclined, warm, ready for the night that included two rerun episodes of *Everybody Loves Raymond,* followed by *The Golden Girls, Seinfeld,* and *Frazier. Life is good,* he thought.

He dozed off moments into *Raymond.* But for the phone ringing, he would have remained there until bedtime. He wiped drool off his chin. He had one phone, on the kitchen wall. Also out of reach. His wife was still in the basement. He tried to remember just how much laundry she had in the basket. If he calculated right, she might be appearing on the top of the steps by the third ring. Third ring, fourth, fifth ring. More laundry than he thought, confirmed when he heard her yell from the basement, "Pick up the damn phone, Looney!"

"Hello!" he yelled, ready to give hell to someone trying to sell him insurance.

"Looney?"

"Who is this?"

"Tommy."

"Tommy?"

"Yeah, me, your brother Tommy."

"Hey, what's up? Why are you calling?"

"Does there have to be a reason? Can't I just call?"

"Yeah, you can, but you never do. What's up?"

"Listen, I'm coming in to see Mom. Can you pick me up at Kennedy?"

"Kennedy, Jesus, I hate that place!"

"It's not far from you."

"I know, but the traffic is terrible. When are you coming in?"

"I land at five on Sunday."

"Five!" Looney shouted. "Christ, that's late. Do you know what traffic is like to Kennedy on Sunday night? I'll be sitting in traffic!"

Tommy cut him short. "Not five at night, five in the morning."

"Five in the morning!" His voice elevated. "I'll have to get up at four. Christ, I got to go to work. I've got things to do. Why so early?"

"I got a ticket on my frequent flyer miles, and the flights are restricted." He was sorry he'd offered the explanation. "Listen, forget it. I'll take care of it."

"You sure?"

"Yeah."

"Okay, because if you're stuck, I could change some things around . . . if you really wanted."

It's five in the morning, moron. What could you possibly be doing?
"No, I'll be fine. Will I see you?"

"I don't know. When are you leaving?"

I didn't get there yet. "I may stay for Christmas," Tommy said.

"Christmas?" Looney did some quick calculations. "Jesus, that's a couple of months from now."

"So, will you be down to the neighborhood?"

"Yeah, I should be down to see you. Where are you staying?"

Tommy hesitated, not believing his answer. "At Mom's, I think. It'll be good to spend some time with her."

"You're staying at Mom's? Where are you going to sleep? Does she know?"

"Not yet," Tommy admitted. "I thought I'd surprise her."

There was silence on the line. "Yeah, you'll surprise her for sure."

"So, will you be down, or maybe I can take Mom and come out there for dinner," Tommy suggested, more so to twist balls. It worked. He heard Looney gag. "Are you all right?"

"Fine, fine," he said, coughing. "No, I said, of course, I'll see you downtown. I'll talk to you."

CHAPTER 10

Back at the ICU, Jake Rossini opened his eyes again. The first face he saw was Bernadette's, complete with a fifties-style beehive hairdo. She leaned in to kiss him. His mouth was dry.

"Jake, Jake. Can you hear me?"

There was another voice. "Mr. Rossini, I'm Dr. Page. I was your surgeon. I want you to know that everything went very well. You're a lucky man, you have your wife to thank. You are lucky to be alive. Do you hear me? Dr. Guinness is here as well. He's our staff psychiatrist. He's here to help you deal with any issues you may have."

"What are you talking about? Where am I?"

"You're in the hospital, Jake. You collapsed. They had to perform surgery immediately. Do you recall anything?"

Still confused, he looked toward Bernadette. "Why are you here?"

The doctors exchanged glances.

"Jake," she said. "I'll take care of you."

"No," he said. "No. Please go." His voice was hoarse, his eyes watery.

"He's still under the effects of medication," Dr. Page offered.

"Get her out of here, get her out of here!" Jake yelled.

Bernadette began crying. She turned and ran out the door.

"Mr. Rossini, you've been through a traumatic, life-changing event."

Yes, my marriage, Jake thought.

"It's only natural for you to be bitter. How's the pain? Can we get you anything for the pain?"

"Sabrina," he said. "Where's Sabrina?"

The doctors looked at each other.

Dr. Page said, "Mr. Rossini, your wife, Bernadette, has been here with you. She has saved your life by giving us permission to amputate your leg."

Those words were clear. It was all clear now. That wasn't a dream. He reached down his right thigh again to nothing. His screams were whimpers now, mournful whimpers.

"Mr. Rossini, I know how you must feel. But please know, with therapy you will be up and around in a few months. As soon as you're home, we can arrange for that therapy."

"Home?"

"Yes, because of your lack of insurance you will have to complete your treatment at home. Is there anything you need now?"

"Sabrina," he said. He pointed to the closet. "My wallet," he said. The doctor obliged. He got the wallet and looked for Sabrina's phone number.

"I will call her for you," he said.

Later that day all heads turned in the lobby of Aventura Hospital. Sabrina, looking like she just stepped out of the pages of *Seventeen* magazine, sashayed through the halls. She wore a revealing miniskirt, white kneesocks, and a halter top.

"Jakeypoo?"

She walked over to his bed. "What are you doing here?"

"Sabrina, thank God you're here." He reached his arms out to her, but she stayed her distance.

"I hate these places," she said. "They're like . . . hospitals." She blew a bubble and continued chewing.

"Sabrina, I hate them, too. How are you, baby?"

"Great," she said. "And what's new with you? You need a shave."

"I don't know what happened. Best I can remember I collapsed and woke up here. They performed surgery."

"Really," she said. "That sounds, like, serious."

"It was; there was an amputation."

She blew a bubble. He saw she was confused. "That's because I had sugar," he explained. "It was out of control."

"I use Equal," she said. "You should use Equal from now on. Well, I have to go."

"Wait, wait, please sit down and stay awhile."

She looked around the room. "I really don't like these places. They gross me out."

She sat in a chair by the window, peeking through the blinds. "So, did they take your appendix out or something?"

"My appendix?" He shook his head. "No, no, it was an amputation. My leg, they amputated my . . ." He couldn't finish the sentence.

Sabrina digested the information as she eyed his shape beneath the covers. Her eyes came to rest on the bottom of the bed where one foot was visible. She began to gag. She spat her gum out, and ran to the bathroom. He heard her choking.

"Sabrina, are you all right? Are you okay, baby?" he called to her. There was no answer.

"Listen," he said. "I thought I might be able to crash at your place until I get back on my feet." That sounded odd, even to him.

She appeared in the doorway. She was pale. "You mean you have no foot?"

"I don't know. From what I understand they had to amputate above my knee to stop the infection from spreading."

Sabrina was pale now and ran back to the sink. As she coughed and gagged, he continued talking, louder to be heard above the gastric demonstrations. "I thought I could come back to your place and recover."

She appeared in the doorway again. "Jake," she said, "I don't know how to tell you this, but we are so over. It's been coming for a long time. I was going to tell you that there's been another man in my life."

"Sabrina, I want to marry you. I'm divorced now. I'm free."

"Married? I don't want to get married."

"Don't you understand? We don't have to sneak around anymore."

"I didn't mind sneaking around. It was so fun."

"But I thought . . ."

"Listen, Jake, you were a good guy and what we had was real, but not forever. It had to end. You had to know that. There were signs."

"Signs?"

"Yeah, like warnings."

"I guess I missed them."

"I guess," she agreed. "You must know the sex wasn't great anymore. I used to scream, but not lately. Edgar makes me scream."

"Edgar?"

"Yes, he drove me here. He's downstairs waiting." She walked over to the window. "See," she said, "there he is in his Maserati Quattroporte. I'd better go." She waved to Edgar.

He reached his arms out to her. If he could hug her once, she would come to her senses, he was sure. She did not advance to the bed, but instead puckered her lips and sent a kiss in his direction. His mouth remained open as she turned and left.

His head collapsed back into the pillow. He was drained. The pain was getting worse and was coming from all directions. There was pain in his heart and pain in his body, pain in a leg that wasn't even there. He was angry with himself. *I really did it this time, didn't I?* he thought—*fixed things really good.* With a deep breath he took stock of his situation. He increased the morphine drip. He recalled the days when he had it all: cars, houses, a wife, women on the side, money, clothes, jewelry, and more women on the side. He recalled the days when just his mere appearance in a restaurant's lobby would get managers and waiters scurrying around. He was larger than life, a presence.

He saw a dome-covered plate and plastic utensils alongside his bed. He could never live without the necessities of life—without money and all it bought; without his leg and all it meant to his dignity. He reached for the knife and cut a slit into his wrist. The plastic knife was dull, and he hardly broke the skin. *I can't even do this right,* he thought. He went back and forth in a sawing motion until blood appeared. Then he closed his eyes.

The attempt failed, but it bought Jake an extra two days in the hospital, this time in the psychiatric ward. Not enough time, as Dr. Guinness saw it, to unravel a lifetime of self-esteem issues, with underlying self-loathing and a touch of self-indulgence with signs of depression; but without insurance, it was the best they could offer.

"Isn't there anyone you could call, Jake?"

Jake sat in a wheelchair facing the window, wearing a hospital gown. "Jake, you are more than your limbs. You're a person with more value and worth than the sum total of your appendages."

He was unresponsive. "Is there someone you could call, Jake?" Dr. Guinness asked.

It was an interesting question. He went down the list. He couldn't call his brother Tommy; his wife, Bernadette; his father-in-law, Pauly; or Sabrina. *Maybe Edgar,* he thought sarcastically. No. That left Looney.

Looney answered; and after some small talk, Jake got into his situation. It was a one-way conversation ending with, " . . . so they had to take my leg off."

"Christ, Jake! Why didn't you take care of yourself?"

He sounds genuinely concerned, Jake thought.

"Just a bad break, that's all," Jake assured him. "I had a lot of irons in the fire. Things were beginning to click. A few more months, I would have turned a corner with the Blue Note. It was the talk of the strip. I've still got some things going. I have some big-time investors reaching out to me. Things will turn around."

"Well, good; good for you, Jake. I'm sure you'll bounce back. You'll be back on your feet in no time."

Right, asshole, Jake thought. He realized only his idiot brother would use that analogy, but this was not time to piss him off. Instead, he swallowed hard and summoned all the tact he could. "Yeah, yeah, no doubt I will. In the meantime, though, I was thinking about a place to stay for a while until I'm able to get around. I thought I might crash in your basement. There's a bedroom and bathroom there, and it would be easier for me." There was silence. He expected it.

"Looney, Looney, are you there?"

"Uh . . . yes, yes. Jeez, Jake, I don't know. You know, we were planning a trip to Hershey next week; and my son will be coming home, and he'll need his room; and Penny's mother might stay with us for Thanksgiving; and my car is in the shop and . . ."

"Looney, Looney," he said. "Enough, enough. I'll talk to you soon."

"Are you sure?" Looney said. "'Cause if you want. I could juggle a few things around . . ."

Juggle this, he thought grabbing his crotch. "I'll figure it out."

"Okay, then, and hey, good luck with that leg thing."

"Yeah, thanks."

"Where will *you* be staying?"

"Not much of a choice now. Mom's, I guess."

"Mom's? Where are you going to sleep?"

"Our old room, why are you asking?"

"No, no reason," he said.

"Right, see you soon." Jake hung up.

As the day for his release came closer, Dr. Page kept asking, "Is there anyone we can call? Anywhere you can go?"

"Home," he said. "I'll have to go home."

PART
V

CHAPTER 11

*T*ommy's travel plans changed at the last minute. His frequent flyer miles were canceled along with his credit cards. He voiced his displeasure with the system. "Those points were banked, bought, and paid for," he argued. He thought about getting louder, but had already gotten the attention of the TSA; and the last thing he needed was to have his briefcase searched.

Tommy was forced to take the scenic route. He boarded a Greyhound and headed home. Looney wouldn't have to pick him up after all. It was Tommy's first trip on a bus, and he was resigned to rough it with the little people. His carry-on duffle bag stayed with him, as did a small attaché. It held an array of heart meds and the sum total of everything he had left; sixteen thousand dollars, in cash. Vanna overlooked *that* shoe box, although she found three others that Tommy had stowed away for a rainy day. Come the revolution, he would say, cash will be king.

This was to be seed money. He would use the time on the bus to put a plan together. *I'm not afraid of work, never was,* he thought. He knew the bottom had dropped out of the construction business, and he also knew things weren't much better in New York. But he still had some friends, some connections; and if worse came to worse, there was always Don Pauly Fazzula—the very one he ran away from.

New York, that's where he would stage his comeback. *Like the song said,* he thought, *if you can make it there, you'll make it anywhere.* Tommy was not accustomed to being down-and-out. He knew he would have to find a way to parlay the cash in his hand, to rebuild his empire, his life. It wouldn't be easy; it never is in New York. He'd have to mend some fences, kiss some asses. He thought about his mother: *She'll be so happy to see me again.* He called and told her he was coming home, or tried to. He rested his head, reclined his chair, and fell asleep recalling the conversation with no beginning, no end, and no understanding. "What are you doing, Mom?"

"What can I be doing?"

"I have some good news for you."

"I don't need new shoes. I don't get out much."

"No, Ma, not shoes . . . news."

"What's shoes news?"

Get to the point, he thought. "I'm coming home, Ma."

"Who's this?"

Right, he thought. *I can't wait.*

He thought about some positive things about being home. Maybe she'll make meatballs. That was a good memory. He and his brothers would wait as his mother fried meatballs in a skillet. The smell of the meat frying in a pan with oil, parsley, and garlic opened his nasal cavity. Still hot, a few of the meatballs would be commandeered and placed into a wedge of seeded Italian bread. She yelled, but she somehow always made enough to withstand the pilferage. The remainder would be put into the pot of red sauce simmering on the stove. His mother made a great sauce; not bad for an Irishwoman, his father would say as he loosened his pants after a Sunday dinner. That's when her hand knocked a glass of water into his lap as she cleaned the table.

"Christ!" his father would yell.

"Oops," she'd say with a wink in his direction.

Tommy had a lot of time to think on the bus. He had a slight headache and his hand ached. He had not been back in some time, a few Christmases from what he could remember; even more, he conceded. There always seemed to be a reason that prevented him from going east. His mother understood. He was busy, working, working. It was a trait she instilled in him. He would have no reason to go east at all, if not for her. He left that rat race for a reason. The stress was killing him. His demolition business was thriving, but the bid system kept him up nights.

The various trade unions were controlled by five crime families. The largest contractors in the world competed for every skyscraper built or torn down in the city. No building in New York City went up or came down without the nod from a Mustache Pete or in his case, Don Pauly Fazzula.

He sat in on many meetings held in the backroom of a dingy café on Sullivan Street where multimillion-dollar decisions were made.

The discussion among mob hierarchy, a study in eloquence, usually started and ended with one of the ball-scratching *goumbas* saying, "It's my turn. This job goes to my boy Tommy."

Soon after "winning" a bid, Tommy would be introduced to six to twelve of the closest relatives and friends of the *caporegime*. The mousse-haired no-shows appeared once a week for their paychecks. Sometimes just one of the fellas was sent to pick up the checks for all the others. With the price of gasoline, that was more economically practical while ensuring that only one of the group of ne'er-do-wells had to actually get out of bed and do something. Tommy knew the game. His bid always included 15 to 20 percent for the boys on Sullivan Street. It ensured that the dumpsters kept moving, that the concrete kept flowing, and that there would be no union problems.

The system worked for the most part, but Tommy never knew if he was stepping on someone's toes. That's where the stress came in, as he explained his decision to his brothers.

"I've got to get out. If I accept a bid out of turn, I could wind up in a cement footing, never to be found or be found slumped over the wheel of my car. They could use me to send a message to other freelancers thinking of disregarding the contracting rules in the ever-changing mind of these mob elders."

"Ah, you're crazy," Jake argued. "These are honorable men."

"And you are a moron. Honor went out the window with these guys long ago. And what do you know about the endless favors that become more and more difficult to fulfill? I don't sleep anymore."

"You should be proud," Jake said. "You have a much-deserved reputation on the street as Fazzula's muscle. You earned it."

"Thanks," Tommy said.

Fazzula was an expert in carrot-and-stick diplomacy. Hit someone with a stick, and he gave you all his carrots. Tommy began to get nervous of what he was capable of doing to achieve success. His muscular frame and large hands came in handy to the Don who had a knack for discovering young talent. Tommy found out at an early age he wasn't above throwing a punch to deliver a message from the Don. Sometimes just the sight of his intimidating, huge body was enough to convince a would-be freelancer to reconsider; but more often than not, he'd be forced to wield the stick. There seemed to be more and more that needed his special brand of convincing. And for his ruthlessness, Tommy Rossini was on a fast track—fast track to a heart attack.

As the bus rolled along, the light posts along the interstate morphed seamlessly into the line of fluorescent lights on the ceiling of the linoleum hallway leading to the operating room at St. Vincent's Hospital in Greenwich Village. He was thirty years old when he felt his insides trembling and sweat pouring from his body moments before feeling a vise squeezing his chest. He remembered sensing he was in a tunnel. He recalled stories of near-death experiences where there were reports of a tunnel leading to a great white light. Was he there now? Was this it for him? A woman surfing the gurney alongside him intruded on his moment. "Is there anyone we can notify? Stay with us. Is there anyone we can notify?"

A cracked sternum and a triple bypass later, he felt as good as new; that is, if one could be considered as good as new with three quarters of his heart muscle dead.

As he recovered, a gang war raged on the streets—a murder on Elizabeth Street followed by a shootout in a café on Mott, followed by a
body found in a trunk on Prince Street. He was able to connect the
dots. Infighting, house cleaning, a purge was taking place. He was
safe in a hospital for now, and that's when he made the decision. He
would leave New York, where more and more would be asked of him.

He took his expertise and street smarts and headed for greener
pastures, Arizona. With the excuse of his medical condition, and a
note from his doctor, Fazzula and Co. granted his request for a medical leave. The *goumbas* were sorry to see him go. He was a good
earner, and his intimidating frame had come in handy more than
once during delicate union negotiations. That was thirty years ago.
It was the best move he had ever made, notwithstanding it having
caused the occasional nightmare of his mother crying on the sidewalk as he waved good-bye.

In a few days he would be home. He patted the attaché. It would
have to last a while until he got back on his feet.

At New York's Port Authority, the armpit of Manhattan, Tommy
Rossini was already having second thoughts. He had forgotten the
madhouse that was New York. He looked at the skyline; no sky. The
air was thick with smog. The street littered with trash. The little hot
dog pushcarts with the quaint Sabrett umbrellas he remembered were
now grotesque aluminum menageries selling everything from roasted
chestnuts to gyros, from sausages to pastrami, from Thai to curry, all

with corresponding hawkers and all of it buried in a foot of trash. He was getting nauseous from the competing odors that rose from the greasy grills and steaming pots.

As he took in the sights, he stepped off the curb, oblivious to the bus barreling toward him and to the blaring horn swallowed up in a cacophony of other sounds. Only a last-minute tug from a pick-pocket saved him.

"Christ!" he yelled. He looked at the man. "Thank you," he said. "You saved my life."

"Hey, ya gotta be careful," the man said as he brushed Tommy off.

"Thanks, thanks," he said as the man kept walking.

The revelation came to him, not a moment later. He checked his back pocket; his wallet was gone. Christ, he said, as his eyes roamed the crowd. His savior had melded into a pedestrian sea, with his wallet. He punched the air, mad at himself for not knowing better. *How appropriate,* he thought, *in the first minute home I'm practically run down—splattered across a row of fast-food concessions—and pick-pocketed. He was good, I'll give him that,* he thought. Gotta love this town. The laugh is on him, though. Those cards are canceled, but he did get a good snakeskin wallet and three hundred dollars. Not a bad day's work.

After the near miss, he stretched, as every bone in his body registered their disapproval with his mode of transportation. His lungs took in a gulp of exhaust and returned the favor with phlegm, registering their disapproval with his destination. He cleared his throat and hailed a taxi. Four cabs cut across three lanes of oncoming traffic vying for his business. The winner stopped at his feet. The taxi took off before the door closed, sending him careening backward into the springless backseat. As it made its way down the West Side Highway, the taxi fought for every advantage in the vehicular jungle. It was coming back to him, the madness. The Hudson River was restless, with whitecaps slapping the hulls of freighters transporting cargo. New Jersey lay across the river, dark, gray, and uninviting. As the taxi approached lower Manhattan and Canal Street, Tommy leaned forward and stared farther south to where the Twin Towers once stood, but were no more. Visible only by their absence, still a gaping hole in Manhattan's horizon years after they fell.

"Those bastards," he said out loud.

"Excuse me?" the driver said.

Still staring, he repeated, "Those Muslim bastards."

The driver turned his head, face to face with Tommy; and only then did Tommy notice the colorful knit kufi. He looked at the license on the partition, Mohammed something or other. He leaned back. *Great*, he thought. "Maybe I'll get out here," he suggested.

Mohammed had the same idea; he pulled over to the curb on Varick Street.

Tommy took a twenty from his jacket pocket, handed it through the driver's window, and waited for change. Instead, the taxi sped away. Then he realized he had left his attaché on the backseat. His seed money was speeding down the West Side Highway, kidnapped by a terrorist. "Bastard!" he yelled, his cries lost amidst the hum of cars, trucks, horns, and helicopters all conspiring to create the city's symphony. He waved to a police officer in a passing cruiser. The officer waved back. *New York's finest*, he thought.

Now, in New York for twenty minutes, he had less than when he left Arizona. The city extracts a toll. Not a good start!

Walking east brought him further into a time warp. Each step propelled him deeper into a valley of antiquity. A far cry from the expanse of the west. This was a neighborhood of walk-up five-story brick tenements surrounded by expressionless glass skyscrapers built on steel pilings drilled deep into the island's bedrock. They stood aloof, cold and unfeeling, like the palace guard ready to repel intruders. He saw it now, as if he had discovered it for the first time. His old neighborhood, an archeological dig, relics left untouched by all encroaching modernity, silent testimony to a distant past. Here too, in this Old World corner of Manhattan, the clock had not moved, like in Pompeii or Herculaneum. Rusted wrought iron fire escapes clung to chipping brick façades on turn-of-the-century buildings. Widows and homebound, with aged faces, their torsos framed in window panes, shared ledges with pigeons and stone gargoyles cemented in time, frozen like one-dimensional black-and-white photos.

On the sidewalks, white-apron-clad vendors hawked fruits and vegetables; and behind the windows of the same shops with sawdust-covered floors, old-fashioned butchers boned legs of veal and wielded scaloppine hammers with a deftness passed through the genes of their fathers and their fathers' fathers before them. He paused by Forzano's Italian Imports. The windowpane became a time machine. He spotted the owner where he had seen her a thousand times before. She was unmistakable, for he had imagined her every night, a mental picture of her had been embedded in his mind. He studied the woman, seeking hints of the girl he left behind. She had aged well. Gray highlights had taken the place of auburn. He was back on the tenement's roof, tar beach, with her in his arms. Beneath a blanket of stars and with only pigeons as voyeurs, he pressed between her legs, never feeling so free, so alive, so in love. This was the way he left it, wishing now he had never left at all.

But leave he did. He left her, the streets, the life. And now he was back, not by choice. He stood on the corner of Mulberry and Grand Streets, and looked up at the building where it all began. In a three-room apartment that had not changed in one hundred years. Due to the unlikely union of his parents, this was home.

CHAPTER 12

An unlikely union, because as he understood from dinner-table banter, the 1948 marriage of Margaret Sheen and Carlo Rossini was, in his father's jargon, a long shot. It was considered a mixed marriage between a dago and a mick. "My friends were betting on the under and over," his father would quip.

"I should have listened to my mother," his mother used to respond, with a wink.

The story was recounted often at the dinner table, and it was never the same. Carlo and Maddie used the tale to jab at each other. Tommy sensed an underlying playfulness between them, or hoped he did. It seems beer and wine flowed at their reception held at the Knights of Columbus meeting hall on Grand Street. "As if alcohol could dull my father's pain," Maddie used to say.

"He certainly thought it could. Drank enough of it," Carlo would remind her.

The Sheens were none too happy with their daughter's choice of a husband. They would have preferred she had stayed within her tribe. The Rossinis felt the same way.

The Sheens moved from the Mulberry Street tenement where they had resided since the building was constructed in 1908 up to the Inwood section of upper Manhattan, leaving their daughter to fend for herself among foreigners. "They couldn't wait to hightail it out of town," Carlo joked. That's when a glass would spill into his lap.

"Oops," his mother would say as she winked at him, "it was an accident."

The Irish-Italian mix was a fiery one, a clash of cultures. Maddie Rossini learned to enjoy a glass of red wine, and Carlo learned to chase a shot of Jameson down with a cold beer, or two, or three. "Always drink a beer," he advised his boys. "You don't want to get dehydrated or get a hangover." Tommy remembered that the advice usually came as he and his brothers watched their father heaving into the kitchen sink.

Carlo was an unskilled laborer. It didn't take much skill to work as a low-level numbers runner. He lived from day to day and struggled to put food on the table. What he earned often went on a hunch, a sure thing at Belmont; and often his hunches were wrong. That left Maddie to make sure there was some steady source of income. She cleaned the school cafeteria by day, and at night she did piecework on a Singer sewing machine for a local garment factory.

Tommy remembered that every Friday after the last race was

called, Carlo left the café to prepare to take his family to his cousin's Lake Ronkonkoma bungalow. It was a weekend ritual. He'd proceed to the garage on Broome Street, a few blocks north up Mulberry. Exactly three hours later he'd return with his pride and joy, a classic late-model Bonneville, mint condition, burgundy with leather seats and electric windows. A few last wipes with a cloth rag while Maddie gathered her boys, and they were off to their weekend getaway. Ronkonkoma, on Long Island, was a safe haven away from the madding crowd; and Carlo would help his cousin complete his dream house. There were always repairs to be done on the house. "One of these days," his father would say, after a glass of Chianti, "I'm gonna buy my own dilapidated bungalow and retire there." Carlo Rossini retired early. Not in Ronkonkoma.

Carlo Rossini was Hollywood handsome. He had a medium build, dark eyes, and shiny, sleek black hair. As a bookie he was all over the streets, making stop after stop. He was, by reputation, a ladies' man. A well-deserved reputation as his son Tommy discovered on the day his father died. Tommy paused as he climbed the stairs to his mother's apartment, his mind floating back to that very moment. He relived that day when he was called upon to break the news to his mother. He paused against the banister, which swayed beneath his weight. The hallway's peeling painted walls closed in on him. He felt an internal tremor, a pounding in his chest, sweat beginning to form on his brow.

His father died on a Friday afternoon. Tommy was in the aisle at Falco's grocery store stacking Ronzoni macaroni on the shelf. Like a solar eclipse, the man who appeared at the end of the aisle blocked the ceiling lights and cast a long shadow. Thinking back now, the undertaker was a blur to him. He was tall and lanky, with a black-and-white striped bow tie and black-and-gray striped pants, and was known and feared by the entire neighborhood.

Mr. Sotto called Tommy out from the grocery store. He put his arm around his shoulders and walked him a few blocks north to Mott Street. He was babbling something about the special responsibilities that befall the oldest boy in a family.

"But my brother Jake is the oldest, Mr. Sotto."

That fact was a mere technicality, as Sotto explained, "Yes, but not by much, and I can't find him. That makes you the oldest . . . available."

Mr. Sotto paused in a doorway on Kenmare Street. "Tommy," he said, "you're a man now, and a man has to take responsibility and step up."

Tommy nodded, still wondering why he was called from work. He got the answer.

"Tommy," Mr. Sotto said, "your father has died."

He remembered how odd it was to hear those words coming from the undertaker. Like some Japanese Godzilla movie where the soundtrack never matches the lip movements of the actor. But the undertaker said it again and again.

"Tommy, do you understand?"

"He can't be dead," Tommy explained. "We're going away for the weekend this afternoon, like we always do."

Sotto bent lower and was eye to eye with Tommy. His hands braced Tommy's arms and squeezed. "I need you," he said, calmly, "as the oldest boy, to make an identification of your dad, so I can bring him back to the funeral home."

"But I'm not the oldest," Tommy reminded him. "Really, I'm not."

"Follow me," Mr. Sotto said. He began walking up the stairs, one flight, two, three flights, then through a darkened hallway, where he knocked on a door. It opened just a crack, and he heard Sotto whispering. The door opened all the way, and the undertaker turned toward Tommy and waved him forward. He took his elbow and led him through the door, into the kitchen. There was a woman in a robe sitting at a kitchen table. A cat sat on the ledge of the windowsill, eyes like neon. It jumped across the table and scurried into a back room. Her head was down. She was crying. He gave way to the pressure on his arm and walked into another room. It was dim, the cat sat on a bureau alongside the bed. There was a body under the covers. Mr. Sotto gently pulled the sheet down, just below the graying face of Carlo Rossini. The cat hissed.

"Is this your dad, Tommy? Is this your dad?"

The cat hissed. Tommy didn't answer. He wanted to run. He stared and stared, beyond the colorless cheeks, the blank expression, the eyes wide open, his mouth, too, as if he wanted to say something. That made some kind of sense.

"Tommy, is this your dad?"

He didn't answer. He wanted to pee.

"Tommy, you're the man of the house now. You've got to step up."

"That's him," he said, but there was no sound. He tried again. "That's him," he said again.

"Do you know who your dad's doctor is?"

"Curillo, Dr. Curillo. He's the family doctor."

Sotto covered his father's face with the sheet. "Good work, Tommy." Sotto led him out through the kitchen, clutching his arm. The woman was still crying. She looked up at Tommy.

"He rang the bell and wanted to know if he could use the bathroom . . ." she said.

Him, too?

Sotto kept pulling Tommy out the door, not wanting her words to sink in. Back on the sidewalk, Tommy sat on the stoop, and Sotto sat next to him.

"Tommy," he said, "we'll have to tell your mother."

"Yes," he said, "my mother and my brothers."

"Right, Tommy." He paused. "Now, what exactly should we say?"

Tommy looked up at him.

"I mean," Sotto said, "how important are *all* the facts in a situation like this? You're twelve now, Tommy. It's your call. What do we tell your mom? Where did Dad die?"

Tommy was beginning to get the picture. He knew nothing about marriage and relationships, fidelity, infidelity; until now. All he knew was this ain't right.

"We can't tell your mom everything, can we?" Sotto said.

Why not, he thought. *It's plausible, isn't it, that when he went to get the car, he had to go to the bathroom, so he stopped in a random building, pushed a random doorbell, asked to use the john; got undressed, got into bed, and left a naked woman crying. Sure, that works, sure it does.*

"I can't tell my mom where he died. But she's pretty smart, sir. Do you think she'll believe . . . How . . ."

Sotto took a deep breath. "I'll take care of the details with Dr. Curillo. He's a friend. We'll work out the details. The important thing is that Mom should never know. I can come with you, Tommy. We can say that he passed out on the sidewalk and died instantly. It happens every day in this city. We can tell her that. It might be best not to break her heart any more than necessary. She'll have enough to deal with."

Tommy nodded. "Yeah, yeah, I agree. She can never know this."

"It's our secret, Tommy, just you and me."

"And her," Tommy said, pointing up the stairs.

Sotto nodded. "Oh, Angie? Not to worry."

He recalled walking up the very stairs where he now stood, the undertaker behind him, a gentle push each time he paused on a step, making retreat impossible. He recalled not wanting to go further, not wanting to tell his mother. There was no turning back—especially with the undertaker's hand pressed against his back! He was the eldest *available* son, as it was explained to him.

When the Bonneville didn't appear in front of the building at the predetermined time, Maddie Rossini got a chill up her arm. Her concerns were validated when Tommy came into the apartment with Mr. Enrico Sotto behind him. Tommy knew his mother well. Maddie *was* a smart woman, more than able to add two plus two. No Bonneville and Enrico Sotto—it equaled trouble.

From that point on, in the dark of night, whenever Tommy closed his eyes, he'd recall his mother's screams when he broke the news. Her cries of "how," "why," and "where" went right to his bones. He recalled the pressure of the undertaker's hand on his shoulder, steadying him. As for her questions, Dr. Curillo would answer the "how"—massive coronary; the priest would address the "why"—God's will. No one would ever address the "where." His mother never stopped asking why or how; but at some point, she stopped asking where. Maddie Rossini was a smart woman, and that was when he heard her say those words. He stood clinging to her black dress at his father's graveside, tears flowing, his nose running. It was more of a whisper to herself, as he recalled it now, she said, "There's no fool like an old fool."

A few steps more, and he ran his hand across the very spot on the concrete hallway that he punched that day. He remembered running from the apartment and slamming his hand into the wall and hearing a cracking noise. Sotto ran out behind him, grabbed him, and cradled his hand.

"It's broken," he said. "We've got to take you to the hospital."

Instead, he ran wincing in agony, burying his hand in his chest, and ensuring the details of that day would always and forever be associated with the pain from bone chips and scar tissue, a memory never to be dulled by time or distance.

He jiggled those fingers as he continued up the narrow flight of stairs to the second landing followed by the malodorous smells emanating from dented metal trash cans behind the stairwell. He paused by the door and took a deep breath. He had to be careful. His mother was in her eighties now, and a sudden surprise could be dangerous. He imagined the shock on his mother's face, the joy at seeing him might easily cause her heart to palpitate. He prepared himself to quickly quiet her down and reassure her. Another breath. He gave a tap and opened the door to find his mother sitting by the window alongside the table, the very place he'd waved good-bye to her years earlier. She looked up at him, the ghost of his mother.

"Mama, I'm home."

She studied him. "Who are you?" she asked, then went back to reading her Bible. The pages trembled in her hand.

He moved in closer. "Ma, it's me, Tommy, Tommy Boy."

She looked him over closer. "Did you bring the groceries? Put them over there, and put the change in the jar."

Tommy scratched his head, only then did he notice the aide standing by the sink.

"Hello," she said, "I'm Dory. Don't mind her, she's forgetful sometimes. It comes and goes. Maddie, this must be your son Thomas."

"I don't have a son Thomas. I left him in Bayonne."

"Sure you do, I've been away," Tommy said. "But I came back to see you."

There was a blank expression, no color on her once-porcelain skin. No luster in her eyes. Then enlightenment as a smile spread across her face, a flicker of sparkle from two gold teeth, and her blue eyes gleamed, reminiscent of the mental picture he carried of her.

"Oh, Tommy, my Tommy from New Jersey."

Tommy took a deep breath. *Good enough,* he thought. "Right, Mom, it's me, Tommy, back from New Jersey."

"It's a miracle," she said. "I'm sorry, so sorry, Thomas."

"Sorry for what?" he asked.

She nodded, extended her hand. Her fingers traced his face, studying it by braille. Then she closed the Bible, using a memorial card of a deceased friend as a bookmark.

"She's a special woman," Dory said.

"I guess," he said as he stared at a pile of memorial cards on the windowsill. *They didn't make the cut,* he thought. On the wall other laminated memorial cards were taped, row upon row, each with a small picture of the deceased along with dates of his or her birth and death and, a prayer: May the Martyrs Come to Welcome You. Souvenirs from every wake she had ever attended. The morbid hall of fame, ghosts of friends and family long dead surrounded her.

"They are a source of comfort," Dory said.

Tommy nodded. "Italian wallpaper." He looked around the apartment. There's little redecorating that could be done in a three-room cold-water flat. It was a far cry from his more recent mailing address. Wood-paneled walls, a toaster oven, and the sum total of all her possessions neatly piled on the windowsill alongside her.

"What time is it, Dory?" Maddie asked.

"Almost noon, dear."

Maddie made motions to rise, but her body was not cooperating. Tommy realized the extent of her condition. As she stood, lost in the folds of a simple dress, he guessed that she didn't weigh ninety pounds. Her body was skeletal.

"Time for church. So much to thank God for," she said. "Give me a hand."

"I told her the priest would be happy to come here."

"It's not the same," Maddie said. She steadied herself holding on to Tommy. "Do you want to come?"

"Next time, Mom."

"You used to come, all three of you."

"I remember, Mom. We were kids then. Next time, I promise."

Dory steadied her as her body tried to melt backward into the wheelchair. "We'll have to hurry," she said. She turned to Tommy.

"When her meds wear off, her body shuts down. It's the Parkinson's," she whispered. She buttoned Maddie's sweater and placed the walker in front of her. Inch by inch, with Dory's help, Maddie made her way to the door.

Maddie looked back. "Will you be here when I get back?"

And then some, Tommy thought. "Yes, Mom, I'll be here."

"Don't wake up your brother. He's trying to sleep."

Tommy was saddened by his mother's physical condition and mental confusion. No doubt his brother was sleeping somewhere, but not here. "Not to worry, Mom."

Maddie passed him, stopping to reach her arms around his head and kissed him. "I'm glad you're here and not in Bayonne."

Tommy remained at the table and looked around. He picked up the phone and dialed information for the Taxi and Limousine Commission. A loud noise coincided with a door opening behind him. He froze for a second, dropping the phone back into its cradle. He turned around to the source.

"What the hell are you doing here?" he said.

Wedged in the doorway was Jake, sitting in a wheelchair. Jake maneuvered the wheelchair back and forth, trying for the perfect angle that would allow it to pass into the kitchen.

"What do you think I'm doing? I thought it would be a good idea to get away from the good weather, the fresh air, the golf, the restaurants, the booze, and broads and come up here to see Mom."

Tommy studied him closely. Jake's normally reddish complexion was replaced with a pallid hue. His once-full head of red hair had receded. He was wearing a jogging suit, and Tommy, still stunned, stared. There was something missing. He stared until he saw it. The right leg of the suit was folded under his thigh. Tommy's mouth dropped open.

"Your l . . . le . . ."

"Oh, right," Jake acknowledged. "Didn't I tell you, or did I? Gee, let me think. Ah, yes, I do think I mentioned that I was in trouble and had a problem with my foot. Yes, now that I think of it, I did mention it."

"You're putting this on me?"

"Who else?" Jake asked.

Tommy fell backward into a chair and took a deep breath, running his hands across his temples. "Christ," he said, "Jesus."

"And," Jake asked. "What prompts your return to paradise?"

Tommy did not answer, except to say, "I need a drink."

Knowing nothing in the apartment had changed, he opened a cupboard above the sink where an array of multicolored shot glasses sat on the shelves. Jake reached into a cabinet under the sink and pulled out a bottle of Stock 84 brandy. The bottle was nearly empty, prompting a look from Tommy.

"Mom," Jake said. "She's good for a shot every now and then."

Tommy filled the two glasses.

"What will we drink to?" Jake asked.

Tommy did not answer. He couldn't think of an appropriate toast. They tapped glasses and downed the drinks.

Jake coughed.

"Hey, maybe you shouldn't be having liquor. Are you on medication?"

"Yes, but who cares. I'm better off dead anyway."

Tommy did not want to indulge him, but felt his silence might be interpreted as subliminal agreement. "Hey," he mustered.

"Why? It's true. My life is over."

There was no rebuttal.

"What am I supposed to do now? I'm stuck here. I can't get up the stairs in the building. I can't get down the stairs. Even if I could, I'm not supposed to be in New York. I was warned not to come back. I'm fifty-five. I'm broke, living with my mother, living on social security disability. I've lost my license to practice, and who would want to go to a one-legged foot doctor anyway. You see, I'm better off dead."

Probably, Tommy thought. "Hey, now," he said again, adding "now." "Look at all those young men coming home from Iraq with missing limbs. They're up and around and active and productive."

"And younger and in better shape."

He had thought it through, Tommy observed. "You'll get help. There are programs available, I'm sure. You've paid in all those years."

Jake put his hand up to stop further conversation. "Right, I waited for the prosthesis; and when it finally came, it was the wrong leg. I can't walk with two left feet. So much for government help. Now the other one shows up, and it's two inches short; and I'm not going to be able to balance myself on it anyway. I just know it. I tried and couldn't do it."

"Whatever," Tommy said. "I'm not your babysitter."

"Well, that's it. That's all you can say?" Jake asked.

"I've got my own problems and can't be a part of your soap opera."

"Where will you be staying?" Jake asked. "The Plaza, the Sheraton, the Tribeca Grand? Maybe I could crash with you. I'm suffocating here."

Tommy poured a bit more brandy. Jake refused. "No, I think I'll stay here for a while."

Jake's eyebrows jumped up on his forehead. "Here, like *here*. Where? There's no room here."

Tommy looked into the bedroom. It was like a museum. Nothing had changed. It was small even when he was small. But bunk beds and a Castro convertible were enough to bed him and his two brothers in those days. The window overlooked an alley, and there was a closet his father had fabricated.

Tommy walked in and opened the closet. In his day, Jake was a fashion plate. Now his last worldly possessions were hung, meticulously, in military fashion, with three inches between each suit, sports jacket and pants. Dated, but immaculate. Tommy opened his bag and pulled out a pair of jeans and a few shirts. He tossed them across the chair.

"Hey, aren't you going to hang those up?"

Tommy didn't answer. Jake rolled back into the room, reached up into the closet. He folded his brother's pants and hung them and his shirts on hangers. "You see this? This is a hanger," he said holding it up to his face. "You're a slob, you always were a Goddamned slob."

Tommy didn't answer.

"What's going on, Tommy? What are you doing here?"

"Looking for work," he said.

"Work? Construction? This town is spoken for. Why here? I thought you were on fire out west. There's very little going on, and what is being built goes through Fazzula."

"I know. I may have to call on him. We were tight once." He noticed Jake's eyes open wide.

"Once, like before I left his daughter," he reminded him.

"He's a businessman, one thing has nothing to do with another," Tommy said. "I hope," he added.

"That's what *I* thought," Jake said, "But I was wrong."

"Finally, an admission," Tommy said. He sat at the table, and Jake rolled up to the other side.

"What's going on, Tommy?"

"I wish I had an answer. It seems I made some bad investments, hard to understand, really. Somehow, some way, my investments got involved as collateral for these loans and *poof*, like dominos, it all came down. I trusted the wrong people. I didn't pay attention. Now I'm under investigation. Feds want to know if I was a victim or part of the scam."

"Christ."

"Right, and what about you, is there anything put away?"

"Are you kidding? I'm getting a check for disability, hardly enough to pay for these pills I have to take. Look at the size of this one," he pulled a pill from his pocket. "It would choke a horse."

"A horse's ass, in your case."

"Did I tell you how funny you are?"

"Not recently," Tommy said. "Is there anything to eat here?"

Jake rolled to the refrigerator. "Pizza," he said. He pulled out a package wrapped in aluminum foil. "Heat it up," he said.

"Pizza?"

"Get used to it, brother," Jake said. "It's the main staple of our diet. We order a lot of pizza. Leftover crust is good for breakfast. You have to dunk it. It's cost-effective."

"You're kidding me, right?"

"Wish I was, brother. I can tell you it's better than cat food."

"What's with her anyway? She doesn't look good at all."

"Parkinson's," Jake said. "There's nothing that can be done. Dory told me her body and mind are not in sync. Her mind says 'walk,' but her body can't carry out the order."

"What about drugs?"

"Sure, she takes a pill and then she's convulsing, shaking all over. There's no happy medium, no way to measure."

"Is it hereditary?"

"With my luck, probably," Jake said.

Tommy sat in his mother's chair and looked around. This was command central for his mother. Everything she would need during the course of the day was within arm's reach. He opened a small file box on the windowsill that contained her bills. All very organized. There was also a large poster board near the phone with emergency numbers written in large red type. He found a pen and paper and started to write down numbers. "We have to take stock," he said. "What about Mom?"

"Mom, are you kidding? She's on social security, and Dad didn't get a pension from being a bookie. After her medicine and the rent, she's broke too. Medicaid pays Dory, not enough if you ask me. They threaten to remove her weekly. They didn't figure on her lasting this long either."

Tommy jotted some figures. "What's the rent?"

"Two hundred," he said. "That's why the landlord is waiting for her to die. He can get two thousand for this apartment. The prick checks on her once a week. He makes believe he's checking on the apartment, but he's checking to see if she's still breathing."

"Two thousand for this matchbox?"

"Believe it," Jake said. "This neighborhood is primo these days.

We got three Rockettes living on the third floor, they pay twenty-two hundred. There's a news anchor on the fifth, what a body, she pays the same."

"I can't believe it. Three rooms?"

"Believe it. It's Little Italy, all the nouveau riche want to live downtown now. That's why the landlord stops in. He can't wait for her to die. Last week I had to hide for twenty minutes while he was in the hallway."

"Why?" Tommy asked.

"If she dies, the apartment is his. He can rent it at market rates. But if I'm here for six months, I can't be thrown out. That would piss him off big time. I'd be entitled to stay until I die, and he couldn't raise the rent. It's the law."

Tommy rubbed his aching hand. "No wonder nothing has changed down here in two hundred years," he said. "So you're in hiding?"

"Yep, on the lam, not only from him, but from Fat Pauly too. He sent word I was not to return to New York. But I had no choice. He made sure that every door closed."

Tommy put the pen down. "I may have to go see him."

"Are you crazy?"

"What choice do I have? I've got to earn again."

"What if he asks about me?"

"I'll tell him I haven't heard from you. I don't know what I'll tell him."

"No you can't. I won't let you."

Tommy ignored him. He picked up the phone and dialed the

Taxi Commission, hearing, "If you want to speak English, press one." He did, to hear, "If you want to speak to reservations, press two; to speak with mechanical, press three; to order an application for a medallion, press four; for all other business, press five." He pressed five.

Click. Disconnected. "You motherless . . . !" Tommy thought about calling the police; but it would be hard to explain cash, and it would cause a whole lot of other problems if he tried. He was starting to accept he wouldn't see the money again.

Maddie returned after an hour, clinging to the walker as Dory steadied her into her chair. "Only three people in church," she said, "and they were chinks."

Dory made her comfortable in front of the window. She sat at the table and reached for her pill dispenser. Dory readied a glass of water as Maddie looked through the colorful assortment. "The blue one?" she asked.

"No," Dory said. "Blue is in the morning. It's the pink one now."

Tommy and Jake watched as she ran her fingers through the medical cocktail, then with Dory's help steadying the walker, she inched her way into her bedroom. She stopped just before entering and looked at her sons. "Dory, tell me the truth."

"What is it, Maddie?"

"Am I dying?"

"Dying? Well, not on my watch, dear one."

Maddie nodded. "I've been trying to figure out why my sons came home. Only a funeral brings family together."

"They just came to see you, Maddie, dear, and you are very much alive. Your boys are precious, just precious."

"Yes," she said. "Gems." She stroked Jake's head. "What did you do to yourself?" she asked. Jake's head slumped into his chest.

A knock at the door froze all of them in their place. Jake began rolling into the backroom.

PART
VI

CHAPTER 13

*P*atzo approached the gate of Woodlawn Cemetery in the Bronx. He was tired this Sunday morning. The café where he worked was busy, and he didn't lock the doors until 3:00 a.m. But this was his duty, his routine. On the second Sunday of each month he'd leave the confines of lower Manhattan for a trek to the Bronx. The IRT Lexington Avenue subway line would take him to Grand Central Station where he'd board the Harlem line Metro-North train up to the last stop in New York City, Woodlawn. There it was a two-minute walk to the Woodlawn Cemetery.

He was comfortable here, surrounded by the dead. He reprised his mother's words: "The dead can't hurt you, only the living." He carried a bouquet of flowers in one hand and a container of coffee in the other. He was surprised this time to find someone sitting in the very bench where he sat to pray and think and wonder. *Damn nerve*, he thought as the rightful owner of that bench. Undaunted, he approached the grave and placed his flowers and turned to sit. This was his turf. If anyone left, it would be the stranger. He thought it odd and disconcerting that in a cemetery of more than four hundred acres, a stranger had to intrude on his solitude. He did not feel threatened by the man or the black late-model Impala in the distance. The driver made no move. An audience of pigeons surrounded the man as he tossed crumbs from a paper bag.

Patzo sat and sipped his coffee and took a better look at the man from the corner of his eye, surprised when the man spoke. "Good morning."

Patzo just nodded.

"Cold morning, you were wise to bring coffee."

Patzo just nodded again and stared at the headstone.

"You're a good person," the man said. "I can tell."

"What makes you say that?"

"You honor the dead. That's important. You are a faithful visitor."

"How do you know that?"

"I know a lot," the man said. "What's your name?"

"They call me Patzo."

"I know what they call you; Patzo, as in 'crazy.' But I don't think you're crazy. Besides, your real name is Carmine, Carmine Luca."

Patzo stared at him now. "Do you know who I am?" the man asked.

Patzo nodded, his eyes opened wider.

"How do you know?" the man asked.

"I've seen you in the newspapers."

"Ah." The man smiled. "I'll bet you're smart enough to believe only half of what you read."

"I don't read, just look at pictures mainly."

The man nodded. "Well, that's not important. What's important is that I know about you. I know you come here often to visit your mother's grave; and although there are three names on the stone, only your mother is in there. Your father and brother were never found."

Patzo fidgeted now and placed his cup on the path and stood.

"Don't worry," the man said. "I know you come here and pray and ask yourself a million questions, mostly about your father and brother. I know you put their name on the stone so you'd never forget them. That's why I like you. As I said, you honor the dead and I may be able to help you."

"How's th-that?" Patzo asked.

"Do you mind if I call you Carmine? I don't like to call anyone Patzo even if they are crazy, and I don't think you're crazy; far from it."

Patzo liked the compliment. His breathing eased. "So why exactly would you want to help me?"

The man adjusted the brim of his fedora. "Why not?" he said. "What good is all the wealth and power if you can't use it for good? In the end we are all the same. Only our good works go with us. Look around," he continued pointing to the grave. "Your mother, a simple woman, yet she shares the same earth with Herman Melville, Fiorello LaGuardia, Duke Ellington. In the end we are all equal. So why not help someone along the way?"

Patzo was listening, but still a bit confused. "Fiorello . . . ? How exactly can you help me?"

"I can offer you closure. It is closure that you seek. I can tell you a story that will answer your questions about your father and brother. And if after hearing the story you believe me, you and I may be able to help each other. How does that sound? And if you do, maybe one day your father and brother will share this hallowed resting place with your beloved mother."

"And that Fiorello guy?"

The man laughed. "Yes, him too." He patted the bench. "Come closer, Carmine, come closer."

Later that day Patzo picked up groceries from Falco Brothers Grocery Store to deliver to Maddie Rossini. She was good for a dollar tip. A dozen or so odd jobs like that a day, and it added up. There was a renewed bounce in his step. He whistled as he walked through the aisle. With a dollar bill he paid for a quart of milk. On the way out he nonchalantly helped himself to a loaf of bread, a box of macaroni, and a box of Entenmann's cake, nimbly placing the items in the bag with the poise of a master of prestidigitation.

Maddie's door was always unlocked. Not today, as he discovered by banging his head into it.

"Ch-Christ!" he yelled as he rubbed his temple. He tried turning the knob. "Hello. H-hello."

Tommy looked through the peephole and saw Patzo rubbing his head.

"It's only Patzo."

"He can't know I'm here," Jake said. "He'll tell Fazzula. The kid can't keep his mouth shut, never could."

Patzo's position in the café gave him unrestricted access to whispered conversations.

"Well, I got to let him in," Tommy said. "He'll get suspicious if I don't."

"I can't believe he still shops for Mom."

"He knows how to stretch a dollar," Maddie explained.

Tommy opened the door. In came a young man with uncombed hair, faded jeans, and antique Keds sneakers.

"Hi, Patzo," Tommy said.

He stared at Tommy, his eyes wide. "Tommy, Tommy, is that you? I haven't seen you in y-y-years." He dropped the grocery bag on the table and threw his arms around him.

Jake had only made it halfway into the bedroom. "And Jake, is that you too? Hey, you guys, what are you doing in town. It . . . it's been years. Jesus, just when I thought the day couldn't get any better."

Tommy said, "Just here to see Mom. She's not doing well, as you must know."

"I'm not doing well? I knew it," she said to Dory.

"It's only an expression, dear one," Dory said. "Come, let's get you a nap."

"Okay," she said. "There's certainly been enough excitement for one day. I kind of like it." She moved into the bedroom. "Patzo, don't forget the change."

"I won't, Maddie. We did good today." Patzo put coins into a jar behind Maddie's chair. "Boy, it is gr-great to see you guys." He looked at Jake. "What happened to you, Jake?"

"A little accident," he said.

"Jeez, Patzo, it's good to see you too. What are you doing these days?"

"Same old stuff," he said. "Nothing new."

"Where are you living?"

"I'm still with the 'guy,'" he said. He bent his nose with his finger.

"Really?" Tommy said.

Patzo nodded. "What choice do I have? He lets me sleep in the back. Gives me a little money every week."

"Well, I give you credit for hanging in with him all these years."

"Yeah, he yells and cusses; but I let it go in one ear and out the other. I bide my time. The worm turns, you know."

"Listen, Patzo, you gotta do me a favor."

"What is it, Jake?"

Jake approached the table. "Don't mention to anyone that I'm here. I mean like to Pauly or anyone else. Don't mention that I'm in town."

"Don't worry," Tommy said. "Patzo is still loyal to me. Aren't you, Patzo? He would still be a virgin if not for me. I got him off his nut, got him laid." He turned to Patzo. "Do you remember that day? You just finished playing basketball and stopped for ice cream with your friends. I saw the bunch of you guys and decided to take you to Madam's. It was quite a sight when I showed up at the whorehouse with a bunch of kids, Patzo in short pants, had a basketball under one arm and an ice cream cone in the other. Madam looked at me like I was crazy, but she let them in. Five seconds later, they were men. Do you remember, Patzo? That kind of makes me your godfather, doesn't it?"

Patzo was flushed. "Yeah, Tommy, I remember, I-I remember."

"I'll never forget," Tommy continued. "He got an asthma attack, and the madam sent one of the girls down to call me. We thought he was gonna drop dead, but he would have died happy. Right, Patzo? He actually got so excited he passed out. I got one of the girls to give him mouth to mouth, which led to another go round on the merry-go-round."

"Y-yes. I remember, I was tw-twelve."

"Right, you became a man that day."

Maddie called from the bedroom, "Did you get my Lotto tickets?"

"I did, Mrs. Rossini." He took them from his pocket and placed them on the table. "And your change is in the jar, like you always want it. It's in the jar. B-boy, it's been a long time since I saw you two guys together."

"Right, Patzo," Tommy agreed. "Now, listen, I need a little favor. I don't want you to tell anyone—*anyone*—that my brother is here. Do you understand?"

Jake was fidgeting in his chair.

"Do you promise, Patzo? If you want, I'll set you up again."

"I d-don't think the madam is still alive," he observed.

"Not to worry, I'm sure the business is still going. But you gotta keep quiet about seeing Jake here. Do you understand?"

"Sure, s-sure I do. I understand. You can trust me. I'm no stool pigeon flunky for Fat Pauly. He's a sick man. He shoots cats in the alley. That's why there are no cats in the neighborhood. People blame the Chinese restaurants, but it's not them, it's Pauly, I tell ya. He kills the cats." He looked at his watch. "Hey, I'd better get back. I gotta sweep the café and wash Pauly's car."

"Lips are sealed?"

"S-sealed," Patzo said. He kissed Tommy and Jake on the way out.

"Hey," Tommy asked. "Speaking of pigeons, do you still have that bird?"

"Pippy?" A big smile came across his face. "Oh yes, he's my

buddy. Poor bird puts up with a lot of abuse from that animal boss of mine, but yeah, he's my buddy."

As Patzo left Jake was beet-red. "You are a genius, a real genius. That guy can't keep a thing to himself. If Fazzula finds out I'm here, I'm dead. I'm a dead man, a dead man," Jake said. His head sunk onto his chest.

"Cool your jets. He's not telling anyone. He's solid. And what's the difference; you said you're better off dead."

"You're funny."

"Well, I'm not trying to be." Tommy stood up and went to the window and peeked through Venetian blinds and watched Patzo scurry up the street into the café. "Still, I could never understand why that kid is so loyal to Fazzula after what happened."

"Maybe he doesn't know," Jake offered.

"He's slow, he's not stupid. The whole neighborhood knows Fazzula ordered the hit." He thought for a moment. "Doesn't make sense," he said.

"Life in the streets," he said. "Fazzula knows how to push buttons. He's a master of getting people to do what he wants."

"You should know," Tommy said.

"And you're any different? Anyway, what choice does the kid have? Even if he knows about what happened, what could he do? He's too stupid to do anything. He's helpless. It's the deal he's made with the devil in return for a roof over his head."

Tommy fingered through the lottery tickets on the table.

"How many of those does she buy?" Tommy asked Dory.

"Oh, five or so. She wins a few dollars and buys more. It keeps her busy."

Tommy was doing the math.

Maddie's voice came from the bedroom. "Dory, I got to go to church to book the masses."

"We just did that, Maddie. You've got the masses booked for the year. All the dead will be prayed for." She looked to Tommy. "Your mother has memorial masses offered for your father, grandparents, your Uncle Rick, your Aunt Bea, and I forget who else."

"Tony, the old janitor," Maddie reminded her from the bedroom.

"I thought she was deaf," Tommy said.

"Selective hearing, I guess," Jake said.

"Oh yes," Dory remembered, "she's right, the old janitor gets a mass, too."

"She has a mass offered for the janitor?" Tommy asked, his eyebrows high on his head.

"He was a good man," Maddie explained from her bedroom. "He kept this building spick-and-span. He has no family; someone has to remember him."

"I thought she was deaf."

"She is . . . sometimes," Dory said. "Anyway, that's him. Four in from the left in the third row." She pointed to the memorial cards taped to the wall.

"If these were baseball cards, they'd be worth a fortune," Jake observed.

"What do all the masses cost?" he whispered now.

"What was it? I think seven hundred dollars," Dory said.

"What?" Tommy shouted.

Dory cleared the table of the groceries. "A whole month's social security," she added.

"Maybe I should stay with Looney," Jake said. "I'll be safe there."

"You are so self-indulgent," Tommy said. "Is that all you can think about? Did you just hear how your mother is spending her social security?"

"I'll help you pack," Maddie offered.

"Aren't you tired, Ma?" Jake shot back.

"That's why I'm in bed," she said.

Tommy wiped his brow. "Seven hundred," he repeated in disgust. "I got to go. I got to go see Fazzula. Maybe I can get a feel for what's going on, maybe hook up some work."

Jake rolled his wheelchair to the door. "You have to get by me first," he said.

Tommy reached around for the handles of the wheelchair and rolled Jake effortlessly across the room.

"You're gonna sell your soul too!" Jake shouted.

"It depends on how much I can get for it." Tommy said. "And besides, you did."

Johnny Pump knew that his boss would not like the news, but he had to be told. He strolled into the backroom, putting up two fingers. Patzo understood. Fat Pauly sat in his barber chair, reading the *New York Post*.

"We need to talk," Pump said.

Fat Pauly licked the tip of his finger, and used it to turn a page.

"It's important," he added.

Pauly closed the paper and sat at the table. Patzo brought two cups of espresso. "Left, right; left, right," he muttered as he jiggled the cups in his hands.

"What's with him?" Pump asked.

"What do I know? He's not only a moron, he's a *dyslectic* moron."

Pump got back to the matter at hand. "We got a problem," he said. "There's a witness. Puts us at the scene."

Without reaction, Pauly sipped the coffee. "Does this taste right to you?"

"Yeah, fine."

"And you know this how?" he asked.

"We got someone inside the Fifth Precinct, Bella. She's part of maintenance—mops floors and whatnot. She thinks they have a witness. Olivetti was interviewing him."

"Him?" Pauly traced his finger around the rim of the cup. He relived the events of the early morning when he directed the monsignor's body be dumped. He thought about the street, quiet, no traffic, no pedestrians. His mind's eye scaled the tenements floor by floor, fire escape by fire escape.

"Do you want to know who . . . ?"

"I already know," he said. With that the last remnants of espresso flooded down his throat.

"I told you to let me handle it. It was too risky."

Fazzula put his hand up. "This was personal. Plus it's in my own backyard."

"There's something else," he said. "We got a visitor in the neighborhood from out west. Been here a couple of days."

Pauly's raised his eyebrows at that news. "Where is he staying?"

"He walks toward Tribeca at night but circles back to his mother's apartment."

"It's getting *crowded* in there," Pauly observed.

CHAPTER 14

In the property room of One Police Plaza, the sum total of personal effects of the Right Reverend Monsignor Matthew Burns lay spread across a table at the instructions of Santo Olivetti. He did not know what he was looking for, but he would know when he found it. He combed through boxes of files, coming across pictures of the good monsignor on a Las Vegas vacation. He was with Wayne Newton in one photo. There were other pictures of him in Atlantic City with Donald Trump. He did not wear a collar in any of the photographs. In another box he found racing forms from Belmont Raceway and Aqueduct as well as numerous losing stubs from OTB. It would seem from the paraphernalia that the monsignor was an avid sports fan—football, baseball—willing to put his money where his mouth was. Or, Olivetti thought again, *someone's money*.

Olivetti was putting a mental picture together of a wayward priest who crossed the line from saint to sinner. There was one other thought that occurred to him. *One man controlled all the gambling in the New York metropolitan area.* He leafed through a scrapbook, coming across another photograph. It was an old black-and-white of five men wearing tuxedos, standing shoulder to shoulder. He studied the photo: a young Frank Sinatra with his arms around an equally baby-faced Fat Pauly Fazzula and Vito Carozza, another renowned *caporegime.* And there at the end of the line, he saw a baby-faced Burns. From the jacket he noticed the photo was taken at the Westchester Premier Dinner Theatre just before the last curtain dropped. The history of its demise was well documented. Embezzlement, fraud, and mob infiltration. This picture was interesting for that reason. He was leaning more toward sinner than saint. Olivetti stared at the young priest in the photo. Burns had some very interesting friends.

Fat Pauly Fazzula could be found conducting business from his storefront café on Grand and Mulberry Streets at any time during the day. Fazzula's was a local institution serving espresso, cappuccino, fresh pastries, and paninis. It was a legitimate source of income for a man who needed to show a legitimate source of income. The café was open to the public; the backrooms were by invitation only. Patzo utilized one of them as his bedroom. There was a small private kitchen for intimate gatherings, private catered dinners by invitation only, and a walk-in refrigerator with more than enough space for perishables.

For fresh air and exercise, Pauly would take business associates for a walk up the east side of Mulberry and down the west side.

His business meetings were often interrupted by fawning followers who stopped to say hello, plant a kiss, and double-pump his hand in return for a slight tap on their faces or a simple squeeze of their cheeks—a blessing for the masses! He understood his power, often quipping, "I should get a papal ferula. That's what I'm missing."

Pauly was unimpressed by federal surveillance teams monitoring his movements daily. His "here I am" attitude infuriated his would-be captors and made him an all-the-more-lauded trophy. Tommy knew that he was dealing with a smart man. Fazzula bragged about being one of the few crime bosses with a college education, a business degree from Fordham. With the help of the Jesuit education, he was able to maintain a criminal enterprise beyond reproach from the IRS, the federal forensic accountants, and the Organized Crime and Drug Enforcement Task Force. He'd often boast, "I was taught by the best crooks. The key is, always *over*pay your taxes."

Tommy knew he would have to be just a little bit smarter. Ever on his guard not to have Fazzula smell blood in the water, for that's when the sharks gather.

On this November afternoon Tommy strolled past the café and peeked his head in. Patzo was cleaning the display window. His parrot sat perched in an open cage staring at a television. Patzo nodded to Tommy. A small group of men played cards at a back table, stopping only to glance at Tommy. Tommy returned the acknowledgment.

He saw Fat Pauly, as he had often seen him, in the private back-room of the café, reclining in a barber chair. The doors were wide open as Tommy remembered Pauly liked them, believing that closed doors made his enemies curious, and he had nothing to hide. He was, after all, a legitimate businessman who made a fortune as a consultant and a real estate developer and who also enjoyed operating a little café, just for the heck of it.

He was covered in a black cape, his pants visible on a hanger behind the door. His toes were separated by pieces of Kleenex tissues. His arm stuck out from the cape as an Asian woman, wearing a traditional flowered dress, applied a coat of clear polish to his nails. She had shiny black hair pulled back in a bun and long, dark eyebrows.

Tommy recognized her as Lucy, Fazzula's geisha. She did his nails, laundered and ironed his shirts, which he did not trust to a commercial laundry, and she performed a number of duties that kept the orchid in her hair fresh. She hadn't changed much—the face of a porcelain Japanese doll, the body of a Buddha.

She was careful not to get in the way of Favio, the barber who meticulously ran a straight razor across Fazzula's throat. A position of trust.

The barber then wrapped a hot towel around Pauly's face and pressed it with his hands. Tommy stood in the entrance to the backroom, surprised to hear Fazzula say, "Do I have a visitor?"

"Hi, Pauly," Tommy said.

Pauly waved his pamperers away. "Enough, Favio. Lucy, come back later." The barber removed the hot towel and adjusted the lever that brought the chair upright.

Fazzula adjusted his eyes. "Tommy, Tommy Boy Rossini. How are you?" Fazzula said.

"Good, Pauly, I'm great."

"You son of a gun, how long has it been?"

"Jeez," Tommy said. "I lost count."

"Come over here, you son of a gun you." Tommy walked over and reached for Fazzula's hand while placing a kiss on his cheek.

He pointed to a chair, "Sit, sit, *amico mio*."

Tommy sat at Fazzula's right arm, his chair lower than the barber chair, giving Fazzula the height advantage. Fazzula wanted it that way, he was sure.

"So, I hear you've made a fortune out there. Nevada, right? You son of a gun, never thought of sending a little something back."

"Arizona," Tommy corrected him. "I've been in Arizona."

"Right, Arizona. I got reports. Said you're the biggest developer out there. I always knew you had what it takes. You got it up here." He tapped Tommy's temple. "Not like that piece of shit brother of yours. How is that prick?"

So much for subtlety. Tommy shrugged. "Who knows? I lost touch with him."

"You know," Fazzula whispered. "He disrespected me very bad, very, very bad."

"Yes," Tommy said. "I got bits and pieces from my mother when all that went down; but you know, he's got a one-track mind—could never talk sense to him."

Fazzula nodded. "Didn't you introduce him to my Bernadette?"

Tommy backed away. "Well, technically, but at your request, as I recall." *It was good to get that on the record*, he thought.

Fazzula ran a finger across his polished nail and nodded. "So," he said, changing the subject, "What brings you east?"

"Me, oh my mother." He shifted in his chair. "She's not well, you know, and I haven't been back in a while, so I thought it was time."

"Good, that's good." Fazzula leaned forward and pointed at him.

"You're a good son. Not like that prick brother of yours. He turned out to be a real scum. You got another brother, don't you?

"Yeah, Looney; I mean, Phil."

"Right, right. He was slow, wasn't he?" he tapped his temple, making little circles.

"No, no, he's normal . . . kind of."

"Well, where are you staying?"

Tommy thought for a split second. "I'm at the Tribeca Grand."

"Of course," Fazzula said. "Nothing but the best. Will you be in town long?"

"I don't know when I'm going back. Probably soon, I left so many things up in the air."

"I'm sure. It's not easy when you're running an empire like you are. You gotta have eyes behind your head. Everybody is looking to screw you, to take what you have, what you built. They win your trust, then screw you. Like that prick brother of yours."

Jeez, a bit obsessed. Let it go already, Tommy thought. "Don't I know it?" he agreed.

"Hey, what kind of a host am I? You're here a half hour, I don't even offer you coffee." He discovered something on his nail, brought his finger to his mouth, and bit, spitting the offending nail into the air. *Some things, like class, they can't teach at Fordham,* Tommy thought.

"Lucy!" he yelled. The manicurist rushed to Fazzula's side and filed the errant fingernail.

"Hey, that's okay. Another time, though. I'll stop in again, maybe tomorrow."

"It's a deal," Fazzula said. He leaned forward, presenting his face for another kiss. Tommy rose and obliged.

"Hey," Tommy asked, "how did you know I was in the room?"

Pauly smiled. He pointed to the antique tin ceiling. "I saw your reflection," he said. He loosened the cape from around his neck, revealing a gun in his hand. "You can never be too careful," he said. "I've learned the lessons of Albert Anastasia. Shaves can be hazardous to your health. You know, this is the chair he was shot in. I bought it at auction. It serves as a reminder to me: Never let your guard down."

Tommy nodded. "That's why you're still on top," he said.

After Tommy left, Pauly wiped remnants of shaving cream from his face. Patzo brought him a cup of espresso and the *New York Post*.

"Can you imagine that," Fazzula said. "Tommy Boy Rossini. I haven't seen him in some twenty-five years. Can you imagine? You too. Right?" he asked. "You haven't seen him for years."

Patzo put his head down. "Right," he said, "I haven't seen him."

Fazzula sipped his coffee, and began thumbing through the paper. "Well, what kind of friend are you?" he asked. "You don't see a guy in years, and you don't even give him a big hello and hug or nuttin' when he comes in? You don't even make a fuss."

Patzo shrugged. "I was cleaning the window. I didn't recognize him."

"Right," Fazzula said. "He's gained a few pounds, hasn't he?"

Patzo nodded and walked away. Fazzula followed, coming to the edge of the doorway, twirling the remnants of his coffee in the cup. "Johnny!" he yelled.

Johnny Pump put down his winning hand and rushed into the backroom.

"Yes, boss."

"I want you to pack a bag."

"Where am I going?"

"Arizona," Pauly said.

CHAPTER 15

Tommy walked down Mulberry Street, passing the courtyard of Church of the Most Precious Blood. A brick walkway led to brass church doors. He adjusted his eyes to the darkness. The church was quiet, save for piped organ music. It was empty save for a few believers kneeling at various statues. Precious Blood was an Old World church built in 1866 by the Franciscan Order. It was intended to be the spiritual home to Italian immigrants.

Ornate gold-leaf-painted ceilings enveloped the marble altar and flickering candles reflected off mosaic walls. Tucked in dark corners were small private chapels. He saw a man in a black cassock and coat sitting in a pew. On the wall was a fresco of a group of men, one with his arms outstretched.

"Hey, who runs this place?" Tommy asked.

The man looked up. He was young, fair, with a baby-faced, reddish complexion, light eyes, and bushy hair. "Excuse me?" His voice was soft and nonthreatening.

"This church," Tommy said. "Who's in charge? Who runs this operation?"

"Well, I am Father Bryce Gleason. I am the interim pastor. Can I help you?"

"The pastor," Tommy said. "You look like an altar boy." Tommy cracked his knuckles.

The priest smiled. "Yes, well, they promote us sooner these days," he said. "Fewer and fewer men choose the priesthood, so there's plenty of room for advancement."

"Is there someplace we can talk? This place gives me the creeps," Tommy said.

"Does it?" the priest asked. "Because it gives me such a sense of peace and reassurance." He shrugged. "Sure we can talk. I was just finishing afternoon prayers. I find this place most conducive to prayer. There is spirituality here among the saints." He looked up at one fresco. "*The Incredulity of Saint Thomas,*" he said referring to the painted wall. "It's a masterpiece by Caravaggio. Do you know of Caravaggio?"

"No," Tommy said. "I've been out of the neighborhood for a few years."

"No, no," the priest answered. "Caravaggio was an artist, a Renaissance artist. This is a replica of his painting where Jesus revealed himself to Thomas after his Resurrection. The original hangs in the Sanssoucci, in Potsdam. Even the Apostles had doubts. Can you believe it? This is my favorite place." He ran his hand across the wall.

"I've seen the original, marveled at how he used light and shadows. And there," he said pointing, "*The Baptism of Jesus* . . ."

"That's all very nice, Father."

"I'm sorry, I was rambling. How can I help you?"

"I'm Tommy Rossini. I'm here about my mother."

"Rossini," he said. "Maddie's son? Is she all right?" The priest stood up. He was tiny compared to Tommy.

"Uh, yeah, yeah she's fine."

The priest extended his hand. Tommy shook it, swallowing up the small hand in his considerable palm. "Your mother is a devout woman," the priest said as he pulled his hand back. "She is a woman of faith."

"Yeah, well, she's also a woman on a fixed income."

Gleason raised his eyebrows as Tommy continued. "Now, I understand she dropped a few hundred dollars here. What's that all about?"

"Oh," he said, as he sat back in the pew. "I believe you're referring to the memorial masses your mother has celebrated during the year."

"Memorial masses?"

"Yes," the priest explained. "She has mass dedications on the anniversaries of all those she loved. She has a mass dedicated for your father, your grandparents; you have an uncle that she offers prayer to. It's her special devotion."

"And what exactly happens during this mass?"

"Well, the name of the deceased is mentioned during the prayer of the faithful."

"You mention their names?" Tommy repeated.

"Yes," he said. "In prayerful memory."

"Not for nothing, Father, but these people have been dead for a long time. If they ain't in heaven yet, then a few more prayers here or there are not going to help. My father especially, I don't think a mass will help."

"Prayer is very powerful," he said. "Never underestimate the power of prayer."

"That's all well and good, Father. Believe what you will, but the bottom line is that my mother is not as sharp as she once was; and you can't go by everything she says."

"Your mother has been a wonderful patron of this church for many years. Look here." He paused by a grotto where there was a statue. Water flowed into a pool at the base. "That's John the Baptist baptizing Jesus." Then the priest pointed to some brass plaques with names inscribed on them: IN LOVING MEMORY OF CARLO ROSSINI. "When your father died, your mother contributed five hundred dollars to repair the motor. She kept the grotto running."

"What did you do with the rest of the money?"

"Excuse me?"

"Come on, who are you kidding? A little motor? I don't think it cost five hundred dollars."

Gleason laughed. "Probably not," he said. "But some of the money goes to the general upkeep of the church; and of course, we have to give a percentage of our collection to the Diocese uptown."

"So you gotta kick some upstairs."

He laughed. "Yes, now you get it, you understand."

"What's not to understand, Father? The Mafia works the same way, kick up to the boys on top, everybody eats. So a church is a little crime family kicking up, like a pyramid scheme."

"Tommy, no," Gleason said. "But it takes money to run the church, to continue its good works."

Tommy looked at his watch. "Sure, I'm sure it does. But it also takes money for my mother to live. So I'm gonna come back tomorrow. I'd appreciate it if you would return this memorial mass money. I'd hate to think you took advantage of an old lady."

Father scratched his chin.

Tommy turned to leave. "And another thing, Father, don't mention any of this to the old lady. As I said, she's confused."

Gleason called out to him. "Mr. Rossini," he said. "Do you believe in good and evil?"

Tommy thought for a moment. "Only in evil, Father. I believe in that."

Tommy ducked into a building and made his way to the boiler room. It was musty and damp. By the light of bulbs dangling from suspect wires, he turned left and right and left until he recognized the basement of his building. He walked up the stairs to the door leading to the hallway. It was locked. "Christ," he said. In a swift motion, he kicked the door just below the knob. It flew open, sending a lock and bolt flying in the air and ricocheting off garbage cans. He slithered up the stairs to the apartment to find that door locked as well.

He knocked. "Who's there?" It was Dory who asked. He heard rumbling and commotion inside.

"It's me," Tommy said, but barely in a whisper.

"Who is it?" she asked again.

"Me," was the same reply, a little louder.

He heard muffled voices, until, "Who is it!" his mother shouted.

"Damn it, it's me, Tommy," he said louder still.

Dory opened the door. Jake was peering from the bedroom.

"The landlord was here for a spot check," Dory said.

"I thought he might have come back," Jake said. He wheeled himself back to the table.

"He's a real bastard, that one," Maddie said.

Tommy shrugged. "I'm missing something here."

"Mr. Bile, the landlord," Maddie explained. "He's waiting for me to die. When I die, he can get two thousand a month for this apartment. And I don't want him at my wake. I swear, I'll haunt you if I see him at my wake."

"Don't worry, Ma, I guarantee you won't see him at your wake."

"Good," she said. "Anyway, I'm not ready to go anywhere yet, so I hope he's patient."

"Oh, he's patient," Jake reminded her.

"Good, because I'm not going anywhere." She continued fumbling through her rosary beads.

"Maddie, would you like a glass of warm milk before bed?"

Her face contorted. "Warm milk? No. Milk never put me to sleep." Her eyes opened wide with a twinkle. "I'll have a half glass of wine, though. That helps me sleep."

Tommy laughed. "Why not? Let's all have a glass."

Dory reached for a gallon of CK and poured as Tommy examined the label. *Nothing highlights my fall from the top better than drinking this rotgut,* he thought.

After a few sips of red wine, with Dory on one side and Tommy on the other, they assisted her into the bedroom. A portable commode sat alongside her bed.

"Thank you," she said. "Don't get old," she advised. "Everything is reversed, children have to take care of parents, and it's not normal."

"It's okay, Ma. You were there for us, we're here for you."

"And don't fight with your brother. You don't know how lucky you are to have brothers. You're lucky to have family. In the end, family is all you'll have."

"Right," he said.

Jake appeared in the doorway, and she stopped and stared at him. Her hand came to rest on his head. "Tomorrow, Jake, tomorrow are you going to get out of that chair? Are you going to try and walk?"

Jake's head slumped onto his chest. "Yes, Mom; tomorrow."

She kissed his head and closed the bedroom door.

Jake's wheelchair banged against the doorjamb, catching his fingers. He winced in pain.

"Christ, what a racket. A guy can't think around here," Tommy said. "And your mother is right. It would be easier if you just tried to walk."

"Everything is so easy for you."

"Some things are," Tommy said. "You lose a leg, you learn to walk with a new one. You don't sit on your ass feeling sorry for yourself."

"We weren't all born with your skills."

"Guess not," Tommy agreed.

Jake wheeled himself to the table. Tommy sat with his head in his hand.

"How did it go with Fat Pauly? Did he ask about me?"

"Not in so many words, I heard him say mostly the word 'prick,'" he replied.

"What did you say?"

"Yeah, I told him we've lost touch."

"Did you ask him for work?"

"Are you stupid? You don't just go into Pauly Fazzula's café, after all these years, and ask for work. That's like asking for a favor. He'll sense your slightest desperation and then it's all over. No," he said, "it has to be his idea. You got to make him think you're doing him a favor. I'll go back tomorrow."

"But he asked about me, right?"

"I told you he did," Tommy said.

"I wish you'd reconsider."

"Do you have any better ideas? Do you realize we're broke? I don't like being broke. I'll do whatever it takes."

Jake didn't answer. He rolled back from the table and lined himself up with the doorway, trying to find the right angle. "Christ!" he yelled as he jammed his finger.

During the night Tommy tossed and turned, struggling with the blankets. He rose and tiptoed two steps over to Jake's bedside, holding a pillow between his calloused hands, fluffing it like an accordion. He placed the pillow over Jake's face and applied pressure. As breath left his lungs, Jake's leg began kicking at the covers, his torso convulsed, his arms grasped to remove the encumbrance from his face. There were muted cries of hysteria until Tommy removed the pillow.

He stared straight down into Jake's colorless face. "If you don't stop snoring, I'll kill you. Do you understand? I'll kill you," Tommy said. "I can't sleep as it is. You're either crying in your sleep or snoring. I can hardly close my eyes."

Jake struggled to regain normalcy in his breathing. "You crazy heartless bastard. You could have killed me." Jake's breathing stabilized. "You stupid bastard, I'm telling Mom what you did."

"Boohoohoo," Tommy mimicked his brother. "I'm gonna tell Mom, boohoo. You big friggin' baby."

"I'm not a baby."

"Are too."

"Well, you could have killed me." He readjusted his covers. "I was dreaming that Fat Pauly had me tied to a chair, and he put a plastic bag over my head. You could have killed me."

"You snore," Tommy said. "Knock it off or *I'll* put the bag over your head."

In the morning, after a cup of coffee, Tommy kissed his mother and said, "I'll be back in a few hours."

"This package came for you this morning." She slid it across the table.

"Why did you open it?"

She shrugged. "It was delivered here. I thought it was for me."

He reached into the open package pulling out dozens of envelopes, unpaid bills, and a divorce decree signed by a judge in Vegas.

"Is everything okay, Tommy? There are a lot of bills in there."

He rubbed his brow.

"She left you." Maddie said.

"Ma!"

"I never liked her."

"You never met her. You didn't know her."

"Believe me, I knew her."

He stuffed everything back into the large envelope. "Everything is fine, no problems."

"You're only having coffee? That's not breakfast. You got to eat something." She picked up a piece of bread. "Dunk it, it'll be easier to eat, or we can toast it."

"I'm not hungry. I'll be back."

"Be careful," she said. "I'll be here."

"You're going through with this?" Jake said from the doorway.

There was no answer as he left.

Tommy walked into the basement of the building and retraced his steps, leading to the sidewalk a block away. He was on his way to Most Precious Blood hoping he wouldn't have to get physical but fully aware he would if it came to that.

CHAPTER 16

When Maria Forzano saw three men walk into her shop on security monitors, she removed an envelope from her desk and walked into the showroom. The men dispersed. Two saleswomen stood frozen in place. She saw panic in their eyes.

"Take a break," she said.

"Maria, will you be all right?"

"Sure, just take a break."

Forzano's was a staple of the Little Italy neighborhood, owned and operated by the Forzano family for three generations. It specialized in Old World antiques, from furniture pieces to trinkets, imported from Italy. She approached one of the men and stood eyeball to eyeball with him. He had a ruddy complexion highlighted by a scar running from his right ear to the center of his cheek. It had not healed well. He picked up a Murano figurine and examined it. Suddenly he fumbled it. "Ooops," he lamented as it fell from his fingers, shattering across the floor.

"I'm so sorry," he said. "But I guess you know accidents happen, especially in this neighborhood."

She did not flinch. "I'm well aware of the dangers on this street. It's filled with low-life, worthless, brainless, Neanderthal wannabes. Despicable pieces of excrement abound."

He nodded. "Yeah, well, my boss is always very helpful to people who feel threatened."

"And would your boss be Paul Fazzula?"

"One and the same," the man said. "And he sent me in here to let you know that if you should ever need help of any kind, he would be more than happy to assist."

As he spoke, the sound of glass objects shattering on the floor began to take on a rhythm.

"Hey guys," he said, "you gotta be more careful." He looked at her. "You see what I mean? Accidents happen."

"Oh I know," she said. "That's why two months ago when I had a break-in and my office was destroyed, I put in a security system. I installed it just in time to catch a picture of this man at three in the morning." She pulled out a photo downloaded from her security camera of a man carrying a gift-wrapped box approaching the front door. "You see here," she said pointing, "it's dated and time-stamped. Technology is amazing. Do you recognize him?" She gave the picture to him. "I want you to give this to Mr. Fazzula. I bet he'll recognize him. Anyway, when I opened the box and found a fish, a dead fish—trout, I think—I mean, really, does this stuff still work? Someone is watching too many movies. I mean, we're not in the Dark Ages."

She saw him recoil as he studied the photo. "So, here," she said, "Why don't you give this picture to Mr. Fazzula. I bet he recognizes him. Tell him I've upped my insurance, so 'up his.'" Before turning to walk away, she said, "I'm going to ask you to leave; but before you do, please smile and wave and say good-bye." She pointed to an innocuous ball-shaped device in the ceiling. "Technology is so amazing these days."

The scar-faced man looked to his companions. A subtle move of his head, and they followed him out.

CHAPTER 17

*T*ommy's steps echoed on the marble floors of Church of the Most Precious Blood. A group of the faithful filled two pews nearest the altar. In unison they prayed the rosary, with a Gregorian cadence that resounded throughout the vaulted ceilings.

"Hey, anybody see the guy who runs this place?" His voice shattered the solemnity.

He was met with a resounding "shush" and evil eyes as all heads turned. One man pointed to a small alcove behind the altar. "Father's office is that way," the man said.

Without the benefit of genuflection or a spritz of holy water, Tommy walked across the altar into the sacristy. There he saw a sign for the office. A woman sitting behind the desk typing was startled by his entrance.

"Can I help you?"

"Yeah, what's his name, Father, Father . . . ?"

"Father Bryce," she assisted.

"Right, Bryce," he said. "Where is he?"

"He's taking an important call at the moment. Do you have an appointment?"

"Kind of," he said. "Tell him Tommy Rossini is here."

Her eyes perked up. "Are you Maddie's son?"

"I am," he said.

"So nice to meet you. I'm Sister Michele. Your mother is a holy woman."

"So I hear," he said. He looked her over, head to toe. "Aren't you supposed to be wearing a costume or something?"

"A habit?" She laughed, correcting him. "Oh, we've changed those habits a long time ago."

He nodded. "I liked it better the old way," he said. "It was easier to disseminate a chick from . . . In any case, be a doll and tell Bryce . . . Father Bryce, I'm here."

Her cheeks reddened. She walked to another door, opened it, and stuck her head in. He heard her speaking. She turned to him. "Mr. Rossini, please have a seat. Father will be a few minutes." She motioned him to a chair outside the priest's office.

"I've got some chores to do," she explained. "It was nice to meet you. My love to your mom."

She left, leaving the office door open just enough. He could hear one side of the conversation, garbled though it was. From what he garnered, the priest was worried about something. The man on the other end was a detective by the way Bryce addressed him, and the priest was insisting he still felt safe. The call ended, and Tommy jumped back from the door. In a moment Father Bryce appeared. "Mr. Rossini, please come in."

Tommy sat in a chair across from the priest. Books lined the shelves of bookcases, and periodicals were stacked high on his desk.

"I came by for that little matter we discussed yesterday."

"Ah, yes," the priest said. He opened a drawer and pulled out an envelope and handed it to Tommy. "You can count it if you like," he said.

Tommy scoffed at the suggestion. "Father, jeez, I trust you. Jeez, if I can't trust a priest, then who can I trust?"

He tucked the envelope into his pocket and rose to leave.

"Are you sure about this, Mr. Rossini? We were going to help a lot of people with that money, the poor, the homeless."

"I have the same intention." *Me being the poor and homeless,* he thought. "And maybe it might be time to question your God. I mean, why are there people who are poor and homeless and sick and what have you? It doesn't look like your God has returned the favor," he said. "Otherwise, there would be no sickness or things like that."

"Oh, I don't know. God is not the cause of evil, but He may be the cure."

Tommy began walking away.

"Mr. Rossini," the priest called after him. "I will pray for you. I will pray for your conversion. I will pray you are born again."

"Thanks, but once is enough." He turned back. "And by the way, if you see my mom in church when you're saying mass, be sure to give a shout-out to my father and to whomever else she wants prayers said for. She shouldn't know what transpired here."

As he opened the office door he saw Maria Forzano waiting. "Maria," he said.

She studied him for a moment. "Hello, Tommy."

"You two know each other?" Gleason asked.

"We did," she said, before Tommy could answer. "A long time ago." She walked past Tommy. He felt a chill. "I brought you the proceeds from the silent auction," she said. "More than we expected. I'll leave it on your desk."

"You see," Gleason said, "sometimes God winks. Just to let you know He's there."

"Well, I'm glad He finally pitched in."

"So, you know Maria," he said.

Tommy only nodded.

"She's a special woman, an inspiration to me, actually."

"Really?" Tommy asked.

"Yes, she makes my crosses seem small."

"You have crosses, Father?"

The priest turned to Tommy and walked him toward the door. "We all have crosses to bear, some more than others. She helped me through the first few months after the disappearance of Monsignor Burns. She was a rock. And believe me, there are so many things going on now. She's like my backbone. She also works in Oasis House, a shelter for women we run over on Twelfth Street. It was part of St. Vincent's Hospital. It's a struggle to keep it open now that the hospital is closed."

"St. Vincent's is closed?"

"Wow," the priest said, "you have been away for a long time. Anyway, that's another story. So, how do you know her?"

"Like she said, it was a long time ago."

"Well, you are blessed. She too is a woman of such faith and devotion to God."

On the sidewalk Tommy slipped into a doorway and opened the envelope counting seven hundred-dollar bills. Satisfied, he folded the envelope in half, then half again, and arranged the bills around it. He put the enhanced wad into his pocket and walked down the street. He paused momentarily, reminiscing; the old restaurants were still there, new ones too; lots of new ones, and along with them the hordes of tourists. He stopped for coffee at Caffè Napoli, surveying the streets as tourists walked and pointed in awe at the tenements and their relic inhabitants.

He continued walking alone with his thoughts and found himself outside Forzano's. There, practically where he left her years ago, he saw Maria Forzano. She walked from item to item rearranging them on the shelves. Turning each item ever so slightly to get maximum eye appeal, directing a saleswoman to do the same. Her image danced off antique mirrors, and reflected in the thousand pieces of cut crystal that surrounded her. She had changed, from pigtails to a woman, a simple beauty—olive-skinned, in no need of cosmetics, and natural highlights in her hair; more beautiful than he remembered. A woman, still with the hint of the girlish innocence that he recalled. He took a deep breath and walked in.

"You were always good at marketing," Tommy said. "You learned well from your father."

Maria stopped what she was doing, but didn't turn around. "When did you get back?" she asked.

He moved to face her without answering and stared into those hazel eyes, recalling them filled with tears so many years ago.

"Your father always knew what people liked," Tommy said. "He was a stickler too. Everything had to be just right on the shelves, and the place had to be spotless. He taught me how to sweep: 'Turn the broom on an angle to get into the cracks on the sidewalk.'" He smiled as he recalled it, his eyes never leaving her. "How is he, how is your old man?"

Without looking at him she murmured, "Can't tell you, they haven't found his body."

His head fell. He felt blood drain from his head. "I'm sorry, I didn't know. He was a good man, always good to me."

"And you returned the favor, didn't you?"

"I tried to explain. It was business. I was young, stupid . . . I tried to stop . . ."

"Well, I guess you didn't do a good enough job, so they sent someone else to finish it."

"Maria, I'm sorry. I didn't know."

"Right, it was only local news. He wasn't important enough to make national headlines."

"I wish I had known."

"What for? You couldn't send a flower; there was no wake. There was no body."

Tommy wished he could crawl into a box. This was not what he had in mind for their first encounter after an eternity. He studied her up close.

"You look wonderful," he said, realizing how ill-timed the comment was.

"Why are you here? Or shouldn't I ask? Let's see if I can guess. Paul Fazzula's former enforcer shows up out of the blue just after the body of a murdered priest is found on the church steps. Have you been paid yet?"

Tommy shook his head. "I don't know what you're talking about. I don't know about any priest . . ."

"Why, then?"

"It's a long story. I got in just a day ago," he said. "Mom, you know; she's not doing well."

"Ah," she acknowledged. "I see her going to church. I don't know how she finds the strength."

"Me either," he said. "How have you been, Maria? I'm sorry I never kept in touch. I really am. When I left . . ."

"You don't owe me an explanation," she said.

He stared at her. "You are more beautiful than I remember. What are you doing now?"

"Enjoying my inheritance," she said.

"Some things never change," he said.

"You haven't changed much," she observed. "A little tanner, maybe."

"Right, except for thirty pounds and a lot more snow on the roof," he said, pointing to his head. There was an awkward silence. "I thought about you a lot over the years. I should have called or written . . . or . . ."

"Don't sweat it," she said. "I didn't expect it and wouldn't have answered. You left without a good-bye or forwarding address. For the longest time, I thought you were dead and after awhile, you were to me."

Tommy looked up and down the street, at one restaurant after another, and tour buses bringing hordes of tourists to sample the

Italian delicacies and culture. "I can't believe what happened to this neighborhood," he said, more so to change the subject.

Maria nodded. "There's nothing like a few Mafia murders to boost tourism, but you would know how that works. We're famous now. It's okay. Crime is good for commerce."

"Some things never change, I guess," he repeated for a lack of anything substantial to say.

"Well, in any case, I have to get back to work." She took a push broom and walked out to the sidewalk. He followed her.

"Just like your father," he said. "He was a fanatic about cleaning the sidewalk." His words sounded hollow. He knew he had made a mess of this encounter.

～

As they spoke, a midnight-blue Mercedes moved like a shadow on glass, stopping in front of Tommy. Inside, Fazzula was finishing a cell phone conversation with Johnny Pump. The information was simple and informative.

"So that's it, boss," Pump said. "That's all I found. The office was buttoned up tight; a pile of mail outside the door, bills mostly. I went to a few job sites, all shut down. Looked in the local paper, a ton of creditors are looking for him; and the local constabulary would like to talk to him too. He probably took it on the lam, probably had to."

Fazzula nodded. "You done good, Johnny, come home. It's just what I suspected."

"What are you going to do now, boss?"

"I told you, I'm going fishing. I'm going to enjoy this."

Pauly Fazzula's face became visible as the tinted window whispered open.

"Tommy, Tommy Boy, I'm glad I caught you. Hello, Maria. Anyway, stop by the café. Let's have a cup of coffee, or lunch maybe. I want to talk to you about something."

"Sure, Pauly. I'll come over, probably tomorrow."

"You do that, kid. Tomorra."

With that assurance the window whooshed up, and the car pulled away.

"I guess you're right," Maria said. "Some things never change. You feed rats, they get bigger."

Tommy gazed around Mulberry Street, his mind drifting back. The crowds of neighborhood people and tourists were spilling off the sidewalks onto the narrow street. Small boys chased one another, darting about and through the crowd. The street was full of chanting fruit and vegetable peddlers and vendors selling hot Italian sausage and peppers and hot dogs, New York style.

He muttered, "You're right, things don't change." He kept his eyes on the street scenes. "There's so much . . . so much . . . "— Tommy was groping—"I dunno . . . so much . . . !"

Maria said, "Electricity?"

"Yeah, yeah, that's one way you could put it. Like, so much energy."

He turned back to her, and he found her eyes in his. The orbs were locked and expressing themselves silently, and Tommy suddenly felt a bit choked up, maybe even overwhelmed.

"You were always so smart. Coming up with stuff . . . to finish my thoughts."

Now he struggled with the awkward silence. Finally, he said, "Hey, would you like to have an afternoon espresso at Caffè Napoli?"

She simply looked at him, and then started down the street. A thaw? Maybe. He quickly caught up, happy at the implicit agreement.

As they got settled, Maria's eyes were again deep into his. "What, Tommy?"

His only reply was a raised eyebrow, not sure where she was going with this. "Just surprised you'd sit with me, that's all."

"Why?" she asked. "What do you think? It's coffee, nothing more. We're not going to go off running across the meadows."

Tommy was hurt by the sarcasm, yet he had no way to really express himself. "No," he said, "I don't think that. Just looking at you . . . it . . . it takes me back. I need to explain . . . I . . ."

"What, Tommy? About my father? Or about you leaving without a good-bye or explanation? For the longest time I thought you were dead. Didn't know if you were in a landfill or witness protection."

"I didn't know, Maria. I didn't plan or want to harm him. They just done it. I . . . And afterwards I was so ashamed. I couldn't look in the mirror, nonetheless your eyes. I ran."

Her eyes seemed to sparkle just a bit. Was it a tear? Tommy leaned forward. He was earnest. But nothing came out. Finally, Maria said, "Why don't we just be nice to each other, while you're here, okay?" She sipped her espresso. Looking over the rim of her cup she asked, "How long are you going to be here?"

"I dunno. I have business problems."

"Have you had a happy marriage?"

"Huh?" he asked, caught off guard.

"Your marriage. Has it been good?"

"Well . . . I guess the truth would be no, not so much."

She peered at him. "You never change. Still the Tommy I remember. Always in control, always trying to make everything appear good whether it was or not. You hated to talk about problems or trouble. Always acting like you're in total control of your life. Classic; what the Italians would call *Un uomo con la pazienza di Giobbe*."

He sipped some espresso, lapsing pensive. Eventually, in a lower-than-usual voice, said, "I'm talking now. I guess you find out a lot about people when the chips are down."

"You're telling me!"

When he looked up at her, she seemed sad. He was too, realizing that he had let the good one get away.

"I gotta go," he said.

"I'm sure," she said, "your old friends are waiting. I'm sure they missed you. With my father gone, maybe you'll be sent to pay me a visit this time."

"That's not fair," he said.

She turned and walked toward her shop, leaving him standing alone on the sidewalk. He made his way up the street. Then he did something he had not done decades ago. He looked back.

Tommy walked past restaurants and coffee shops along Little Italy. Mulberry Street had indeed become a mecca. Maria was right, even bad publicity is good. A mob murder at a sidewalk café guaranteed press, which brought out the curious, prompting more restaurants to open. Even Fazzula's once "member's only" café was transformed and opened to the public.

The word on the street that it was owned by the famous Don Pauly Fazzula made it possible to charge five dollars for a cup of espresso. A small price to pay for starstruck average Joes to be in the presence of real bad men. He was bothered by Maria's suggestion that he was involved with the murdered priest. He had committed many sins, but that wasn't one of them.

The next day, as Tommy opened the door to Pauly's café, the first thing he heard was Pauly yelling at Patzo. "I told you to put that friggin' pigeon in its cage and clean this display case! There's bird shit all over the glass. He's shittin' on the pignoli cookies."

"Asshole, asshole," the parrot said. "Kill the asshole."

Patzo became beet-red as Fazzula threatened a move toward the bird.

"Where'd he learn that?" he demanded to know.

"He just heard it on television, Pauly. That Jerry Springer show, the guys say it all the time. I swear, I swear, Pauly."

"Get him in his cage and get to work."

Patzo extended his arm. The parrot walked across the bar, and perched on his arm. He walked it over to a cage. "Asshole," he whispered.

"Asshole, asshole," the parrot repeated.

Fazzula stopped in his tracks, turned slowly, and repeated, "Shut it up, and clean the showcases."

"I-I did clean them," Patzo said.

"Well, clean them again; and get that pigeon out of my sight before I make soup out of it."

Patzo hugged Pippy tight to his chest and scurried into the backroom.

Fazzula was an imposing figure. He was dressed in a double-breasted sharkskin suit that accentuated his large barrel chest with a hand-painted silk tie expertly draped from his neck and a blinding white-on-white shirt with a long collar that hid the knot.

"That kid never learns," Fazzula complained. "How about lunch?"

"That works for me," Tommy said.

Fazzula came from behind the counter and inserted his arm around Tommy's. "We'll go up to Paolucci's," he suggested.

Paolucci's Restaurant, a family-owned tradition on Mulberry Street, was filled with patrons. Traditional red-and-white-checkered table-cloths, empty Chianti bottles hanging from the bar. Black-and-white photographs of everyone from Joe DiMaggio to Joe Gallo lined the walls. There were few dignitaries who had not dined at Paolucci's. The décor had not been updated since the grand opening in 1947, and that was part of the charm. Fazzula often commented that Mr. Paolucci had dust brought in every week to maintain the atmosphere. Fazzula had a standard seat in the back, facing the door. He was a welcome sight to Mr. Paolucci and to all the waiters who knew a good tip was in the offing.

Fazzula ordered, "Bring us a cold antipasto, cheeses with the Auricchio provolone; is it sharp?"

Mr. Paolucci brought his fingers up to his lips and kissed them.

Fazzula nodded. "Good, good, and you know, the usual. And how are the peppers? Are they hot?"

Paolucci delicately kissed the tips of his fingers again, assuring him in impeccable broken English, "They'll open *u s*."

"Perfect," he said, "and I'll do the osso buco." He looked over to Tommy. "You remember the osso buco, don't you, Tommy?"

Osso buco was a signature dish of Paolucci's. "My mouth watered for it every night, for years," Tommy agreed.

"Good choice. And the marrow is good for you. Anyway, they don't know how to cook out there. It's the water. Can't make sauce or Italian bread without the right water. It's the water." He broke off a piece of twisted seeded bread that had been brought to the table. "Hey, where's the earl?"

"*Phil, porta l'olio, subito.* And, the usual wine, Mr. Fazzula?"

"Yes."

Paolucci brought a bottle of wine cradled in his arm like a precious newborn. Just as proudly as if it were, he displayed the bottle before Fazzula's eyes, awaiting a sign of approval. Fazzula stared at the label, and nodded. Paolucci removed the cork with expertise. He smelled it, squeezed it, and put it before Fazzula, as he poured a tasting portion into an oversize wineglass. Fazzula smelled it, felt the cork as well. He tasted the wine, swished it in his mouth, and swallowed. As he went through the ritual, Tommy stared at the bottle. It looked expensive, and he carried it as if he was the protector of the vintage. A red rooster stood atop a colorful label. It was like a work of art. *Art is expensive,* Tommy thought. He tried to see the year but couldn't make it out. He started doing calculations, knowing he would have to pick up this check for appearances' sake.

Fazzula nodded and Paolucci motioned to another waiter, who brought a cut crystal decanter to the table. *Christ,* Tommy thought, *you don't pour Ripple in those.* Paolucci poured the wine into the crystal bottle, then from the bottle into each glass.

"*Cent'anni,*" Fazzula said as he lifted his glass.

Tommy did the same, "*Cent'anni.*"

Fazzula appreciated the wine for a moment then said, "You know," he said, "maybe I misunderstood, but I thought you were staying at the Tribeca Grand. I called the desk last night. I wanted to know if you wanted to come with me for dinner. They told me you weren't registered."

Tommy fought a muscle tremor in his hand; his throat tightened. "Uh," he started.

"Oh," Fazzula interrupted, "don't tell me. I know, you're shackin' up with one of your old girlfriends. She's probably married, right? You got to lay some pipe while you're in town."

Tommy sighed. "You're sharp, Pauly. I could never hide anything from you."

Fazzula laughed. "You dog, you. You're just like your old man. He couldn't keep it in his pants either. What a hound dog he was." He laughed again. "Like father like son."

He could have done without the reference to his father, but Tommy was thankful for the alibi.

"I see you met up with that Maria woman. I'm surprised she's still talking to you."

"Well, it wasn't exactly a great conversation."

"Don't let it get to you. Her old man was stubborn, and so is she. You know, out of all the establishments in this neighborhood, hers is still the only one that doesn't pay a nickel to me; and I can't do anything about it. The old man ran right to the feds when we put the move on him. Stool pigeons, that whole family, stool pigeons. She's been seen talking to Olivetti, another traitor. Who knows who she's fingering? And they do very well in that two-by-four joint. They sell those stupid tchotchkes all over the country. I even tried to stop their supply from coming in from Italy, but she outmaneuvered me. But, as I say, I'm not finished with her. She jogs every day, you know. That can be dangerous. Women get raped and killed all the time while they're jogging. Or maybe gas. She lights up that maganette every morning. I'm thinking gas leak; *vabooom!* Happens all the time in these death-trap buildings. I got a guy who specializes in it. So anyway, I hope you didn't kiss and make up. I wouldn't get too emotionally involved. There's no future in it."

"Well, if it makes you feel better, it didn't go well," Tommy conceded.

"I'll say. But, hey, you did what you had to do. You went too light on him, though. You should've let the guys finish the job. You stopped them. That was not good. I was very, very disappointed in you."

"We were sent to break the place up, not hurt anyone. It got out of hand when he showed up."

"Still, you should have let the guys finish him off right then and there. You had bad instincts."

"Anyway, I understand he went missing," Tommy said.

Fazzula nodded. "Yeah, a shame. But I miscalculated. I thought, deal with him, the kid will fold. I should've figured the other way. With her gone, he wouldn't have any fight left in him. Anyway, more drastic steps were called for after your efforts failed. You were young and hungry in those days. But not anymore, right, Tommy? You've done well for yourself. Got the wrinkles out of your belly."

"Thanks, Pauly. That was long ago." Tommy felt a twinge in his chest as he relived his crimes.

"So," Pauly continued, "how long will you be staying? I know you probably got to be getting back. Business doesn't run the same without you."

"True," Tommy said.

"I'll tell you why I'm asking. I've got a big opportunity and there might be room for you, if you were interested. There's big money to be made. Can I convince you to stay for a while?"

Plates started arriving. Tommy sipped his wine, timing his response, seeking a proper balance between needing work and not showing it. "Jeez, I don't know."

"Well, listen, you think about it. I might be getting a job worth millions, and I could sub it to you. We can all eat. Like the old days."

"What's involved?"

"I can't say any more until I firm things up. It would be nice to know I can count on you. You got the expertise I need."

"Why me?" Tommy asked. "You got a hundred guys at your fingertips."

"I know, I know, but this is perfect for a guy like you. You've been out of the loop for a while, and that makes you valuable for this particular job. Your name doesn't show up when the friggin' city does its search. Remember the time you did that job for me in Brooklyn? That little pipe job. You earned well on that. Do you remember? That gave you your first start. You lost your cherry on that job."

Tommy nodded. It was a memory he tried unsuccessfully to forget. "That was a long time ago," he said.

"I know, but you earned good on it. I'll never forget the look on Carozza's face when he was arrested. It was priceless."

Tommy regretted taking sides in a turf war. He did so, as always, at Fazzula's request. Vito Carozza was a rival to Fazzula, not as much education but just as ruthless. The two dons had a blood feud that went back decades. Each tried to corner any moneymaking industry in New York and control of the unions was the key. A shaky truce was honored for years. Carozza stayed on his side of the Brooklyn Bridge, and Fazzula, on his. It was Fazzula who crossed the line when he heard of a large contract Carozza had secured. Fazzula devised a plan where the city would be forced to pull the contract from Carozza.

Fazzula's request from young Tommy Rossini had seemed harmless. "The building has to come down anyway," he told his young protégée. "Do you have any ideas?"

Tommy suggested a fire. His idea to cut the standpipe in the building's basement was brilliant. Two days later, a fire engulfed the building that encompassed a whole city block. Firemen attached their hose to the standpipe and turned on the water, which flooded the basement instead of filling the hoses. It was impossible to extinguish the flames.

The cut standpipe indicated foul play, and Carozza was blamed. Tommy earned five thousand dollars; and when the city awarded the demolition contract to a shell company Fazzula controlled, he subbed it out to Tommy Rossini's newly formed Rossini Contractors. Tommy's company and reputation grew exponentially from that point.

Tommy could have lived with all of it. It was all part of his plan—ingratiate himself with Fazzula, and his upstart company would be off and running. It all went according to his plan; and except for the death of two firemen, it all worked well.

It was that incident that made him beholden to Fazzula, forever joined in an unholy alliance. He understood his sins would always be held over his head. He also knew that he would have to extricate himself from these ties because, now that he wasn't a virgin, Fazzula would call upon him again, always upping the ante. No job too big, like busting the head of the CEO of a funeral home conglomerate doing business in the city because he was taking a hard line in union negotiations. No job too small, like vandalizing a small gift shop to get the owner to agree to a monthly tribute.

"Did you know Carozza wound up getting ten years for that?" Fazzula laughed.

It was news to Tommy. Bad news!

"Only served eight years; friggin' justice system. You know," Fazzula continued, "I kind of feel bad about that. Me and Carozza . . . well, it's never been right with us since then. Kind of miss that guy. Anyway, how could you have known he did a stint? You went away soon afterward. I'll never forget the look on his face; swore out loud he was framed." Fazzula laughed. "Boy, was he pissed. Still is. To this day he vows he'll find out who framed him. Can you imagine if he ever found out who framed him? I wouldn't want to be that guy."

Another bottle of wine, more bullshit about the good old days, two glasses of brandy, more embellished memories enhanced by time, and a cannoli later, Fazzula nodded to the waiter. Tommy knew he had to make an attempt for the check. He had to appear as if he were on top. But he couldn't figure out the wine. That painted label worried him, the decanter too. He would have felt better had it been a twist-off bottle. The waiter was about to place the leather folder on the table near Fazzula, but Tommy reached for it. The waiter held on to it, but Tommy pulled it from his hand in a mini tug-of-war.

"Thanks," Tommy said, "I got this." He pulled out the hundreds wrapped around the envelope, only slightly shading the roll from Fazzula's gaze.

"Hey, Tommy, think about it."

"I will," Tommy said.

Fazzula reached across the table and pinched his cheek. "That's all I can ask, Tommy Boy."

Tommy felt Fazzula's eyes staring at the wad of money in his hand. The Don's cell phone rang from deep in his pocket. As he answered the call, Tommy looked at the bill. Just as he thought, Chianti, vintage 1988, times two. *That son of a bitch,* he thought. *The waiter will be getting a bit less than the customary tip. No wonder the bastard fought to give Fazzula the check,* Tommy thought. He peeled off three hundred-dollar bills and put them in the billfold.

"Thanks," the waiter said. Tommy wasn't feeling the love.

Paolucci came to the table visibly upset. "This new generation," he said.

"What's wrong?" Fazzula asked.

"Those two," he said. He pointed to a corner table of two young men. Baseball hats did nothing to hide their ponytails and earrings.

They were getting loud. "I tella them we have a dress code, but they told me to 'fucka offa.'"

Fazzula nodded. "Are we all settled here?" he asked.

"Sì," the waiter said.

Fazzula made his way through the crowded dining room, and stopped at the table of the offending customers. He whispered something to one of the men as he took off his hat. Tommy saw the man give Fazzula the finger. *That's not smart,* he thought. Fazzula grabbed the man's finger and bent it backward. The metacarpal bone echoed in the room. The click was followed by an agonizing squeal.

The other man attempted to rise from his chair. He was met with Tommy's elbow in his eye. Then Tommy grabbed both men and banged their heads together. Blood exploded from their brows. They fell to the floor. He kicked them in the stomach and head. They crawled out the door on their hands and knees, presenting themselves for a final kick in the ass that sent them careening down the steps to the sidewalk. Fazzula turned, and brushed off his sleeves and readjusted his cufflinks, then his tie. "Be respectful when you come into my neighborhood, punks." He turned to Tommy. "Tommy Boy Rossini," he said. "You still got it. The animal still lives in you. You're a natural. I knew it." He placed a gentle pat on Tommy's cheek. "Come by tomorrow, we'll talk more."

Tommy watched as Fazzula walked away. He thought about his words, "You still got it, the animal lives." He hated himself. He hated Fazzula for being right. During the altercation he felt something take over. Some raw anger, some animal rage from deep inside that he thought he had conquered. In that moment, he realized he was what he was.

Tommy was feeling things about Maria. Concern. Worry for her safety. It was something he just did not know how to handle. At least not right now. In any case, it gave him an excuse to contact her. He wrote a note and slipped it under the shop door. "Can you meet me? Later today. Our spot at Coney! I have to tell you something."

He stood in the shadow of the Ferris wheel, which was stationary against a gray sky. He stared at the Cyclone in the distance, and imagined hearing the echo of frantic screams as the roller coaster tumbled back to earth. Silent now. He walked alongside the once great pier, dilapidated now, and he wondered if she would even remember their favorite spot and if she did, would she recognize it? He certainly didn't. Coney Island was deserted now, a far cry from the bustling beachside Brooklyn wonderland he remembered. A victim of economic downturn, surrounded now by neighborhoods that had seen better times. The arcade trailers were buttoned down and rusted. The flashing crayon-colored signage was dark; the carnival tents were packed, the cotton candy machines spun no more; no more Orange Julius or Nathan's. The carnival hawkers urging you to "Break one more balloon to win your baby a stuffed animal" had moved to greener pastures. The beach collected debris and attracted seagulls that meandered through rotted driftwood in search of food. A portrait of decay speckled with an occasional jogger running along the water's edge. The shoreline attracted all varieties of trash, and garbage blighted the horizon. Would she even remember and if she did, would she come? "Can you meet me? Our spot at Coney!" He said, "I have to tell you something." Only the very brave or stupid would come to Coney Island now. He figured he was the stupid one and hoped Maria was brave.

Finally, he saw a little Ford pull up to the beach. It was her. Maria turned the collar up on a knit sweater and walked toward him. From a distance he noticed her shapely contours. She was comfortable in her skin.

"Why here?" she asked.

"We had some nice memories here."

She looked out at the North Atlantic. The ocean was choppy and slammed onto the shore. "I like it," she said, "The sea, brooding and full of secrets."

"Remember when we couldn't wait to strip down to our suits and charge into the breakers?

"Well, I don't think my bikini would fit anymore."

He laughed, "And with this spare tire I don't think I'd be charging anywhere."

Now she laughed. "We did have some fun, though. Our picnic basket drew a crowd."

"I'll say. Why wouldn't it? You knew how to pack a basket. Italian bread stuffed with prosciutto, provolone, and salami. Chilled Chianti. It was a mini-feast complete with olives and some dried fruit. You thought of everything."

"We were so young, so naive."

"If it makes you feel better, you still look great. You really do."

Self-consciously, she tightened the sweater around her. "I like to run. I try to every day."

His ears perked up. "Running is hard on the knees. You should think of something else to do."

"And look at you! Mr. Glamour Boy with the permanent Southwest tan. Around here we have to pay fifty bucks for that tan." She flashed a grin that brought him back so far and so quickly. It was a wry little thing that he loved, that curve at the corner of her full lips.

They walked and sat on the remnants of a bench and let the fall breeze wash over them. He tried to keep his eyes off her. She said, "Old Coney Island. Nothing like those trendy places you probably go to in California. Like Malibu?"

He didn't answer. When he did his voice had dropped. "Yeah, right. Scottsdale is nothing but a furnace with a million pools around it to beat the heat, and California is one great big freeway."

She shrugged. "Well, I guess every place has its drawback. I was out there . . . " she hesitated, "with a friend some years ago. I liked it, but for me it just wasn't New York."

He grinned, sensing there was more to the story. "Guess you're just a homebody."

"Guilty," she said.

Tommy just looked at her. He had no intelligent comeback, so said nothing. "Where did the time go?" He said staring out to the sea.

She just looked at him and shook her head. "It was a different time for sure. Anyway, you said you had something to tell me."

"I did? Right, I did. I forgot. It wasn't important. I'll remember."

She stared deep into his eyes. "Tommy, I don't know why you're here, or why you came back," she said. "I can only surmise you were summoned, probably for some big job that only you could do. Or maybe did already. And presto, the monsignor shows up dead. You can't blame me."

"Well, you're wrong. I came back on my own . . . to see my mother. I wish you'd believe me, but I understand why you don't. "

"I don't know what I believe," she said.

"Are you ever going to forgive me? Can you ever fully forgive me?"

"Honestly, I don't know. Sometimes . . . I just don't know. Do you even need my forgiveness? You are who you are. Those are your words."

"I did what I thought I had to do to survive. I didn't ask to be born here, in the middle of all this. But I was born here, and I had to play by their rules."

"Their rules?"

"That's right. These guys, these street guys made the rules; and that's all I knew. We were dirt poor when my father died. But I knew it was wrong, I knew I was becoming something that scared me. Don't you see, that's why I left. It was getting crazy. I was getting involved in something, too deep."

"You had other choices."

"Did I? I did the best I could. I played the hand I was dealt."

"That's a copout . . ."

"No, no, it was the way out."

"Was? And now you're back . . ."

He stood nearer to her now. In a moment, words were not enough. He put his arms around her and pulled her close. He relived the nights her body lay against his, on rooftops under the stars, thinking the world would always be as simple and beautiful as it was in those moments when his very being disappeared into her. "Maybe we can have another chance. Maybe we can have it back. Can you forgive me, Maria?" He kissed her.

"I'm so confused, Tommy. I don't know. I'm just so confused."

Forgiveness was illusive. He did nothing except say, "I'm sorry, I'm sorry."

"We better get out of here before we get mugged. How did you get here?"

"Train," he answered.

She paused. "Would you like a ride?"

When they got back into the city late that afternoon, Maria said, "Did you remember what you had to tell me?"

They were near her apartment, and he said, "Well, I . . ."

"Come, I'm uncomfortable. I need to shower. Come in. Sounds like you need time to get up some nerve to tell me whatever it is."

He couldn't disagree.

"There's a CD player on the bureau and some French wine in the kitchen."

He looked around the apartment. It was immaculate. She lived alone, he surmised, and didn't entertain. No pictures of the "friend" who took her to California. *That's good,* he thought. He looked through the CDs and soon found himself stretched out on her easy chair listening to Bobby Darien with the sound of the shower in the background and his heart racing.

When she appeared in a robe and her hair in a towel turban, his heart skipped.

Later he tried to remember why he never talked about the threat he felt was hovering over her. Life is about moments, and this wasn't the moment. Instead he handed her a glass of wine. "*Somewhere beyond the sea, somewhere waiting for me, my lover stands on golden sand . . .*" He couldn't remember whose idea it was to go into the bedroom, but a good idea it was.

Her lips were soft, with an intoxicating trace of Bordeaux. He kissed glistening beads of perspiration off the nape of her neck. Her scent was dizzying. He was as thoroughly excited as he had ever remembered; awash in a mélange of longing, nostalgia, and pure lust. He was young again. She made him young again. Things heated up fast and, selfishly, he decided that what he had meant to warn her about could wait. He would find a way to protect her. Sure he would.

When he awoke later, Maria was getting dressed. She stretched jogging tights up to her waist. Tommy said, "Where are you going?"

"I told you, I like to run; and I have to get to work early. They are installing some cameras at the store, and I have to be there to make sure it goes right."

Tommy said, "Please, don't run today. Stay. I'll make you coffee. Besides, you already have cameras."

"Yeah, but the goons taunted me the other night; and I told them about the cameras. Even showed them some photos."

Tommy sighed. "So what good is putting in more cameras?"

"Well, we're going to hide these better. I'm putting some in the alley."

"That won't get Pauly off your back." *And cameras don't see gas,* he wanted to add.

She seemed determined, and he knew he couldn't change her mind. But he tried anyway. "Look. You and your place are kinda like a matter of pride for Pauly. You are the only one not paying. Makes him look bad."

Maria rolled her eyes. "That's what you wanted to tell me?"

"Yeah, that and Pauly never gives up. He's maniacal."

Maria bent over to tie her sneakers, causing him to stop for a moment and swallow.

He said, "He has guys that will do anything for him."

"Don't I know that? I just slept with one. " Her tone had changed. *I deserved that.*

"Pauly wants to make an example of you."

Now she stood there with her hands on her hips, her eyes blazing. "And you're going to do what while he does this?"

"I . . . I don't know. I can't go up against Pauly. You know how it works. I'm just a small potato. I have no power. No influence. I can't really do more than warn you. Like I'm doing now."

"So you're just an innocent victim of the system. You grew up around here, you ran with these guys, and now they own you. Is that it?"

He looked at her, surprised at how succinctly she'd put it.

"Well, yeah. That's the way it goes. Nobody can get away from the power of the Don. He has all the money; all the muscle. All you can do is do what he says or run and hide."

"Like you've done for thirty years. You have no control over your life?"

"Well . . ." He thought a moment. "No, I guess I don't."

She picked up her purse and headed for the door. "Well you warned me. Now it's my problem."

"Maria. Wait. I feel like . . . I . . . I don't know what to do."

"Do what you did thirty years ago. Head for the hills."

"Why are you so friggin' stubborn?"

She left, slamming the door behind her.

That went well, he thought.

Later that day he went back to her apartment and waited for Maria to come home from work. He had no idea when she'd be back. It turned out that she came home after eight. She was surprised to find him still there. Her brows shot up at the sight of him.

"I hope you don't mind."

She dropped her purse on a chair. "I'm hungry," she said. "Order from Luna's. They'll deliver. I have a house account." She stopped just before heading into the bedroom. "Strange," she said, "a Con Edison crew showed up at my shop today. Someone reported a gas leak. Do you know anything about that?"

"Me? Uh, no."

When she came out she found the table set. There were calamari, veal scaloppine, and some cheese ravioli. He even found a candle in a kitchen cabinet.

She said, "I can't eat all that."

He grinned. "I also took the liberty of ordering wine."

She eyed him suspiciously. "Amarone?"

"You know me. I always liked nothing but the best. Actually, the wine was compliments of Luna."

Maria ate more than she thought she would, and they both lit into the wine.

They found themselves sitting side by side on the sofa. She in a bathrobe and he in his shorts and T-shirt—that's all he had until she got up and pulled a sweater from a drawer. His eyebrows raised. "My father's," she said handing it to him.

"*Ouch . . . !*"

When one bottle was gone he looked at her with a silly smile. "We look like an old married couple."

"Yeah, maybe we'd be sitting just like this if we had married thirty years ago."

"Yeah, maybe we would have made five or six little Tommies by now."

"Lord no," she said.

They both broke out in a huge belly laugh. It turned into a laughing fit and neither of them could stop. When they finally stopped, choking, coughing, and sputtering, she said, "I needed that. I'm so sick of this crap."

Drunkenly, Tommy asked, "What crap is that?"

She sipped some more wine. "Of trying to run an honest business in a nest of vipers who want to make sure you become as corrupt as them."

Tommy held back on that one, knowing which camp she probably put him in.

Later they fell into bed and feasted on each other like love-starved teenagers, or more likely the long-lost lovers that they were.

When they had sated themselves, at least for now, Tommy said, "So are you a Leno or a Letterman gal?"

Maria shrugged. "Both think they're funnier than they are."

Tommy hesitated. She giggled. "Oh, don't look so stricken. I don't care which one you watch. Take your pick. I'll probably be asleep soon anyway."

"It's funny trying to adjust to each other after so long."

She did drop off to sleep early; but before she did she mumbled, nearly incoherently, "I'm glad you're back, Tommy. Really so glad," she said. Her lips moved, but he knew it was the wine talking.

Maria left him sleeping that morning. He reached over to caress empty sheets. He smelled her pillow and lay there for a moment. Tommy showered and took the leftover food to his mother's. It had been a long time since she'd eaten like that. All the while, he had Maria on his mind.

Getting back with her had turned out to be breathtakingly wonderful, yet now he'd created even more danger for both of them.

In his gut he knew that this "thing" that Pauly wanted to talk to him about would not end well. He just knew it. Pauly wasn't a guy who gave out favors, even to those loyal to him for years. He paid for what you did for him and he paid well, but no favors. He felt the walls coming down on him. He had a gut feeling he was being played, that Pauly was planning to settle all debts in one sweeping blow.

He knew he had to confront Pauly, but he had no idea what he would say. He felt a pain in his chest. If he let on that he was protecting Maria, it would be all over for both of them. No, he had to be cool. The best thing he could do was see what Pauly wanted of him and maybe find a way to turn it against him. With no muscle, no money, and no power he had to live by his wits. *Ha,* he snorted, *that's a joke. As if I had any freakin' wits. If I had wits I wouldn't be in the spot I'm in today.* It was déjà vu. The stress of thirty years ago was back. The same choices had to be made again. He had gone nowhere after all. But this time, lives other than his were in danger. It was time to man up.

CHAPTER 18

Santo Olivetti did not expect to garner much useful information from the old-time, Old World vendors on Mulberry Street. Having a last name ending in a vowel made one reluctant to talk to police. He understood. They had to live and work here, and even perceived disloyalty was . . . frowned upon. If he was to learn anything at all, he would have to be subtle walking into one shop after another, asking nonthreatening, simple questions.

"Hey, that monsignor guy, did you know him?" he asked the fruit vendor.

"Oh sure, who didn't. Wonderful man. Heard some rumors over the years, but he was always nice to me."

"Rumors?" He squeezed a melon and handed it to the man.

"Yep, rumors, liked the ponies, that was the word. Dollar eighty," he said.

With melon in hand, Olivetti visited the pizzeria. "Can you put some hot pepper on that?"

"No problem," the counterman said as he threw a disc of dough into the air, swirling it adeptly in his fingers as it landed, then tossing it again. "He was a good guy, liked poker, from what I heard. I remember one night they went to get him from a card game behind the pastry shop because someone needed last rites. The boys were pissed because he left with their money that night. He said, 'God works in mysterious ways'; that was the joke on the street. But he gave it all back the next night, and then some. That was the story. You want a glass of wine with that?" the man said as he placed two slices of pizza in front of Olivetti.

Then to Forzano's, where the owner had no qualms about answering questions. "Monsignor? He was a man with problems," Maria explained to the detective. "And a man with problems is easy prey to the animals in this neighborhood. He was into Fazzula, into him real deep, everyone knows that, and you don't want to find yourself in that position. I wasn't surprised to hear he disappeared, less surprised to hear he had been murdered. I would bet they bled Burns, milked St. Vincent's dry, and had other plans."

That was productive, Olivetti thought. He ventured further. "And what can you tell me about Paul Fazzula?"

"Pure evil," she said without missing a beat. "He will take your eyes out and eat them if you owe him a nickel. He is evil incarnate."

"You seem to know a lot about him."

"I could write a book. Maybe I will."

"Aren't you afraid?"

"Of course I am."

He turned to leave then paused. He took a photograph out of his pocket. "One more thing," he said. He showed her a photo. "Do you know this man?"

Her eyes opened wider. "That's Tommy. Tommy Rossini."

"He seems to be a new player in all this. Can you tell me anything about him?"

"Like what?"

Olivetti shrugged, "Good guy? Bad guy?"

She looked up from the photo. " I . . . wish I knew," she said.

Tommy stopped by a fruit stand and bought an apple before going into the building. There was much to digest. He thought about Fazzula's reference to his role in the fire. It was problematic. One thing he knew, Fazzula had a method to his madness. The incident was mentioned for a reason.

And he thought about Maria, his first love, both young, naive. He began to get a twinge in his heart as he recalled how it all disintegrated because of the choices he made, and he comforted himself with the thought that he didn't really have a choice. But still, there was an uncontrollable shaking in his hands; and his heart felt as if it would jump from his chest. Sweat formed on his brow, and his vision became blurry. He took a pill from a vial in his pocket and placed it under his tongue. Maddie was seated in her wheelchair by the window.

"Tommy, are you all right?"

"Fine, I'm fine. I've brought some real food. And here; this is for you." He reached into a bag. "Here, Mom, bite into this while I heat this up."

"Jesus, fresh fruit," she said. She bit into the apple as he watched. He took the apple and examined it and gave it back. "Why are you breathing heavy?" he asked. She took another bite.

"Let me see you smile," he said. The glint from her gold teeth was still visible.

Damn, he thought. Then from the bedroom he heard moaning. It was alternately high and low, mingled with grunts and groans. He went to the door but could not get in.

"Jake, Jake!" he called. "Are you all right?"

Maddie turned from the window. "He's fine," she said.

The moaning continued, then he heard muted whispers. "Jake, are you okay?"

"Fine. I'll be right out. I'm getting a manicure."

The bedroom door opened moments later, and he was eye to eye with Lucy. Her blouse was misbuttoned, and her skirt rumpled. There was a blush in her cheeks.

"Oh, hello," she said. "I give brother manicure."

He looked behind her to see his brother fixing his pants.

"Christ!" he yelled at the top of his lungs. "You're the only guy I know who gets a manicure with a happy ending. Are you friggin' crazy? Your mother is out here, and you're doing the *Last Tango in Paris?*"

"She can't hear anything," he said grudgingly.

"Right," Maddie agreed. "I can't hear anything."

Lucy reached for Tommy's hand and stroked his middle finger. "Maybe I give you manicure too," she said as she winked.

"Thanks, but no thanks," he said.

"Well, if you change mind, you call. Jake knows how to get me."

"I'm sure."

After she left, Jake rolled himself to the table.

"I thought you were crazy, and now I know. First of all, what does a 'manicure' cost?"

Jake laughed. "Cost? I've never paid for a manicure. Lucy loves me."

"Yeah, well in case you didn't know, she loves Fat Pauly Fazzula too. Yours is not the only thumb she's polishing off."

"Don't you think I know that? She's my spy, like Tokyo Rose. She tells me what Pauly is thinking and doing."

Maddie turned. "You mean Mata Hari, not Tokyo Rose."

"Asshole," Tommy said to his brother. "As if we don't have enough problems. I think you are crazy."

"Come, boys. Let's eat together." Maddie said. "Jake, come see what Tommy brought home. Real restaurant food."

Dory came into the apartment. "Boys, is something burning?" She ran to the oven where the ravioli and scaloppine had been warming up. She took it out as Jake pointed to a gallon of wine on the counter. Tommy poured some, and all sat around the table. Tommy did not take his gaze off of Jake. He stared and kept shaking his head back and forth. "With your mother in the next room," he said.

"She's deaf."

They finished eating. Maddie said, "What a treat."

"Perfect," Jake noted as he unbuckled his pants. "I always get hungry after I get—"

Tommy smacked him in the head before Jake could finish the thought. Then came a knock on the door. Tommy peeked through. "It's only Looney." Looney, coming in, kissed his mother and hugged his brothers.

"Good to see you guys," he said.

"What took you so long? We're here a week."

"You must be so proud, Maddie, to have all your sons here around you."

"Right," she said. "I should have produced vending machines instead of babies. I'd have a steady income today." She laughed.

Dory laughed. "She doesn't mean it. She tells me all the time how much she loves you all."

"Yes, but who is her favorite?" Jake asked.

"All equally," Dory said.

"Don't put words in my mouth," Maddie said with a hint of a smile.

"Well, who then?" Looney wanted to know.

"You're all different," she said. "Tommy, he's the strong one. I'm glad the abortion was botched."

Tommy choked on his wine. "Abortion! You tried to have me aborted?"

Jake laughed. "Oh, you didn't know that, dear brother? I thought you knew."

"It wasn't like that," Maddie explained. "You and Jake are only eleven months apart. Irish twins. Do the math. The doctor said I wouldn't survive. What did I know? I was young. They took me to some place in New Jersey. In any case, they told me it was over; but you kept growing, and here you are. That's why you're the strong one."

"And maybe that's why you have an aversion to hangers," Jake suggested. That prompted a smack to his head.

"What about me?" Looney asked.

"Pure accident," Maddie answered. "I was blindsighted."

They all laughed.

"Listen," Looney said, "do you want to come over for dinner on Sunday?"

"Dinner? At your house?" Tommy asked.

"You'd better stop drinking," Jake added.

"Your wife cooking?" Tommy asked.

"You got a problem with that?"

"No, no, she's a fine cook." He turned his head away and held his nose.

"I saw that," Looney said.

"Saw what? I had to sneeze."

"Bullshit."

"Boys," Maddie admonished.

"He started," Looney answered. Jake and Tommy put their heads down. "So," Looney said, "is that a yes or a no?"

"And your wife is cooking?"

"If you're going to break my balls then forget it."

"No, no, we'll be nice," Tommy assured him.

"And that goes for my wife too. Don't break her balls either."

"I knew she had balls," Jake chimed in.

"What did you marry, a transvestite?" Tommy asked.

"That's it, forget it. It was a bad idea."

"I'll go if he takes me to visit the cemetery too," Maddie said.

"Do you hear that? We got to take Mom to the cemetery."

"Well?"

"I wasn't counting on having to drive down here to take you. And the cemetery? That's in a different direction altogether."

"Helloooo," Tommy said. "Are you stupid or just ignorant? How are we supposed to get there? I got this cripple Don Juan in a wheelchair and Mom in hers. What do you want me to do, put them on a bus?"

Jake looked at Looney. "You're sorry you asked, aren't you?" Then he turned to Tommy. "And thanks for that, you heartless bastard."

"All right, all right. I wasn't thinking. It's no problem. I'll come down Sunday morning."

"Okay, good," Dory said. "It'll be good to get some fresh country air and to eat something other than pizza."

"Don't count on it," Tommy said. "That goes for fresh air too. We're talking Staten Island here. It's a landfill. "

"Are you gonna start with that again?" Looney asked.

"But I've got to visit the graves," Maddie reminded them.

"By the way," Jake said to Tommy, "your wife called. Tuition is due for her daughter."

"Did she want me to call her back?"

"No, she just said the tuition was due. Send money."

On Sunday morning Jake announced, "I'm staying home. I don't feel like going out. The steps are too much trouble."

"Then I'll stay too," Maddie said. She was already dressed in a powder-blue dress. Dory was putting finishing touches on her hair and placed a flower in it.

"You look so pretty, Maddie. Too pretty to stay home."

"Old. I look old and I'm not leaving him alone. We all go or we all stay."

Tommy pointed to Jake. "Stop the bullshit. You're coming if I have to drag you down the steps."

"I can't, I can't make the steps. And what if Pauly sees me?"

"You're a real *cacasotto*. What if Pauly sees me? What if Pauly sees me?" he mimicked.

Looney, pulling up in front of the house, stopped the car and sounded the horn. Tommy opened the window and yelled to him, "Are you coming up to help me?"

"I'll get a ticket," he whined.

"How do you expect me to get them down without help? Am I supposed to lower him out the window with a rope?"

Looney reached into the car and put the hazard lights on.

Dory walked with Maddie and Tommy, and Looney helped move her down the stairs and out the front door just as a police officer was putting the finishing touches on a summons. Looney abandoned his mother's side and she lost balance. Dory swooped to grab her arms and steady her. Looney was yelling at the police officer. He tore off the ticket and handed it to Looney.

"The city needs the money," he said.

"Christ!" Looney yelled.

Tommy and Dory brought Maddie the final steps across the sidewalk. "What's this?" Tommy asked.

"It's my car," Looney said.

"It's a friggin' Toyota Prius, how the hell are we going to get everyone in a Prius? Are you a moron?"

"Yes, it's a Prius, and it's a hatchback," Looney explained. "And it's a hybrid. Fifty miles to the gallon."

Without help from Maddie, whose muscles were frozen, they placed her in the car. "Are you okay, Mom?"

"I'm fine," she said. "Jake, worry about Jake. Don't let him change his mind."

"Do you have any rope?" Tommy asked.

Looney had rope in the trunk and together they secured Maddie's wheelchair to the roof.

"Now, go around the corner near where Fretta's Pork Store used to be. We need to go in the building through there to get Jake out."

"What are you talking about?"

"I need help with Jake. We can't take him out this way because he's on the lam. He's not supposed to be here."

The color drained from Looney's face. "So if they see him, I could be in trouble too. What did you get me into?"

"Hey, numb nuts, do you want to stand here and argue about him and bring attention to yourself, or do you want to go around the corner and help me? Dory will sit with Mom."

Looney kicked the tire before getting into the car. He drove around the corner and made his way through the buildings.

Jake was holed up in the backroom, refusing to come out. "I can't make the steps."

"What's wrong with him?" Looney asked.

"When the doctor cut off his leg, he slipped and cut off his balls too," Tommy explained. It was loud enough for Jake to hear.

"You think it's easy?" Jake yelled through the door.

Tommy took a deep breath. "Jake, if you don't open this door, I'm gonna break it down and lower you out the window like a piano."

The door opened.

"What's the plan?" Looney asked.

"We carry him unless you can levitate him."

"He weighs a ton," Looney said. "I've got a bad back."

"Well, you can take a pill later. Right now, lift."

They wheeled Jake to the top of the landing.

"Do you have everything you need?" Looney asked. "Did you guys bring a sweater?"

"Lift," Tommy ordered.

"No," Jake yelled. He reached for the banister and gripped it.

"Don't look down, asshole. Let go of the banister."

"No," Jake cried. "I don't want to go."

Tommy reached around him and jabbed his finger into Jake's armpit, causing him to release the banister. He and Looney moved their cargo down the steps, one at a time, pausing only to catch their breath. "It's like delivering a refrigerator," Tommy said.

Minutes later they appeared in the doorway. Tommy looked out and surveyed the street up and down. Except for the police officer issuing another ticket, the coast was clear. He nodded to Looney.

"Christ!" Looney exclaimed. "That's a hundred-dollar ticket."

Before they left the building, Tommy took stock of the car. "How in God's name did you think we could get five people and two wheelchairs into this death trap?"

"I figured Jake would chicken out."

"You figured? You figured? You are a mental midget."

A cold rain began to dampen the streets as the four-passenger Prius jammed with five passengers, two immobile, stacked one upon the other, and two wheelchairs strapped to the roof, sputtered and bottomed out as it turned off of Mott Street onto Canal.

"Do you think we were noticed?" Looney asked.

Shortly after the Manhattan Bridge, Maddie reminded her son, "We're going to the cemetery first?"

"Ma, the weather is bad. Another time, I'll take you. I swear."

"You lied," she said. "You promised and now you're reneging."

"I'm not even sure how to get there," Looney complained.

"You have GPS," Tommy observed.

"Yeah," he said. "It's only good if you know where you're going."

"Take the Van Wyck to Mercer Avenue," Maddie said.

An hour later the Rossinis arrived at the gates of St. John Cemetery in Queens.

"We have to make four stops," Maddie announced. "That doesn't include the flower shop. Pull over there."

Looney pulled up in front of the flower shop.

"Get four bouquets," Maddie instructed. "The five-dollar ones."

Tommy was doing the math. Prepackaged funeral bouquets were neatly displayed on the sidewalk as a vendor conducted business.

"How much?" Tommy asked him.

"Top row twenty dollars, middle row fifteen, and ten on the bottom."

"They all look the same to me," Tommy said.

"They're not," the man said.

Another customer got the vendor's attention. The vendor grabbed a floral arrangement from the woman along with her cash and went inside the shop. Tommy looked around and quickly took four bouquets from the top shelf and tossed them into the back of the car, where they landed on top of Maddie. With her hair done up and a nice dress and now the flowers on top of her, he noted she looked like she belonged in a funeral parlor.

"Let's go" Tommy said.

"Did you pay?" Loony asked.

"Let's go," Tommy said.

Following his mother's instructions, Looney pulled up alongside section 54. "Look out the window and say a prayer, Mom. You don't have to get out."

"No," she said. "It doesn't count if you don't get out. It doesn't count as a visit. I didn't come here to sit in the car. I got to go to the grave. That's why they call it a 'visit.'"

"Ma," Tommy said. "The weather is bad. Can't we just do a drive-by?"

"No," she said. "It's not right."

Jake, Maddie, and Dory were all smashed into the backseat. On cue, Dory and Looney extricated Jake, then Maddie. The rain had worsened, changing to hail. The wheelchair was not an option in the soft ground. Dory, Tommy, and Looney joined their arms together, making a makeshift chair, and carried Maddie down one row of stones then another as she gave directions. At each stone Dory set a bouquet and Maddie prayed.

"This was your Uncle Sebastiano. When you were born we took you to see him right from the hospital. He was a beautiful man. His wife died, she's here too. Margaret. His second wife was a witch. She never made him happy. Never," she said. Then to another row, braced against the wind and searing rain.

"Are we the only friggin' nuts visiting graves on a day like today?" Tommy asked.

"Ma, how many more?" Looney complained.

"Stop here," Maddie said. They stopped at an empty space between two gravestones.

"Ma, who's buried here?" Tommy asked.

"This is your father's grave. We have an eight-grave plot here. Your father won this plot in a poker game. Good thing too. I wonder what graves cost today?"

"How do you know its Dad's? There's no stone."

"That's how I know. It's the only grave in this whole section without a stone. I gave Jake the money to take care of that a few years ago."

Tommy shook his head as he looked back toward the car. "It figures," he said.

"Ma, can we go? My arms are hurting," Looney whined.

"Yep," said. "But remember, this is where you'll bury me."

They brought her back to the car braced against the elements. They were soaked to the bone when they got back to the car.

"Does the heat work in this jalopy?" Jake asked.

"I'm never going to dry out," Tommy said, wiping icy sleet from his head and shoulders. "Put the damn heat on."

"I'm trying," Looney said. "It's draining the battery."

PART
VII

CHAPTER 19

*P*enny Rossini prepared for her arriving guests. Soon, she thought, her quaint home would be invaded, her food critiqued, and her lifestyle questioned. She swallowed two Valium and washed them down with a glass of Pinot Grigio. She put the vial back in the cabinet, then thought better of it and put it in the pocket of her sweater. She looked at her hand. It was shaking. *Calm down,* she told herself, *in a few hours the ordeal will be over. Right.*

The galley kitchen seemed especially narrow. She ran her hands over her hips, choosing to ignore the obvious reason. Squeezing along the counter, she opened the lid of a large pot as gravy meat simmered. She turned the contents with a wooden spoon, grasping for a meatball and bringing it to her nose. It smelled good to her, but she could only hope they were tasty. In another pot, water had yet to come to a boil. At just the right moment she would be able to throw pasta in, and it would cook in minutes. She opened the oven and checked the temperature of the turkey. She was losing track of the sweet potatoes, stuffing, and array of other side dishes. None of which would be enough to satisfy the hobbling gourmets headed to her door. Of this she was sure. She took another swig of wine and peered out the window. The icy rain had turned into snow, and it was sticking. Her window thermostat steadied at 32 degrees, great conditions for a blizzard. The thermostat in the house read 60 degrees. Then a thought came to her. A blizzard might make it impossible for her guests to leave. Another swig.

Meantime, the gypsy caravan of one inched its way along the Long Island Expressway toward the Brooklyn-Queens Expressway and the Verrazano Bridge.

"Can't this thing move any faster?" Tommy asked. "My leg is cramping up."

"Do you see the conditions? I'm going as fast as I can."

"I think you can step it up a bit. There's no one on the road."

"That's because anyone with a brain wouldn't take their car out on a night like this," Jake contributed.

The car slowed as it turned into a quaint hamlet of row houses. "How do you know which one is yours?" Tommy asked.

"Probably the one with no lights on," Jake's muffled voice suggested.

"Great," Looney said. "Now I got Abbott and Costello with me."

He stopped the car in front of an attached structure, indistinguishable from the others around it. A light over the doorway came on as Penny swatted away the last puffs of smoke from her cigarette, attempting to conceal her broken promise to quit. *After tonight,* she told herself. She opened the door.

"Welcome!" she shouted.

There was no answer.

Looney untied the wheelchairs from the roof. Tommy was leaning into the backseat with his arms entwined beneath his mother's. "Dory, is there any way we can get her to help?"

"Don't think so, Tommy. When her meds wear off, it's like a switch. Her body is frozen. I'll give her a pill inside and that might get her moving."

Tommy dragged his mother forward as Looney placed her wheelchair by the car's door.

"I'll count to three," Looney said.

"Do you know how?" Tommy added.

"Come on, boys, come on," Dory chided. "She's half in and half out and she's getting soaked."

"On three," Tommy commanded. "Three!"

With Dory pushing Maddie's feet, Tommy and Looney pulled her torso from the car and placed her in the wheelchair. The slate walkway had turned into an ice rink and the wheelchair had a mind of its own, sliding down the pathway toward the front door. Looney took off after it and fell to the ground. Tommy used Looney's back for traction and caught the wheelchair just before it tipped.

"Hello, everyone," Penny slurred. "Welcome. Hi, Tommy."

"You should have thrown some salt down," he answered.

Once in the house they took Maddie from the wheelchair and

placed her in a recliner. "I'll put this in the garage," Looney suggested as he removed the wheelchair.

Tommy took off his coat and handed it to Penny. "How are the kids?" he asked.

"We only have one and he's fine," she said.

Tommy saw a picture on the table. "Is this him?"

The picture was of a young man at a gala function. He was waving with one hand and held a dozen red roses in the crook of his arm.

"He won an award, as you can see."

"Is he in college?"

"Yes," she said. "FIT."

He repeated it. "F-I-T, what is that, like a bodybuilding school?" He stared at the picture.

She pulled the photograph from his hand. "No," she explained. "The Fashion Institute of Technology."

Tommy raised his eyebrows and pursed his lips. *Don't go there,* he thought.

"He is artistic," she said as if reading his mind.

"Well, don't worry. They're doing wonderful things with that, these days. It's good you caught it early."

Her jaw dropped.

"Hey," he said, trying to change the subject. "How about you, Penny, you look great. Hey, Looney didn't tell me you were pregnant."

"I'm not," she said.

Oops.

Penny bit her lip and went into the kitchen. Tommy looked at his mother. She was shivering. He saw the thermostat on the wall and cranked it up. Moments later the boiler kicked in, vibrating from the basement.

"Hey, who's playing around with the thermostat?" Looney yelled from the garage.

"It's an ice box in here," Tommy protested.

"I told you guys to bring a sweater," Looney commented as he came up the steps.

Looney and Tommy looked at each other. "Jake!" they said at the same time.

Looney rushed out the door and slipped on the walkway again. Tommy used his back for traction again and arrived safely at the car. It was covered with snow. He cleaned off the window and looked in.

"Is he okay?" Looney asked.

"Yeah, if blue is normal he's okay," Tommy said.

"It's about time he had some color."

"Let's get him in the house."

"Yeah," Tommy said. "That should warm him up in no time."

"You know, you're a heartless dick. Didn't I beg you not to break my balls?"

"I didn't break your balls."

"Well, I meant Penny's too."

"She's got balls?"

"Hey, let's not go there again. You're too funny. Just try, for once in your life, to be nice."

"I was being nice. How should I know you had a son who's different, and she looked like she was in the sixth month. And her eyes are glassy, did you notice that? Maybe she's smoking babanya, which is dangerous when you're pregnant."

"She's not pregnant, Goddamnit!!!! Cut it out. You know, I got to live with her after you leave."

"Calm down, you mook. If we don't get him inside, we'll have to bury him in the backyard. Then Mom will come here to visit him once a week."

Looney moved to open the hatch.

Inside the house, Penny opened another bottle of Pinot. It was going down easier. She steadied herself along the kitchen counter.

A long folding table was set with holiday napkins, place settings, a plastic floral centerpiece, and a candle.

"She outdid herself," Maddie said as she was carried to a seat.

"Careful of the table, it's wobbly," Tommy said.

"I know," Looney answered. "I got to fix that leg." He bent down and placed a napkin under it.

"I have some meatballs as appetizers as well," Penny said.

Tommy had already attempted to pierce one with a fork. He tried to bite down on it, but it was hard. He banged it on the table.

"Is someone at the door?" Penny asked from the kitchen.

"You are friggin' hilarious," Looney said.

"Hey, is it my fault? These are more like golf balls than meatballs."

"How do you breathe in this place?" Jake asked. "It's claustrophobic."

"Yeah, this was supposed to be a starter house. Why didn't you move into something bigger?" Tommy asked.

"We're very happy here," Penny said from the kitchen. "We don't need anything bigger."

"She don't like big things," Tommy said. "That's why she married Looney." Jake and Tommy laughed.

Looney put his glass down. "I'm the looney one? You guys were never satisfied, always chasing more and more; and now where are you? You live with your mother, and you're both broke. And you call me 'Looney.'"

"Boys, please," Maddie intoned.

"Were they always like this?" Dory asked.

"Pretty much," she said. An involuntary spasm knocked a glass of water into Looney's lap.

"Christ!" he yelled. Dory patted his lap with a napkin, moving a bit too close to his groin. He began to get flush. He jumped up, hitting the table, collapsing the leg.

Dishes of antipasto and cheese, glassware and stemware drifted like guests on the *Titanic* toward the starboard side, sliding into Jake. He tried to stem the onslaught with his arms wrapped around the table.

At the same time, Penny wobbled into the room with a large bowl of pasta. At the sight of her table collapsing, she tripped, sending two pounds of Capellini Filetto di Pomodoro flying onto Maddie. There was an eerie silence until steam began to rise from Maddie's lap.

"She's burning!" someone yelled.

Maddie, paralyzed in her chair, saw steam rising from her lap and started to scream. Tommy reached for a pitcher of water and poured it on her lap, extinguishing her anguish.

"My meal! My meal is ruined!" Penny cried.

"You're worried about your friggin' meal? You almost cremated my mother," Tommy said.

"What are we going to eat?" Jake asked.

"We'll send out for pizza," Looney said.

The ride home was quiet. Maddie cuddled in Dory's arms. Dory stroked her hair. "You're a lucky woman, Maddie. Your sons love you so. They are precious, so precious."

"Yes," Maddie said. "They're gems, real gems."

The wheelchairs rattled on the roof as the Prius puttered along. The process of getting Jake into the apartment was reversed.

"Hey, thanks, Looney, we had a great time."

"Yeah, let's do it again, real soon."

Once his mother was settled in bed, Tommy said, "I'll be back in a few minutes." Ever aware of the eyes upon him, he needed to exit the building. He waved up to the apartment, bundled his coat against the chill, and walked south certain he would die of pneumonia. Which, at times, seemed a pretty good option.

Back later that night, Tommy twisted and turned beneath the covers.

"That went well," Jake said. His voice pierced the darkness. Tommy did not answer. "Hey, Tommy, did you hear me? I said that went well."

"Right, do you think he meant it when he said, 'Let's do this again'?" Tommy asked.

"Yeah, I think he is going to invite us back in February."

"Really?"

"Yeah. I heard him tell Penny it'll be a cold day when I invite them back."

Jake laughed. Tommy laughed.

They laughed until they started choking, and the laughter subsided into the darkness. It was moments later that Tommy spoke. "Hey," he said. "How much do graves cost?"

"Don't know," Jake said. "Probably two, three thousand dollars."

There was quiet then, "Do you know Mom has eight graves at St. John Cemetery?"

"Yes, and you do know that Dad is in one of them." There was silence. "What are you thinking?" Jake pressed. Tommy didn't answer. "Don't tell me you're thinking of selling them?" No answer. "You're crazy. I know it now. You're crazy. First of all, your father is in one of those graves."

"Well, unless they laid him sideways, there's still lots of empty spots."

"Ghoul, you're a damn heartless ghoul. You'll have him dug up. You're thinking about it aren't you?"

"Look who's talking. You probably blew the monument money on some cheap bimbo."

"That's different, and she wasn't cheap," Jake protested.

"Different this," Tommy said holding his crotch. "Anyway, the old man wouldn't mind. It's not like he left her a pension or anything."

"Ghoul," Jake said again.

The night filled the void. Silence clung to the darkness in the room.

"Do you know the price of gold?" Tommy asked.

"Gold? Why are you thinking about gold?"

"Do you know what it costs?"

"A thousand, I think it hit a thousand dollars an ounce," Jake said.

"What do you think a tooth weighs?"

Jake leaned up on his elbow. "Why would you want to know that?" he asked.

There was no answer, other than, "If you snore tonight I'll kill you for sure. I got to get up early tomorrow. I have a meeting with Fazzula."

"You're going through with this crazy idea?"

"What choice do I have? Don't you understand, we are broke, destitute, we don't have two nickels to rub together, we don't have a pot to piss in, we don't . . ."

"I get it, I get it. But, Fazzula, I don't know."

"Well, I'm not used to being broke."

"Well, think back, brother. We were poor before."

"I know that, but when we were poor we didn't know we were poor. We didn't know what we didn't have. It's different now."

"Remember the things we did to make extra money?"

"I don't particularly remember you doing anything to make extra money. I know what I did."

"The penny jar in the feast. You'd put salt in the water so the coins wouldn't fall straight down, and the people would lose."

"It's not like I was robbing someone I knew," Tommy explained.

"Makes you wonder, though. What would we do for money, where would we draw the line?"

"Hey, 'Chester,' don't be getting all philosophical on me. I don't like dealing with Fazzula, but I like being broke less. It's risky, but I think I can out maneuver him. I know he's about to make me an offer. I'll make a score, a big score, and be able to get the hell out of here again. I just got to make sure he thinks I'm doing him a favor. If I look desperate, he'll eat me for dinner."

"And have me for dessert," Jake added.

"*Tar fat so!*"

"Heartless prick!"

There was no further laughter that evening.

Before leaving the apartment the next morning for his trek through the basement corridors, Tommy searched the small kitchen, looking behind cabinets, and under tables for the secret hiding place where his mother kept the coins.

"You looking for something?" Dory asked. She was in the doorway, about to help Maddie from bed.

"That jug with the coins," he said. "Do you know where it is?"

"Oh, it's empty now. Mom gave it over to the man as she does each month."

"What man?"

"Can't tell you that. Kauf . . . something or other. Just some man who comes by once a month to say hello to Mom."

Tommy had no time to think about this. "Okay, just tell Mom I'll be back later."

"Good!" Maddie yelled from the bedroom. "We're having pizza for lunch."

Tommy was startled by a man holding a broken lock in his hand. He was standing near the basement door, blocking his way.

"Who are you?" Tommy asked. He felt the man's stare, dark inset black eyes looking him over from top to bottom.

"I'm Fuller Bile. I own this building. And who are you and what are you doing in my basement?"

"Ah, Bile," he said.

"And you are?"

"I'm the boiler inspector. I'm with the Board of Health, came to inspect your boiler. Everything checks out, no major violations. You do have a blocked flue, but you'll get a letter and you have thirty days to repair it. Other than that, you're good to go."

"Oh, thank you, thank you very much," he called to Tommy who had brushed past him. "I'll get right on that . . ."

CHAPTER 20

*T*ommy walked into the café to find Patzo screaming at the top of his lungs. Tears were flowing down his face. "Where is he, where is Pippy? Where's my Pippy?"

He ran over to him. "Patzo, calm down. What's wrong?" Patzo was grasping for air. "Calm down Patzo, what's wrong?"

"My Pippy is gone, missing. He did something to Pippy. Where's my Pippy?" he yelled.

Fazzula was unimpressed. He sat at the table shuffling a deck of cards. He spread them across the table then fanned them back and forth, ignoring Patzo's hysterics.

Patzo was beginning to hyperventilate. "Where's Pippy?" he cried.

"Patzo, please, take a deep breath," Tommy said. Then he turned to Fazzula. "Pauly, Pauly, where's the kid's bird? Where is it, come on tell him."

"I warned him . . ."

Fazzula continued shuffling the cards. Patzo fell to his knees, gripping his stomach and wailing.

Tommy asked again, "Come on, Pauly."

"What are you getting, soft on me?"

"The kid can't breathe, Pauly,"

"I don't know about the damned bird," he said tossing the deck onto the table.

"Please, Pauly . . ."

"Last time I saw the friggin' bird it was near the walk-in box. Maybe he's still there."

"Oh Christ!" Patzo yelled. Tommy followed as Patzo ran to the backroom. "It's cold in there and it smells." He opened the door and reached in to open the light. Cold air was visible as it left the insulated confines of the large room. There was a stench emanating from the room. Tommy saw shelves upon shelves mostly empty, stocked with perishables. A few tubs of cannoli cream and in the corner behind a case of antifreeze the parrot lay on the floor. Patzo picked it up and cradled the bird close to his body as he ran from the refrigerator. "Come on, Pippy, come on, don't give up." In a moment signs of life appeared in the bird. Patzo's breathing stabilized as well, and his tears turned to tears of joy as he hugged and kissed the parrot.

"Say something, say something, Pippy."

"Kill the asshole," the parrot chirped.

"Shush, shush, Pippy."

Patzo tried to wave off the bird's commentary. "He's got a mind of his own," he lamented. "Shush, shush, he'll kill you."

"You really love that bird, don't you?" Tommy said.

"Sure do. My mother gave him to me. Don't know what I'd do without him."

Tommy returned to the table, where Fazzula was sitting unfazed. "Go figure," Fazzula said, "The bird got locked in the fridge. How'd that happen?"

Tommy didn't answer.

"I think I'm allergic to birds," he said as Tommy sat. "Anyway, good to see you, Tommy. I hope you have good news. I hope you decided to help me."

"Well, let's say I'm interested in knowing more."

"Good," Fazzula said. "I was hoping you'd say that. Hey, asshole," he yelled to Patzo, "espresso, *subito!*"

There was an echo from the outside room. "Asshole, asshole."

Moments later, Patzo came into the room carrying two cups of coffee. He was talking to himself. "Fazzula; right hand, right hand."

"The bird," Fazzula said, pointing directly at him, "shut him up."

Patzo nodded. Fazzula turned his attention back to Tommy. "Here's the deal," he said. "You see, it's a long story about this very valuable piece of property I acquired for a very good price after a long and lucrative arrangement with one of its principals.

"Well," Fazzula continued. "As you may or may not know or may or may not have surmised, this property was a charitable concern run by a seemingly holy man, a monsignor, as it turns out. He was in charge, has been intimately involved with the mismanagement of that fine institution on behalf of yours truly and some selected close associates. This guy, the holy guy, had some demons of his own, which made him valuable to me. Far be it from me to judge."

Tommy shook his head and shrugged.

Fazzula moved his chair in closer to Tommy. "I've got a little problem you can help me with."

"I'll try."

"You know, I had a very close relationship with the high holy man because he had a little problem with the horses, and various other sports betting. He always did, since we were kids. It seems his closeness to the Almighty did not give him any insights into point spreads, and over the years and under my watchful eye he was into me deep. I let him dig himself in deep. He had a good cash flow in his position. Collect money for a new roof, send me half. A new organ, send me half. Then, to my joy, he got promoted to administrator of St. Vincent's Hospital."

"Why didn't you cut him off?"

"Well, I knew he was in a unique position as the administrator of this charitable concern, a cash cow, and he was helpful to me in many, many ways. Cut him off? Are you kidding? I increased his credit line."

"Okay, so what's the problem?"

"Well, there was none until he got in so deep that he began to sweat and talk about coming clean. Confessing, can you imagine? Like all of a sudden he finds Jesus. I guess that was always an outside possibility, him being a priest and all."

"I guess."

"Anyway, I showed him a way out, kind of blackmailed him into draining this venerable charity. And he agreed. After it went bust,

I demanded one last deal to settle his debt. I'd buy this particular property and we'd be even. Anyway, he got in so deep that there was only one way out. He was going to make sure I picked up the property for a very reasonable price, like practically nothing. It was all set. Anyway, he reneged, that two-timing . . ."

"Sounded like a great deal," Tommy said.

"It was, and still is," Fazzula agreed. "That property in this neighborhood is worth millions. Millions."

"So, what's the problem now?"

"As I said, the Goddamned holy man reneged on me. In the eleventh hour he found religion and reneged on me. He double-crossed me. Can you imagine? A low-life degenerate gambler, stealing from the church poor box to pay loan sharks and bookies. I thought I could count on a guy like this. Go figure. He was about to go to the DA, tell him he was coerced, tell him the whole story and mention names; my name in particular."

"And what do you want me to do? Pay him a visit?"

"Oh no." Fazzula leaned in closer. "I already paid him a visit." He sat back. "No, no, he'll not be a problem anymore." Fazzula leaned back in his chair. "I tried to be reasonable," he said. "I told him unless this deal went through his name would be plastered all over the news, revealing him as the degenerate that he was. But, as seldom happens, I figured wrong. Anyway, he paid the ultimate price. He had to be taken care of. I've beat the biggest crime families in the world and was not about to be taken down by somebody just because he wore a collar. Truth be told, it was a moment of weakness. He came here to give me the news personally. He thought he owed me that much since we had this friendship and all. I couldn't talk sense into him and then, well, I just lost it. You know what it's like when you just lose it?"

Tommy nodded. "What do you want from me, then?"

"It wasn't easy either. After all, he was a childhood friend. We played ball together, classmates for a long time. It wasn't easy. Doing what I did wasn't easy. Oh, yeah, getting back to your question. Well, in the process of getting my retribution I might have been spotted. There might be an eyewitness who could put me at the scene."

"And you want me to pay this witness a visit?"

"Well, a bit more than that."

"I'm listening."

"Kill him," Fazzula said. "I want him dead too. You see," he explained, "I had insurance. I can still pull it off. I've got a contract, but there's a lot of heat on this right now. Questions are being asked about improprieties, and if my name gets dragged in as the suspect that ended a corrupt gambler's life, well, that kind of puts a wrench in the whole thing. This particular priest knows too much. Did I mention what a valuable piece of property I'm talking about?"

"Mega money," Tommy said.

"Right. A whole city block. With just one more pipsqueak, rat, motherless priest standing in the way."

"And you want to kill him? A priest?"

"No," Fazzula said. He leaned back into his chair. "I want *you* to kill him. I got a gut feeling this guy is going to testify to a grand jury. Ever have a gut feeling like that?" He poked his belly.

"This guy jeopardizes everything. We're talkin' millions here. He has the potential to do serious harm to our cash flow. And now the best part: If this goes off, your friends will be very, very grateful.

You'll never have to work again. You can go back west and relax the rest of your life. Never lose anything ever again."

"Isn't there another way?"

"Tommy, Tommy, *bubula*. You know me better than that. I deplore violence unless I have no other options. You think I would kill a childhood friend if I didn't have to?" Tommy looked up as Fazzula continued. "I tried everything, can't budge this *fanook*. He won't listen to reason, and I have sent some emissaries with some pretty direct warnings."

As he spoke, a roach made its way across the tabletop. Fazzula reached for an empty glass and covered the insect, watching with fascination as it realized its predicament.

Tommy nodded. "So with this guy out of the way, the gravy train goes forward."

Fazzula smiled, his eyes still trained on the bug under glass. "You got it," he said. "We milked this cow for years, brought it to bankruptcy because by law, only if the charity went broke, only then could the asset be sold. Ingenious, if I must say so myself. They got all kinds of auditors and lawyers trying to figure out what the hell happened. I'd like to be a fly on that wall. But their trail will end with the dead monsignor. Checkmate!

"Even if they come up with something, it'll be impossible to prove with the number one witness gone. I have the contract to buy, and there's nothing they can do about that. Nothing can stop me, nothing but a little man who may have seen too much. And when you take care of him, it is smooth sailing. And then, and this is the kicker, the place will have to come down and guess who gets the contract to do that?"

"Green Apple Development?"

"DBA Rossini Contracting?" Fazzula added.

Fazzula took a paper napkin and brought it to the candle on the table. He stared at Tommy as the tissue burned then put it under the glass and watched the roach burn. "And a big payday to follow."

Tommy listened. "I'll think about it," he said.

Fazzula smiled. "You won't have to go far. This Goody Two-shoes Samaritan lives up the street at the church. That's like his headquarters. Go see for yourself. Scope it out. His name is Gleason, an Irishman. No one will miss him. When he's gone we'll plant a few stories tying the both of them to church corruption. The whole thing will go away."

Tommy was quiet.

"Well?" Fazzula prodded.

"I'll take a look."

"One thing, though—time is important. My information is that he testifies on Monday. That means you have a week. I think I'd like it to be done with pizzazz, something that will make headlines. Not that killing a priest doesn't make for good copy. I want it to echo all the way to the Vatican. I wouldn't mind if it happens in church on Sunday or even in that halfway house he operates. Can't tell me he ain't tappin' some of that stuff. That's what we'll feed the press." Fazzula reached for a brown paper bag and passed it across the table. Tommy looked in it.

"It's clean," Fazzula said. "Never been used, not once."

Tommy stuffed the bag in his jacket. Fazzula smiled.

Tommy gave Fazzula the obligatory kiss and left. He began walking, sorting out the offer and his predicament. He was desperate to extricate himself from his financial situation. He reprised every word, every intonation, to garner some inner meaning. One phrase came back to him: "Never lose anything again." Maybe, he thought, it was nothing; just an off-the-cuff expression or maybe Fazzula knew more than he was supposed to.

He decided to take a long walk to clear his mind. A gust of wind rumbled off the Battery, Manhattan's southernmost tip, and across Broadway. It reminded him of the roar of adoring crowds who, in the past, lined the Canyon of Heroes. He remembered being on this street as a boy, to cheer the '69 Mets, and earlier, recalled standing on the sidewalk beneath a blizzard of confetti as Neil Armstrong and the crew of Apollo 11 paraded up Broadway. New York was the center of his universe in those days.

He stopped at the former site of the twin towers of the World Trade Center, ground zero, and took a firsthand look at the gaping hole in the ground, courtesy of al-Qaeda. Years after 9/11, still a hole in the ground. He was a city boy, born and raised in the shadow of those buildings. He felt a pang in his chest. Where was God that day? he wondered. He moved on.

His walk took him uptown into the neighborhood where the once-flourishing St. Vincent's Hospital operated in eleven different buildings spanning a city block. It brought back memories of the day he was rushed into the emergency room. He thought about those days and what landed him there and what he had done for money and, more important, what wouldn't he do for money?

He walked around the hospital, thinking about taking one last job. He had nothing to lose. He had already lost it all. He thought of different scenarios, a plan, early morning, or late at night, which would insure the least chance of a witness and thereby collateral damage. Should it be here at the church or somewhere else? Maybe the shelter. Maybe he'd make it look like a robbery. No, Fazzula didn't want any doubt about where this came from. In the church, during mass, or at the shelter, he decided, would have maximum impact and that's what the Don wanted.

As he stared at the building from a hallway, the door opened. A man in a black peacoat with the collar turned up appeared at the top of the stairs. He looked quickly left and right and began to walk. Tommy was drawn out of his observation booth, and the two met eyes.

"Tommy Rossini?" the man said.

"Father?"

"What brings you up here?" the priest asked. "Was there something wrong with the envelope?"

"Ah, no, no, it was all there," Tommy said. "You're not wearing your collar," he observed.

Father did not answer.

"Oh, I get it, Father. Hey, it's all right with me. After all, you're a young guy, you have needs. So, if you found a little something on the side, well that's okay with me. Who am I to judge?"

The priest shook his head. "It's not what you think, Tommy. Come, let's have a cup of coffee."

"I don't think so," Tommy said. He did not want to be seen with the priest, much less get to know him. *Always harder to hurt someone you know,* he thought.

"Please," the priest insisted.

Tommy looked around and turned his collar up. "Not around here," he said. "And you have to pay."

In a coffee shop in Chinatown the two men sat at a table. Gleason fidgeted with the salt and pepper shakers and kept looking out the window.

"So, am I right, Father? Are you getting a little action on the side? Is that why you're so nervous?"

"No, Tommy, it's not what you think. I have stayed true to my vows. But there are things going on that have me on edge."

"Well, for me I think the vows are stupid. I know for me, when there was a drought I couldn't think straight. I mean, they don't want a priest to get married because they don't want him to have sex. They should let you guys get married. Believe me, in six months you won't be having sex. A win-win."

"Well, you have to stay focused, that's for sure," the priest said.

"So, what then? What keeps your mind off it?"

"My life is full. I have much to do."

"Whatever," Tommy said.

"Actually, I was on my way to meet Maria. The woman you met in my office. Oh, what am I saying? You knew her before I did."

"Yeah, I did. A long time ago."

"She's a sweetheart. I told you how helpful she is. She lives for others. She is so helpful, devotes her time to this shelter. It's the only thing that has survived the financial collapse of St. Vincent's and it wasn't easy. We argued successfully that this building in particular is a landmark. Now private funds and lots of hands, good old personal commitment of people like Maria, keeps the doors open."

"This all means nothing to me. Everyone has problems."

"Oh, I agree." Father sipped his coffee. "I've got my problems with the church and all. I too can be disillusioned. You're only back recently. You probably don't know of the excitement we had around here a while back. My immediate superior, Monsignor Burns, seems to have gotten mixed up with the wrong people and he was delivered unceremoniously, like frozen food, to the front door of the steps. It caused quite a stir. You have no idea of the fraud and outright criminality that has been going on."

"Really?"

"Unbelievable. The place has been a private checkbook for some really unsavory characters. This neighborhood has a corrupting influence on people. I have been disappointed by people I believed in and trusted."

"Really," Tommy said.

The priest continued. "Well, the more I looked into it, the more I understood why the parish is in such trouble. The whole thing is controlled by the mob; it's unbelievable. I am in the unenviable position of putting a stop to it." The last words were whispered.

"Well, do you think it's wise to go after people like that? They don't like anyone who rocks their boat, I can tell you that."

"I'm no hero," he said. "Believe me, I haven't slept in months. There's no telling what these people are capable of. But you can't see wrong being done and stand by silently. I've been approached by some people already, some threats have been made. I prayed to God to show me the way. I prayed in that very grotto where we first met and suddenly it came to me. I can't run away, I'm not a hero but I can't run away. It's not in my DNA."

Which, Tommy thought, might soon be splattered all over the

altar. Tommy was connecting the dots. "You probably pissed off a lot of people, Father. A lot of interesting people." He bent his nose with his finger. "And prayer usually don't help with that."

"No doubt," the priest said. "I've seen some things that I wish I hadn't. But I'll survive. And what about you, Tommy, when did you lose your way?"

"I didn't know I had," he said. "And there you go putting your nose in other's people's business."

"Just conversation, that's all."

"Save it. I just don't believe in all this hocus-pocus, all the God stuff. If there is a one, he certainly has a strange sense of humor."

"God doesn't cause bad things to happen."

"What, then, he just watches it happen? Does he get some kick out of it?"

"Or, perhaps, there is a purpose for our trials in this life."

"I know, I know," Tommy said. "God, heaven, blind faith; all convenient answers to questions you can't answer. Sorry, I'm not buying it. I haven't seen anything that would make me believe."

The priest jumped when the waitress asked if he wanted a refill. He sipped the fresh cup. "Faith is not easy. It's a gift. I believe that God is all around us."

"Again, whatever floats your boat is no skin off my back. I've lost everything that I fought all my life to attain, and your God has never revealed himself to me."

"You can never lose your relationship with God, which is the most valuable possession. That is a guarantee. To find him, you must open your heart. God will reveal himself. He's probably trying to get through to you. Sometimes, if you're receptive, you will see God wink. Little signs, little coincidences, just to let you know he has not abandoned you. It's hard to explain."

"Well, Father, you can believe what you like. But I just saw a hole in the ground a few blocks from here. Where was God? How did he let the men who claim to worship Allah get away with that?"

"I don't have all the answers, Tommy. There are angry, greedy men out there."

"Made in God's image?" Tommy asked. The waitress brought the check to the table. "Can't answer that, huh? Don't worry, Father. Coffee's on you." He handed the priest the check. "And you, Father, what made you get into this priest thing? Did you always want to be a priest?"

Father Bryce reached into his pocket and left some bills on the table. "Me? Oh, God no. I studied to be an accountant, but God had another plan for me. Sometimes you're walking in one direction, but God wants you to walk in another."

"Whatever," Tommy said. He rose to leave. "Father, isn't there another place you can keep busy? Maybe this neighborhood isn't the best place for you. You could ask for a transfer. Plus, you won't be pissing off any wiseguys. It would be good for everyone."

"You sound like that detective. He wants to put me in a witness protection program."

"Must be serious."

"I guess it is. I'm in up to my neck."

"Thanks for the coffee," he said.

"I'll pray for you, Tommy."

"Don't waste your prayers on me," he said.

Tommy walked back to the neighborhood. He second-guessed his decision to have coffee with an intended target. It's always easier to beat someone he didn't know. Harder when you have a relationship with the person you're punching. On orders from Fazzula he went to vandalize the shop of a man whose daughter he loved, Maria. *Why?* he wondered. Because that's what it took to survive. He knew it would get done with him or without him. He thought he would be able to minimize the damage. Things went south quickly when the old man came out of the office. That was the choice he made at the time, and he tried not to spend a lot of time rethinking it. But the sight of Maria staring at him from her office as he stood over her father haunted him every night since. He was attempting to pull a goon off the old man, but it didn't look good. He left soon after, unable to look at her again, unable to look at himself, unable to explain the unexplainable. He wished he could now.

But back on Mulberry Street, Tommy took a deep breath and walked into Forzano's Italian Imports. He was startled by a voice behind him.

"They were here again."

He turned. "Fazzula's guys?"

"No, Con Edison. Someone reported a gas leak again."

"Really? That's odd."

"Tommy, is there something you're not telling me?" Her tone had changed.

"No," he said.

"I don't believe you. I can't believe anything anymore. Maybe this was a mistake. We shouldn't have . . ."

"Please don't say that. We have another chance. Believe me . . ."

"I don't know what to believe. A detective showed me your picture and . . ."

"My picture? Who, what . . ."

"Tommy, what's going on? What are you involved with?"

"Nothing, nothing I swear . . ."

"We had such dreams together. What did you become? Why weren't you stronger? Why aren't you stronger? How could you have . . . ?" She didn't complete the sentence.

He put his head down. "I only knew the streets. I only did what I needed to survive. The life was all I knew."

"I survived," she said.

"You're not fair. I left, I got away from it."

"And me as well."

"I was so ashamed, I became someone I didn't recognize, did things that surprised me that I was capable of doing."

"And what now? What choices will you make now? Now that you have a second chance."

"Maybe I only thought I got away. Maybe you can never get away."

Later that day, Tommy stood at the counter watching Patzo wipe the bottom of Pippy's cage. He replenished his water and added seed to his feeder. The parrot watched. Its vibrant yellow and green plumage added much-needed color in the drab café.

"You love that bird, don't you?" Tommy asked.

Patzo turned around. "Pippy?" he said. "He's my buddy. My mother left him to me."

Tommy nodded and asked, "Is Fazzula here yet?"

"Asshole, asshole," Pippy said.

"Quiet, Pippy, shush. You'll get us both killed."

"Hey," Tommy said. "Is the old crew intact? I mean, I haven't seen Johnny Pump. Is he still around?"

"Pump," Patzo repeated. "Oh, yeah, sure. He's still around. Boss don't make a move without him."

Tommy nodded. "Just curious, because I haven't seen him."

"Oh, he's away for a few days. The boss sent him to . . ." He tried to remember. "Ah, Ah, Ha, Har, Har, Harrison, he sent him to Harrison."

Tommy shrugged.

"Ar-ris-zone," the bird said. "Ar-ris-zone."

"Here he is now," Patzo said. Fazzula's car pulled in front of the café.

"Kill the asshole," Pippy said. "Kill the asshole."

"Please, Pippy, please don't."

Fazzula shook some hands on the street before entering. After a few slaps on the back, some hugs and kisses, he entered the café.

"Here's the asshole, here's the asshole," Pippy said.

"Christ, w-w-what am I going to do?" Patzo cried.

Fazzula gave Tommy a big hello. "Good to see you. Did your homework, didn't you? Scoped it out?"

"How did you know?" Tommy asked.

Fazzula laughed. "Ah, I know everything, Tommy Boy. You should know that by now." Tommy nodded. "Good," Fazzula said.

Tommy followed Fazzula into the backroom.

"Prick!" the parrot said.

Fazzula stopped in his tracks and turned to look at Patzo. "Get that pigeon out of my face. I swear I'll make soup out of him. I swear."

Patzo had his hand cupped over the bird's beak. "Please, Pippy, please."

Tommy chuckled and followed Fazzula into the backroom. Lucy was sitting in the corner reading a magazine.

"Come back in half an hour," he said.

She winked at Tommy and left.

The two men sat at a table. "Asshole," Fazzula shouted to Patzo. "Two espresso, now."

From the outer room the bird responded in kind.

"Well, at least you know where the bird picked it up," Tommy said.

"You know," Fazzula confided. "It's not just that the bird has a mouth on him, but he knows when to use the words. I hate pets, always did."

Patzo delivered the espresso. "Right hand, Fazzula; right hand, Fazzula," he said as he brought the espresso to the table and placed the cups in front of the two men, crossing one arm over the other to do so. "Right hand, Fazzula," he murmured. He went back and brought a bottle of anisette under a death stare from Fazzula.

Fazzula topped off his cup with the liquid and did the same for Tommy. He stirred the contents with a demitasse spoon and looked Tommy in the eye. "Does this taste right to you?"

"Fine," Tommy answered.

"Anyway," he said, "my people told me you took a look at the project."

"Yes," Tommy acknowledged.

"So you know, there's a million dollars on the table for you. Kicked in by all of us! The last piece of the puzzle; a diamond in the rough. The key to paradise, right there for our taking." He sipped the coffee.

"Interesting," Tommy agreed.

"If we don't stop this guy from testifying, the whole thing comes down. He's already working with the feds. We had councilmen paid off, and a dozen senators in Albany in our pocket. You understand? It's ours, signed and sealed. Only my arrest puts it in jeopardy."

"But a priest?"

"Who gives a flying . . ." he lowered his voice. "So he wears a collar. It's not a bulletproof vest. He put his nose where it did not belong."

"I get it." Tommy admitted.

"If I let this motherless bum get away with this, *boom,* next thing you know I got every crusader lawman from Syracuse to Staten Island fighting to void the contract. They put me away, the whole thing unravels. He is the only thing standing in the way." Fazzula was ranting now. "They will stop at nothing to stop me. Now I got Goody-Two shoes groups petitioning the courts to give the buildings landmark status. This Mick already succeeded with that brownstone where those whores live. If you pee in the street, they rezone it a wetland. I got to move before these tree-hugging bastards get a head of steam. And, if I get indicted, well, it's all in the crapper. He single-handedly throws a wrench in the whole friggin' plan. He'll cost me a lot of money, not to mention my freedom. I hate that guy. He should have minded his own business."

"He's a high-profile target," Tommy said. "Does a lot of good work, with kids and their mothers and all. It's going to bring a lot of heat."

"Yeah," Fazzula scoffed. "I know. He's opened some halfway house for girls who went all the way." Tommy laughed, a nervous laugh. "Hey, maybe that's a good place to do the deed. Besides, what's the point? You think it's never been done before? That's the problem in this country. We're too squeamish about things like this. Back home, priests are shot every day, from Palermo to Parma, any crusader priest is sure to get a hero's funeral. They still got balls over there.

"They're a drain on society anyway. So, here's the thing. This has to happen soon. For obvious reasons, this has to happen Sunday; maybe on the altar, after mass, or even during mass. The part when he drinks the blood; hey, how's that for staging. Or, as I say, he does a late mass at the shelter. I like it."

"Not much time."

"But that's why this hit is worth a million dollars to you plus what you'll earn on the other end. Let's get it over with. Afterward, you can go back west for a month or two. It'll calm down by then. Give me time to plant a few stories about how he was a degenerate gambler like his friend, who got what was coming to him. I tell you, this is big. There are millions to be made. Are you in?"

Tommy sipped his coffee. "I'm in," he said.

Fazzula slapped his hand down on the table. "Great, great. Monday, I'll have an envelope waiting for you. Call it a signing bonus, a hundred thousand. But that's only the beginning. We'll milk this city dry for a few more years taking these buildings down, then get the contracts to put them up. It's a win-win-win. But it has to happen Sunday, do you understand?"

"I do," Tommy said, forever sealing his bond of marriage to Fat Don Pauly Fazzula.

As Lucy put a finish coat of polish on Fazzula's nails, Johnny Pump listened.

"That's why this truce with Carozza is so important," Fazzula explained. "He's my insurance policy against Tommy."

"If you say so, boss. But, I'd be careful of Carozza. He's got that Sicilian Alzheimer's; he only remembers vendettas."

"My friend, there are no eternal friends or eternal enemies. Make the meeting happen."

The neighborhood was flush with excitement Saturday morning with the rumors of a visiting dignitary. Three sedans pulled up in front of the café; a buzz went through the streets. Four men came out of each car and positioned themselves on the sidewalk, encircling the center car. They looked at rooftops, hallways, under other vehicles in case of an ambush. When satisfied, one man knocked on the hood of the car and only then did the door open. With Johnny Pump at his side, Don Fazzula walked from the café, across the sidewalk.

Vito Carozza came out of the car into the open embrace of Fat Pauly. It was a message to all: the feud was over. They kissed and made up, two titans of the underworld.

Johnny Pump embraced Vito and his entourage, and all followed

Pauly into the café. Pump stood at the bar with Vito's bodyguards as the dons went into the backroom. Patzo did not believe his eyes. The feud between the two was legendary. Carozza was a thin-framed man, weathered by years at Marion Penitentiary. His gait was slower than Pauly's. His hair thinner, grayer. The men went into the backroom, where Pauly pulled his chair out. "Please, Don Carozza, do me the honor. Patzo!" he yelled.

"I know, I know." Patzo prepared espresso, under Pippy's watchful eye. "Asshole," the bird whispered, "kill the asshole."

Sweat from Patzo's brow dropped onto the serving tray. He put the finishing touch on the espressos and placed assorted pastries and a bottle of anisette on the tray and carried it into the room. He stopped at the entrance, noticing Vito seated in Pauly's seat. Pauly had a series of photographs spread on the table as he spoke, pointing and explaining.

"What do these mean to me?" Vito asked.

Pauly noticed Patzo at the door. "Come on, moron," Pauly said. "Are you going to stand there all day?"

Patzo brought the tray to the table, studying the arrangement of cups. He picked one espresso cup and crossed one hand over the other, before placing them on the table. Then he placed the pastry and bottle and removed the tray. As he left, the conversation began again.

"Don Vito," Fazzula said, "you honor me with your presence. Together we will do great things. I know there has been bad blood between us, misunderstandings, small stuff that got out of control. But you and me, together, are unstoppable."

"I am still confused about why we are meeting," Vito said.

"Well, for many years, there has been bad blood between us. I know you believe I had something to do with your legal troubles."

"And you didn't?" he asked

"My word to God," Fazzula said. "But that's not enough. I vowed to find the man who caused you this trouble and not rest until I had."

"And you have some news for me?"

"I do, and I thought this meeting would be a time to reconcile."

"I am listening."

"Many years ago, it seems, I had a young Turk who without my knowledge or permission was trying to get started in business. He had a small company and was bidding on some work. It seems he bid on the job that caused you so much heartache. It seems from my information that he devised a plan that would have the city rescind its contract with you. It is he who cut the standpipes, knowing you would be blamed and his bid was next in line. It has taken me years, but I have found the traitor."

"Who is he?"

Fazzula pointed to the photographs. They were various pictures of Tommy Rossini as he walked the neighborhood. Carozza studied the photographs as Fazzula continued. "His name is Thomas Rossini. Shortly after the incident he ran out west. It wasn't until a short time ago that we were able to put the pieces together. At the time he did this, he was a protégé of mine, but I did not sanction this. This was a move he made on his own. He was a wannabe, a hanger-on."

"You know that I must deal with this now, protégé of yours or not."

"I am fully aware that retribution is called for. That is why I asked for this meeting. I got a tip that he returned. He was spotted, as you can see in these photos. I already have my best people looking for him. He will turn up. Would you like me to carry out your revenge?" he offered.

Carozza shook his head. "No," he said. "It's only revenge if I do it. This is something I must do."

He picked up a photograph that showed Tommy Rossini in front of a brownstone with another figure in the background.

"I know you have vowed to find out who framed you in that unfortunate incident many years ago. I also know you've had suspicions that I was in some way involved. Consider this information as a present to you. I hope you and I can put any bad blood between us to rest."

Vito stared at the picture. "You are certain?"

"*Senza dubbio,*" he whispered. "I just came by this information."

"When you find him, he is mine," Carozza said.

"Of course. I can't say I blame you, Don Carozza. Were I in your position I too would take revenge into my own hands. If for appearances' sake only."

Vito Carozza picked up his demitasse cup and swallowed its contents in one gulp. "You are right," he said.

With equally adoring fanfare and kisses Fazzula walked Carozza to the door and waved as his entourage pulled away. He turned to Johnny Pump. "Do you understand?"

Pump nodded. "I get it, boss. Two birds with two stones, the priest by Rossini and Rossini by Carozza."

"Three birds if you count that rat bastard ex-son-in-law without another crutch," the Don added.

Behind the counter, Patzo put the tray in the sink. A photograph that had adhered itself to the bottom of the tray fell to the floor. He picked it up. It was a photograph of Tommy in front of a brownstone building. He looked back into the room to see if anyone had noticed it missing. There were still six or eight at the table. Confident it would not be missed, he put the photo in his pocket.

Before going to the apartment, Tommy stopped at a fruit stand and looked at the choices. "I'll take two of those," he said to the vendor. The man picked up two green apples, bagged them, and gave them to Tommy.

"I've got a surprise for you," he told his mother. He reached into the bag and pulled out an apple. "Go ahead," he said, "take a bite."

Maddie reached for the apple, examined it, and brought it to her mouth. Her teeth dug into it, barely piercing the skin. Juice ran down her chin.

"Hmm," she said, "delicious." She smiled. It was then he again noticed the glimmer from her tooth, still intact.

"Tommy Boy, don't rush off. Sit, please, sit with me."

"I've got to go, Mom. I'm busy."

"You're always busy. Always running, running. But sit, talk to me. Tell me what's wrong. What went wrong?"

"What makes you think . . ."

"Tommy, you're my son. I know when something is wrong."

Tommy sat next to his mother, and she reached for his hands, cradling them into her own. She stroked the malformed hand. He felt warmth from her hands melt through his palms. He felt no pain, except in his heart as he recalled the day it happened. By the tears forming in her eyes he imagined she was thinking about that day as well. It was a shared heartache that bonded them.

"Whatever it is," she said, "it will all work out. You have to believe. You have to have faith." She reached for the Bible at her side. "He won't abandon you."

He took the book into his hands. "One day I'll buy you a new one. This is torn and broken."

"If your Bible is torn and broken, there's a good chance you're not."

"How do you do it, Mom? How do you maintain your faith? How do you believe?" He handed her the book. "I'm sorry. But I don't feel close to God."

"Tommy, if you don't feel close to God, ask yourself, 'Who moved?'"

He smiled. "You are clever, Mom. That's a good one."

She took his hands again into her own again. "You just have to keep your heart open. God will send you a sign. He'll let you know He hasn't abandoned you. God will wink. When you came home from New Jersey, it was an answer to a prayer. God winked. He let me know he heard me."

"The priest said that too."

She smiled.

He leaned over and kissed the last teardrop from her cheek. "I gotta go."

On Sunday morning Fazzula reclined in his barber chair, reading the newspaper. He stirred his coffee. "Patzo," he said, "have we changed espresso supplier? This coffee doesn't taste the same. I've noticed it for a while now."

"No b-b-boss, same supplier, same espresso. Lavazza."

Fazzula nodded, and finished downing the remnants of the demitasse cup. "Patzo, there's a big white box in the walk-in freezer. It has a bow on it and a card."

"I know, boss. I've seen it. Been there a while."

"Good, I want you to take it to Maddie Rossini's. I want you to do that now."

Patzo knew the box. He had moved it a few times over the last months to make room for other supplies. As he recalled now, it was on a top shelf. He took off his apron and headed to the backroom.

At the kitchen table in the Rossini apartment, Dory was attempting to get a piece of food dislodged from Maddie's throat. Lucy and Jake sat helplessly by. Maddie turned colors until the blockage flew from her mouth, hitting Jake in the head. At that point she began to breathe normally.

"Where's Tommy?" he asked.

"I don't know. He left early."

"Maybe he found a manicurist," Lucy suggested.

There was a knock on the door.

"Fazzula told me to bring this up here," Patzo said. The box was rectangular. "I think they're roses or something, for Maddie maybe, from the Don."

"Who sent me flowers?" Maddie asked.

Dory took the envelope from the box. "They're not yours, Maddie. It's addressed to Jake," she said.

There was quiet around the table. Jake reached for the envelope and took the card out, and read, "I'll take everything you lean on." It wasn't signed.

He untied the bow and opened the box, unwrapping layers of clear, moist plastic. It was clammy. An odor began to emanate. He kept unwrapping until he saw it, a decayed limb, dead flesh, bloody and necrotic, became visible. The sight induced shock. His hands froze. The box fell from off his lap. The limb rolled out onto the floor. A yellow tag identified the limb as that of Jake Rossini from Aventura Hospital. As the horrific scene developed, Maddie's screams engulfed the apartment, echoing all the way into Fazzula's café.

"That bastard," Patzo said. "I'm sorry, Jake, Maddie, I had no idea. I'm sorry . . . Why would he . . . ?"

"It's a message," Jake said. His voice was steady, low. "He knows I'm here."

"That an-an-animal bastard!" Patzo exclaimed.

Jake recalled Fazzula's words in his hospital room. *I'll take away everything you lean on.* It was all making sense to him now. "Tommy's in trouble. Fazzula knows I'm here. He's known all along, and Tommy's in trouble. He's been playing him," he said.

Dory rolled the limb back into the box and covered it, keeping it from Maddie's gaze.

"Tommy's in trouble, that's the real message."

"But what?" Dory asked.

Patzo reached into his pocket and pulled a photo from his pocket. "Look, Jake, I saw this picture of Tommy. Does it mean anything?"

He showed Jake the picture of Tommy standing in front of a brownstone. In the foreground there were pedestrians, and descending the steps was a man in a black peacoat.

"Where did you get this?" he asked.

"P-Pau-Pauly Pauly had lots of them. He met with Vito, and they were talking."

"Vito, Vito Carozza?"

"Yes." It was Lucy who answered. "They had a big meeting."

"But they hate each other."

"Maybe," Lucy said, "but Pauly hates that priest more."

"What priest?"

"The young man, always refuses manicures, sit down many times with Pauly. Last time Pauly real angry." She pointed to the man in the peacoat.

"My enemy's enemy is my friend," Jake said.

Patzo confirmed, "Carozza came, and the two couldn't be happier. It was like they sealed some type of arrangement and are friends again."

Jake stared at the picture. "So what are they planning? How is Tommy involved? I told him to be careful. He thought he could outmaneuver him."

"Johnny Pump is back," Lucy said, "I know he had some information about your brother. He's back from Arizona. Pauly sent him out there to check up on Tommy."

"Arizona," Patzo said, "I thought it was Harrison."

"He played him," Jake said. "He knew all along, and he played him; and now he's gonna pull the string. Dory, dial Looney."

Penny answered the phone, absent salutation, and handed it to Looney.

"It's your brother Jake," she said.

"Looney, you've got to get down here now," Jake said.

"What are you talking about?"

"You got to get in your car and come down here now."

"Are you crazy, it's Sunday. Do you know the traffic on Sun—?"

"Looney," Jake interrupted, "Tommy's in trouble." Silence. "Real trouble," he added.

"I'll meet you on Mott Street."

"No," Jake said, "come to the front of the building. I'll be downstairs in front." Jake handed the phone to Dory. "Get my leg," he said, pointing to a closet door.

"But . . ."

"Get my leg."

Dory and Lucy went into the closet and came out with the prosthesis. With Dory's help, the knee cuffs and belts were secured onto a pylon on his thigh.

"He's been practicing a little after each manicure," Lucy said.

"Should be damned good at it then," Maddie observed.

Jake braced his arms on the wheelchair, and with much effort lifted himself. Dory placed a walker in front of him. Slowly, like a newly awakened Frankenstein's monster, he moved one leg in front of the other. Maddie clutched her chest as he moved; tears ran down her face.

"Get one of my suits from the closet, a white shirt too," he said.

Maria took the steps two at a time as she rushed into Maddie's apartment. She was stunned. "Jake, Jake, what are you doing here? Where's Tommy? Where's Tommy?"

"It's a long story, Maria. I don't know where Tommy is, but I'm gonna find him. I'm gonna find him."

She collapsed in a chair near Maddie, who reached for her Bible.

It was forty minutes before Looney appeared in front of the building. He found Jake standing in full view on the sidewalk, dressed in a fine suit and long cashmere overcoat, with polished shoes and nails, and two mahogany canes.

"Are you crazy?" Looney yelled. "You stick out like a sore thumb."

"It's okay," Jake said. "It's time to stop hiding."

With Looney's assistance, Jake maneuvered one leg in front of the other and sat in the front seat. Looney jumped behind the wheel. "Where are we going?" he asked.

"I don't know," Jake said.

"You don't know? Why am I here? What the hell is going on?"

"Look," he said and handed Looney the picture. "Pauly has been playing with Tommy all along. He knew he was broke, probably knew he was staying with Mom and me. He definitely knew Tommy needed work; and more important, he figured I was counting on Tommy. That bothered him most of all."

"I don't understand,"

"They've set him up, don't you understand? Carozza and Fazzula have set him up some way, somehow. They've been following him," he said as he pointed to the picture. "Tommy said he was getting a big job that would put him back on top, but Fazzula was yanking his chain. This picture has a meaning, a purpose."

"Maybe to frame him," Looney suggested.

"Frame him!" Jake shouted, but then thought about it. "That's not as stupid as it sounds. Maybe Fazzula got Tommy to do something that will benefit him and frame Tommy in the process. Kill two birds with one stone."

Looney looked at the photograph. "Look," he said, "I recognize this building. Let me think."

"Let me see that."

Looney did not hand over the photo. Instead, he studied it. "I've seen this guy before too," he said pointing to the man on the steps of the brownstone. "I read about this a month ago in the *Times*. He's been all over the news, like the troublemaking priest in *On the Waterfront*."

"Well, this ain't no movie," Jake said.

Looney looked at the picture. "He was fighting to get landmark status for the building where they run a shelter. They say this guy knows a lot. They say he can bring down the whole house of cards with information he may have."

"You read the *Times*?" Jake asked.

"That's what you took away from what I just said?"

"Sorry."

"And, yeah, I do. The Sunday *Times,* Business and Real Estate Section; does that surprise you?"

"Actually it does," Jake said.

Looney continued, "Listen, you weren't back yet. A big shot monsignor was on the board of St. Vincent's Hospital. He was murdered, and his body was dumped on the church steps. The DA's office was investigating whether the hospital was run into the ground on purpose."

"Duh."

"Right. And was it with the help of the dead monsignor guy. They think he might have had a change of heart, which prompted his demise. I remember the story now. It was all over the news. I can pull it up." He read off his phone. "Monsignor Burns found after being missing for three months. His body left at the church steps. He was the administrator of St. Vincent's Hospital and under suspicion for being the inside man, helping run it into the ground. They conjecture there was a witness; another priest who is testifying before a grand jury, and the word is this renegade priest has the goods to bring the whole thing down. A grand jury meets tomorrow at the courthouse on Foley Square."

Jake pounded the dashboard. "That's it," he said. "That must have something to do with it. Does it tell you anything else?"

"Wait," Looney said. "Let me think." He rubbed his temples. "Yes, bingo," he said, "the picture I remembered seeing."

"It is a halfway house still in operation on Twelfth Street. No wonder it looked familiar," Looney said.

"That's it," Jake agreed as he looked at the picture of an unassuming young man with a ruddy complexion in the foreground of the photograph. "Doesn't look like anyone threatening, certainly not enough to bring down the Fazzula family, but this must be the priest in question. I wouldn't want to be him."

"Well, I remember reading in the *Times* that the scope of the fraud was staggering, running into the multimillions, not to mention the day-to-day affiliates who had contracts with the hospital."

Who are you? Jake wondered. *And what have you done with Looney?*

Looney took the phone back. "Let's go," he said. He started the car.

"Where are we going?"

"Uptown," Looney said. "This priest knows too much to continue living."

"And I think I know who will take care of that," Jake added.

PART
VIII

CHAPTER 21

*L*ater that morning Tommy sat bundled against the dampness in the catacomb of Church of the Most Precious Blood surrounded by frescos and statuary. The church emptied out after the twelve o'clock mass. He missed two chances to pull the trigger. Just didn't feel right. There was only one opportunity left. He sat staring at the fresco of Jesus and John the Baptist. His mind wandered. He looked at a collection box and realized he had not one coin to put into it. He shook it, wondering if it might yield something to him. It was empty. *Father got here first,* he thought. He stood up and stood face to face with the stucco wall, his hand tracing the outline of Jesus. He thought about what the priest had said about Caravaggio's use of light and shadows. He recognized that he was in a bad place in his life, more shadows than light. He had sunken and drifted into a state of depression brought on by newfound poverty and hopelessness. He understood shadows. An inner anger consumed him as he thought about all he had lost, all that had been taken from him.

As he attempted to leave the church he felt dizzy, his sight was blurry, his eyes twitched. A twinge went down his left arm. He recognized the signs. He steadied himself against the grotto wall, pressed his face against the marble feet of Jesus. The cold felt good. Then his legs buckled beneath him. He crashed right at the foot of the grotto. His mind was fuzzy. Only the humming of the motor kept him focused. His shirt was soaked, his face wet with sweat. He hoisted himself up to the sound of the motor. Kneeling, he saw crystal-clear water flowing into a pool at the statue's base. It sparkled and danced before his eyes under incandescent lighting. He reached for the digitalis in his pocket and placed one under his tongue. After a minute, he cupped his hands and reached into the grotto. He felt a cool sensation as he drank from the well. Then he splashed water from the pool onto his face. His breathing steadied. His head fell into his hands. God, he whispered, dear God, dear God, I've made a mess of things. What am I to do? Forgive me, forgive me. He took a deep breath, filling his lungs with air. The numbness subsided, his breathing stabilized. He knew he had dodged a bullet.

The sun was setting over the Hudson River, taking with it any semblance of warmth or light. Jake and Looney circled the block on Twelfth Street. The street was relatively deserted; lights were shining from within the townhouse.

"Should we park?"

"Not safe here," Looney said. "They have pictures of Tommy, which means they're following him. They might see us too. I'm sure if that building blows up, someone will send a photograph of Tommy casing the building and God knows what else."

"I'd like to see what's going on in there," he said.

Looney parked the car a block away. "Wait here," he said.

"Are you being funny?" Jake asked.

"Huh? Oh! Sorry." He turned his collar up and walked toward Twelfth Street. He looked both ways before walking into the courtyard and up the front steps, peeking in the window. He saw dozens of people, women and children gathered around the altar where a priest was celebrating mass. Looney doubled back to the car.

"What's going on?"

"There's lots of people in there. A mass is going on."

"Any signs of Tommy?"

"No, not yet." Looney ran his fingers through his hair. I saw his old girl in there, though. That Maria dame. Do you think Tommy would actually . . ."

"Kill a priest?" Jake finished the sentence. "Let's see, he's desperate. He keeps giving Mom an apple to eat, hoping her gold tooth will come out; he wants to exhume your father's body and sell the grave; his wife sends a truckload of bills and judgments every other day, and he has hit bottom. Duh, let me think."

"Are you shittin' me?"

"Wish I was, little brother. You'd be surprised at your brother's exploits back in the day."

"I'm going to see if I can get closer. We need to be closer to see him in time to stop him."

The Prius moved down the street where Looney found a parking spot near a park.

"Does the heat work in this thing?" Jake asked.

"You cold?"

"No, I'm just curious. Of course, I'm cold."

"That means I have to keep the car running. Do you know what gas costs?"

"I thought it was electric."

"It still needs gas too . . ." He heard Jake's teeth clatter. A second later Looney started the car. "How did I get myself mixed up in all this?"

"You were born into the Rossini family."

"Right."

"Hey, maybe you could use a little excitement in your life, boring as it is."

"Yeah, boring is okay. I like boring."

Jake rubbed his hands together. "Don't you ever wish you had more?"

"More than what?"

"More than you have," Jake said.

Looney thought for a moment. "No," he said, "I'm satisfied. Never expected too much from life. I'm comfortable, the house ain't much but it's mine, no mortgage. Got a few dollars saved, not much. Live day to day mostly."

"Is that it? Is that all you want?"

"No, sometimes I think of buying a bed-and-breakfast in Vermont. I'm handy, and Penny can cook; and we could lead a simple life."

"Your wife will be the cook?" Looney gave him a dirty look. "Just asking," Jake said.

"You're getting to be like Tommy." He pulled a magazine page from his pocket and looked at it. "You see this? This is my dream." It was an aerial view of a small lake house in a bucolic setting. Jake took the picture and stared at it.

"Doesn't look like you can earn much in this place. It looks small."

"I don't need much. I'd be satisfied. It's in foreclosure. Can buy it from the bank on a short sale and assume the mortgage," Looney said.

"Who are you and where is my brother Looney?"

"I know, I know, I'm stupid, right? Everyone thinks I'm stupid."

"Well, yes," Jake said. "And you're watching too many Bing Crosby Christmas movies."

"Hey, that's my dream. What can I tell you?"

"So, if that's what you want, why not do it?"

"Still need some front money," Looney said.

"You're afraid," Jake suggested.

"I didn't say that. I said I don't have the money or the know-how to run a business and the money. I don't have the money."

"But you do have the money. You're just afraid," Jake said. "Sell your house, it's free and clear, and go make the investment."

"Nah, I can't risk it. Can't take the chance."

The thought was interrupted by a knock on the window, startling both men. A woman with thick purple eyeliner and underdressed for the cold, with high heels and Christmas-red hair. She leaned into the car, her breasts flowing inches away from Jake's face.

"You guys looking for a good time?" she asked.

"We're brothers," Looney explained.

"Kinky!" she said and sashayed down the street.

"If there was more room in this car, I would have taken her up on it," Jake said.

"Right," Looney said.

"You know, I really miss it. When I was on top of my game, I was getting laid two, three, four times a day. I couldn't get enough."

"Really," Looney said.

"Yeah, really. You don't believe me?"

"No, it's not that. It's just I didn't figure Bernadette to be so . . ."

"Who said anything about Bernadette? I had broads throwing themselves at me. Bernadette? Yuck. What about you? You get a lot of action?"

"That's a little personal."

"Come on, I'm your brother. You can tell me. I can keep a secret."

Looney ran his hands on the steering wheel. "Penny and me are married a long time. She's more into cuddling now."

"You cuddle? You don't get laid?"

"I didn't say that," he protested. "We have sex."

"Well, like how often, like twice a week?" There was no answer. "Twice a month?" No answer. "Jesus, once a month?" No answer. "Christ, Looney."

"Hey, if you must know, it probably averages once a year now."

Jake was amazed. "Once a year! How the hell do you live like that? How do you keep track? What if you forget the date?"

"Well," he admitted, "I kind of time it with changing the batteries in my smoke detector."

"Jesus, if I was getting laid once a year, my smoke detector would always be going off."

"Listen, I don't want to talk about this anymore. It's none of your business."

The two men lapsed into silence; half hour, forty-five minutes, an hour. "Maybe we should call the police," Looney said. "Give an anonymous tip."

"And what if Tommy is in there?" Jake said.

"Christ, I can't believe he would do such a thing."

"Don't ever underestimate the dark side. Tommy was on a fast track with Pauly. He could have had his button if not for the Irish blood."

"Still, this doesn't seem like him."

"It wouldn't be the first time."

"What . . . ?"

"Did he ever tell you how he was involved with that fire years ago? Two firemen died?"

"No," Looney said. "What are you talking about?"

Jake told his brother the story of how an upstart contractor committed his first sin. Looney listened in disbelief. ". . . and that's why Fazzula always held a trump card over his head," he explained. "Pull the car into that alley. We'll stake out there. Hopefully we'll see him in time."

Meantime, at the café, Fat Pauly Fazzula sat watching the New York Jets lose. Fazzula checked his watch. The five o'clock mass at the shelter would begin soon.

Patzo brought a tray of espresso and set it on the table. "I didn't ask for that," he said.

"I know, boss. I just thought . . ."

"Stop thinking, moron." Patzo left. Fazzula drank.

Back on Twelfth Street, Jake and Looney sat shivering. Jake looked up and down the street. It was deserted, and the temperature had dropped. The car's heater was not functioning at full capacity.

"What do you expect?" Jake asked. "It's a Prius. A piece of shit."

"Yeah, well I got five thousand from Uncle Sam to buy this. It was a good deal."

"The government gave you five thousand to buy a car?"

"Yep!"

"So why did you buy this? Why not a Mercedes or Lexus?"

"I don't need a fancy car. This car serves my needs."

"Right, unless transportation with heat is one of them. And why yellow?"

"It was a floor model."

The two stayed quiet, peering out the windows, which were beginning to fog.

"How long do we stay here?" Looney asked.

"I don't know. I hope he's not inside already; in the basement, maybe."

"What would he be doing?"

"Don't know, cutting a gas line, pouring gasoline; I don't know how he'd do this."

"I think I'm getting sick," Looney said.

In a moment both men jumped, as there was another knock on the window.

"Christ," they said in unison. The driver's-side door opened and Looney covered his face to shield against bullets.

"Ass," a voice said. "It's me."

Looney brought his arms down to see Tommy staring at him. "What are you two *jamokes* doing here?"

"We came to stop you," Looney said.

"It's a setup," Jake added.

Tommy squeezed into the backseat of the car. His body got stuck between the seat and roof. "Who buys a car like this?"

"And the government gave him five g's, to boot."

"You got five g's, and you bought this piece of crap?" Tommy asked.

"Would you guys just leave me alone? Yes, I bought this piece of crap. That was my choice. I like crap."

"Anyway," Jake said, "it was a setup. Fazzula set you up. He knew all along that you lost everything. He sent Johnny Pump to check you out."

"And you don't think I knew that?"

"How would you?"

"A bird told me," Tommy said. "When I asked Patzo where Johnny Pump was, he answered "Harrison." But Pippy pronounced it a little differently, *Ar-ris-zone*. I put my money on the bird. Figured Fazzula sent him out there to check on me."

"So you weren't going to do the hit?"

"What do you think I am? A heartless animal?" The brothers did not answer. He settled back. "Actually, I came closer than I would have liked to think possible," he admitted.

"Christ," Jake said. "What stopped you?"

"Don't know."

"Now what?" Looney asked.

Tommy took a deep breath. "Now the fun begins. "When Fazzula finds out the priest is alive, he'll want to speak to me. It will be the last time I speak to anyone." He took the gun from his pocket and stared at it. He brought it to his nose and smelled the barrel. "Hey, that monsignor guy; how was he killed?"

"A bullet to his head," Looney said. "That's what I read."

"See, Tommy, I told you he reads." Jake looked at his watch. "Anyway, he probably knows already. Probably has some goons close by waiting for an explosion or something."

"What are you going to do?" Looney asked.

"Don't know; don't know yet."

"Tomorrow, he is set to testify. Fazzula's plans will go down the tubes. He'll be arrested by noon."

"He is going to be pissed," Looney said. "You cost him big time."

"You're brilliant," Tommy said.

"He reads the *Times*," Jake added.

"Let's go home," Tommy said.

As the car moved away, Jake asked, "Hey, Tommy, guess how many times Looney gets laid?"

Johnny Pump brought the bad news. "The priest lives," he said.

Fazzula threw his cup against the wall and slammed the table. "I want you to go to Carozza. Give him Tommy's address. Tell him we found him."

As they approached the building, Looney looked for direction. "Are we taking him in through the back?"

Tommy shrugged and looked to Jake. "No," Jake said, "I said I'm through hiding." He opened the car door. With a brother on each side, they made their way into the apartment to find Dory sitting alone at the table. She was crying.

"Where's Mom?" Jake said.

Dory put her head in her hands. "She was taken to the hospital. I tried, Lord knows I tried, but . . . there's been a lot of excitement around here. What she saw . . ."

Jake explained, "Fazzula was kind enough to keep my amputated leg in cold storage until it had maximum effect. It was delivered here this morning with a nice card."

"Christ, he's not human," Looney said.

"Really?" Jake said.

"Let's get over to the hospital," Tommy said.

Dory put her hand up as she composed herself. "It doesn't matter," she said. "There's nothing you can do. Mom has died. I didn't know how to get in touch with any of you."

The three men staggered and collapsed into chairs.

"It was shortly after you left. It was so surreal, so peaceful, really. She wanted an apple, begged for it. I gave it to her, she ate a few bites, then closed her eyes, just closed her eyes. I called an ambulance right away and gave her an aspirin. But it was too late. They worked on her, but I knew, I knew." She sobbed.

"No good fuckin' deed goes unpunished," Tommy said. "Thank you, Jesus!"

Coffee percolated on the stove as Tommy and his brothers sat around the table in dim light. The table was littered with reminders of Maddie's presence just hours earlier. A pill case, a hearing aid, bottled water, spent Lotto tickets, lots of them, and greeting cards she had received, torn at the binding. They cried, hid their tears, cried, blew their noses, and cried some more.

"Whenever she received a card," Dory said, "she'd cut it in half, write a note on the blank side, and send it off. She recycled. It was cost-effective."

They all laughed at that, it described their mother. There was a piece of stale bread, half eaten, pecked at, as a mouse would, and an apple with a bite taken out of it.

It was Tommy who brought them back to reality. "We've got a lot of problems, guys. First, we've got to bury Mom, and that will cost some money—money which we don't have. Second, it will only be a matter of time before Bile finds out she's dead, and he'll be knocking on the door. Last, but not least, Fazzula will be looking for me very shortly."

"And me too, for that matter," Jake said. "There may be more than one funeral to plan."

"Maybe we can get a family discount," Tommy said.

"How can you make jokes?" Looney said.

"I wasn't joking. Dory, where is the loose change Mom hoarded in the jar?"

"Oh, I don't know. She saved the change, and every month a man came by to pick it up. I told you that."

"She gives a stranger the money?"

"I guess; I thought she knew what she was doing."

There was a commotion outside the door, a voice saying, "Asshole, kill the asshole." No sooner had they all looked up when Patzo burst in the door with Pippy in his hand.

"G-guy-guys, you got to help me. You got to help me."

"Patzo, calm down, calm, be calm." Tommy brought him over to the table. "What's going on?"

"It's Fazzula, he's on the warpath. He was chasing Pippy with a broom in one hand, a gun in the other. I swear, bullets were flying. Pippy was defiant, cursing at him. He took out a gun and fired two shots, but I pushed him and grabbed my Pippy. You got to help him. You got to hide him here."

"Yeah, he should be safe with us," Jake said. "What's one more bird with a price on his head?"

"Fellas, you don't understand, I'm not afraid of Fazzula. I'll take care of him, but in the meantime you got to hide Pippy."

Dory brought a bottle of brandy to the table and poured some for Patzo. "Calm down, boy," she said. "Breathe."

Pippy made himself comfortable in the middle of the table as Patzo regained his composure. The bird's suspicious eyes surveyed the new surroundings. Patzo, too, looked around the apartment. He saw lots of red, swollen eyes, crumpled tissues. Something was missing.

"Where's your mom?" he asked.

Tommy, Jake, Looney, and Dory all started bawling again.

"Uh-oh," Pippy said. "Uh-oh."

Tommy broke the news, "Patzo, Mom's gone," at which Patzo began to cry.

"Jesus Christ," Pippy said.

"Maddie, Maddie's dead? How, when?"

"Just hours ago," Tommy said. "Look, Pippy, I mean Patzo, we got a ton of problems. We'll watch Pippy, but you got to do us a favor. You got to tell me what's going on in the café. Who meets with Fazzula."

"That's no problem. I'll take care of Fazzula and Pump too. Pump was there just before I left."

"Did you hear anything?"

"Fazzula closed the door. He never closes the door. I heard yelling. He's on the warpath, I tell you."

Looney poured another round of drinks. "My heart is racing," he said.

"Patzo, can you do this for us? Can you pull it off?"

"I-I can do it. I'm not afraid of that scumbag." He leaned in to kiss Pippy on his plume and left.

"You're a genius," Jake said. "Now we have to take care of a friggin' bird."

"Fellas, Mom's in the morgue. We got to find a way to get her out," Looney said.

"I'll call the undertaker, get him started," Tommy said. "I'll have to find a way to pay him. We've got to be practical."

"What do you mean, practical?"

"I mean we can't spend a lot of money considering the fact that we don't have any."

"Well, I'm not putting her in a cardboard box," Jake objected.

"She deserves better than that," Looney agreed.

"Hey, numb nuts, I'd like to get her bronze, but we ain't got no money. Which word don't you morons understand?"

"I'll take care of it," Jake offered.

"And just how will you do that? Are you holding out on me?"

"No!" he shouted. "I'll write him a bad check."

Pippy remained perched on the edge of the table. His gaze followed the conversation as it moved from brother to brother. During a lull, he walked toward the partially eaten apple and started pecking at it.

"And we got a hungry bird to feed on top of it," Tommy said.

"I didn't know birds liked apples," Looney observed.

They all watched as the parrot pecked at the apple with single-mindedness. His antics took their minds off their immediate problems, until Pippy found what he was looking for. From the apple, he removed a piece of gold and dropped it on the table. Tommy, Jake, Looney, and Dory stared as a gold tooth rolled back and forth.

"What's that?" Looney asked.

Tommy picked it up, examined it. He picked up the apple and found another gold tooth lodged within. "That's Mom's funeral," Tommy said. Then he looked up. "Thank you, Mom," he said.

Lucy walked into the apartment with her manicure kit in hand. "I heard the news. Your mother was beautiful spirit," she said. "I thought you might need comfort. I give you and brothers manicure."

"Me first," Jake said.

Tommy smacked him in the head. "Nobody's getting a manicure. Are you crazy? Your mother's dead."

In the middle of the lecture there was another knock on the door. Dory looked through the peephole. "It's the landlord," she reported.

Color drained from everyone's face. Jake started limping into the backroom, followed closely by Looney. Tommy mouthed instructions, throwing Lucy into the recliner chair and covering her with an afghan. "Say nothing," he ordered. He took Pippy and placed it on

Looney's arm. The bird immediately climbed to his head. With Jake, Looney, and Pippy in the backroom, Tommy said, "Dory, let him in and just go along with whatever I say."

Mr. Bile stood at the door for a moment, surveying the kitchen. "Hello, Mr. Bile," Dory said.

"And you are?" he asked.

"Oh, she's Dory, my mom's caregiver. You've met her," Tommy answered pointing to the body sitting covered in the recliner. "She does a great job," he whispered. "Mom's sleeping now, sleeps most of the day. You know, those meds knock you out."

"She looks like she got fat," he noticed.

"Oh, a ton of sweaters, she's always cold. No circulation, you know."

"And who are you?"

"Me, I'm her son, L-L-Looney. They call me Looney, but my name is Phil. I came in from Staten Island to visit my mom."

He felt Bile's eyes starting right through him.

"Have I ever met you? You look familiar."

"Met me? No, I don't think so. I don't get down too often. You know, with traffic, and parking is really difficult."

"You look familiar," Bile said again.

Tommy just shrugged. Bile turned his attention to the recliner chair. "So, she's not doing well?"

"You know those old-timers have a strong will, come from strong stock."

"You're telling me," he said. He noticed two wheelchairs side by side in the kitchen. Tommy read his mind.

"One has thicker tires, better for the street, and this one is better for around the apartment."

"Come to think of it, you have brothers, don't you?"

"Yes, two; one is in Arizona, the other Miami. They never get to New York."

Bile scratched his chin. "Was there an ambulance here last night?"

"Oh," Dory said, "I called the ambulance. Maddie swallowed something, and it got stuck. By the time they arrived I had it dislodged."

Bile nodded. "Well," he said, "I'll be going. Nice to meet you," he added. "You sure we never met?"

"I would have remembered," Tommy said.

Bile turned to leave.

"Another asshole!"

He stopped, frozen in the doorway. "Did you hear that?"

Dory and Tommy looked at each other. "No," Tommy said. "I didn't hear anything." He looked to Dory. "Did you hear anything?"

"No," Dory confirmed, "I didn't hear anything."

"All clear," Tommy announced.

Lucy unwrapped herself from the blanket and stood to stretch. "Did he call me fat?"

The crew settled around the kitchen table. "We need a plan," Tommy said.

"It's like everything is happening at once," Jake said.

"That's because everything *is* happening at once," Looney said.

"Lucy, I need you to go into the café. Is Fazzula due for a manicure?"

"I tried this morning, but he was in no good mood. Not like him, shout, angry at everyone, even his new friend Carozza."

"All right, I want you to go back and just hang in. Let me know what you hear, what you see. Dory, I want you to go to tell Father Bryce that Mom has died. We'll have to get her a funeral mass. And oh, ask him how much it will cost. Seven hundred, I'll bet. They always get even. All right, all right dolls," Tommy continued. "Go, do what I said."

The women left the apartment as the three men huddled closer around the table.

"What now? What now?" Jake asked.

"I wish I knew."

On Monday morning the atmosphere was thick in Fazzula's. The Don's eyebrows were crossed. "Stay out of my way," he warned Patzo. "And that bird, if I see him again, I won't miss. I promise."

Patzo said nothing. He went about his business, wiping down the counter with a damp rag. He avoided eye contact with Don Fazzula.

Johnny Pump came in with some news. "We have more pressing problems to deal with. I got information from my contacts downtown. That prick priest is scheduled to testify at one o'clock. That ain't good."

"I know," Fazzula said. "But he's gonna be late, very late."

Pump's eyes opened wide. He smiled. "I understand," he said. "I knew you had to have a plan B. What are you thinking?"

Fazzula gave a whistle. Eight men dressed in identical gray overcoats and gray fedoras appeared. "Let's see what you have," Fazzula said. At that the men opened their overcoats. Each brandished a Glock .45. "You know what to do." One man nodded and left as the others followed.

Pauly stared at Patzo before leaving the café. When the room was quiet, Lucy appeared from an enclave where she had been able to hear the conversation.

"Patzo," she said, "this is important. Go to Tommy. Tell him that the priest is in danger. Tell him something will happen to him at the courthouse at one o'clock. Tell him about the men in gray. Tell him everything you heard."

Patzo dropped his rag and headed out the door. He turned back to gather some seeds from a stash behind the counter.

Patzo hyperventilated the whole story at the kitchen table. "I saw them, all dressed in gray overcoats and gray hats, ten or twelve of them. They had guns, lots of guns."

"So, what's it to me? I got my own problems," Tommy reacted.

Patzo shrugged as he petted Pippy. "I miss you, Pippy."

"What's wrong with you? You can't let this go down," Jake said.

"It's not my fight. We've got our own problems here. He's already pissed. He'll come looking for us next. Gleason is a casualty of war. So are we. Not that I didn't warn him. I told him to get transferred, to run. I warned him."

"You're not thinking right. You're not that kind of guy," Jake said.

"Since when did you get so brave?"

"I don't know," Jake admitted. "I guess I just discovered right and wrong."

"Right," Tommy said, "just in time." He grabbed his jacket and jiggled the gold teeth in his hand. "I'm gonna sell these and go make funeral arrangements. That's my only concern now, not the priest, or buildings, or anything else except to get my mother out of the morgue."

As he opened the door he spotted Fuller Bile coming up the steps. He rushed back in the apartment and threw the afghan over Jake's head and moved his chair into the corner by the window. "It's Bile," he said. "This friggin' guy is persistent or suspicious. Just shut up and play along."

Patzo opened the door and Bile looked into the apartment. Tommy motioned for him to speak softly. "Mom's still sleeping," he said.

Bile looked at the covered figure. "The heat hasn't kicked on this morning," Tommy said.

"Is that all she does? Sleep?"

Tommy shrugged. "Mostly, now; doctors say the end might be near." He saw a half smile. His eyebrows perked up. "It's like a vigil here," he continued. "Just waiting and waiting for the inevitable," Tommy added.

Bile looked at the parrot. "You know we don't allow pets in this building," he said.

Patzo opened his mouth, but Tommy jumped in, saying, "Oh, Pippy? No, Patzo just came to visit Mom and thought the bird might cheer her up. It's like a comfort bird."

"Asshole," Pippy said.

Bile looked at Tommy. "Are you sure I haven't seen you before?"

"Sure you did. You stopped by yesterday."

"No, no, some other time."

"Not that I recall. I would have remembered."

With a wave of his arm, Bile exited. Jake unwrapped himself. "I'm sweating like hell under there."

"Good work," Tommy said to Patzo. "You did good."

Tommy headed up toward the Bowery, where there were various pawnshops that would buy the gold in his pocket. From there he'd go to see Mr. Sotto. It was a brisk day.

As he walked he thought about what was going to happen just a few blocks south at the courthouse in Foley Square. *None of my business,* he thought. *Not my problem. I'm headed in a different direction.* Lost in his thoughts and lost in a pedestrian flow, he was detoured, block after block. A Con Ed truck blocked one route. "Gas leak," the flagman said. A fire on Spring Street sent him in another direction. Construction on a subway sent him in another. The maze of alleyways and the twisting, turning streets mirrored the confusion that battled for supremacy in his head. The Cyclone at Coney Island was in his head, thoughts also twisting and turning; what ifs, maybes, lost love, lost wealth, dead priest, dead mother, all jumbled. Another obstruction, another detour. One of New York's Finest advised him, "Sorry, Mac, can't cross here."

"What the hell . . ."

"Paving the street. Great city, isn't it?"

"Yeah," Tommy said. "When it's finished, it'll be great."

The detour led him to walk farther south muttering to himself as one detour after another brought him full circle. He was lost in thought until he realized he had walked in the opposite direction than he intended. "Christ!" he shouted to a policeman directing traffic. "How can I start out in one direction and end up in another?"

"Life is funny that way, Mac," he said. He recalled the priest making the same observation about walking one way and winding up another.

He heard screeching. He turned his head in time to see a bus barreling toward him. He heard the pop and noticed the front right tire of the bus had blown. The bus swerved into the curb inches from his face. The brakes screeched. Then, as if in slow motion, it went crashing into a hydrant. Its forward momentum jolted Tommy, sending him falling backward onto the sidewalk. He was stunned, groggy, and barely conscious. He remembered a torrent of water spraying into the sky, brown and rusty with a nauseating putrid odor. His last thought was, *They cook hot dogs in this?*

Tommy lay on the street. He opened his eyes to see a cadre of Roman Catholic priests encircling him. One knelt at his side, bringing him to with gentle slaps while others made continuous signs of the cross.

"*Dio mio! Dio mio! Scusatemi,* I'ma so sorry." The bus driver patted Tommy down, looking for broken bones. Tommy held on to the gold teeth.

"*Scusatemi. Sta bene?* Forgive me. Are you okay? Are you okay, sir? I'm so sorry, so sorry. *Mi sono sperduto.* I got lost and turned all around and was just trying to get this group . . ."

"It's okay," Tommy said. His breath was labored, and his hands were shaking. "Could have been worse." He patted his body to make sure he was intact. "Who are these people?"

The driver stuttered, his hands shook. "I am so sorry. I am new to this tour bus gig and got turned around and was trying to make up for lost time." It was an Italian accent coupled with broken English. Ten, fifteen, twenty Catholic priests, a holy sea of black suits and white collars were deep into prayer around him.

"Hey," he shouted, "I'm not dead."

"Grazie a Dio!" "Sta bene?" "Che disgrazia!"

"I'm fine, no problem," Tommy assured them.

"Thanka God," one said. They helped him to his feet.

"Right," Tommy said. "God, thank God."

"You take picture," a young priest said. He handed the driver a camera and posed with Tommy in front of the bus.

"Anch'io," another said.

"Sta bene?" one asked.

"I'm okay," Tommy assured them.

"Ah, grazie, Dio," he said as he placed the sign of the cross on Tommy's forehead.

He turned and spoke to all the others. They all made the sign of the cross collectively.

"Christ, *come si dice,* I'm in deep doo-doo now," the driver said. "I blew it. These priests are supposed to meet up with a guide for a tour of ground zero. I'll be fired for sure."

The battalion of priests spread out along the street and sidewalk, breaking up into small groups. *"Restate assieme!"* he shouted. "I'ma screwed."

As Tommy regained his composure on the sidewalk, he looked across the park. His detours had taken him into Foley Square, home of the federal courthouse. He could see the courthouse through the trees. He looked at his watch, 12:45. In a few minutes Father Bryce would be going up those steps and would probably be carried down. Stubborn bastard!

Listen," Tommy said, "tell them to follow me. I can help you."

"*Ascoltate. Ascoltate. Fate questo per me.* Listen. Listen. Do this for me." Tommy nodded. "*Attenzione. Ascoltate. Seguite questo bravo uomo.*"

With that the priestly troupe formed double lines, and Tommy began walking with a legion of priests holding up the rear. Like Patton leading the Third Army into the Black Forest, he waved his hand, sweeping it over his head and pointing south. "This way," he said.

As Tommy and his entourage approached Foley Square, he held his arm up, stopping their forward progress. He needed to reconnoiter the situation. He had an idea of what to look for and spotted it. The courthouse was awash with people, walking up and down, in and out. On the top steps he spotted five, six men as he could make out. They were all dressed in the same gray overcoat and matching gray fedoras as was reported. He recognized them as the hit team and conjectured as to how this would go down. They would probably come down the steps as Father Bryce walked up. They would open fire and witnesses would be confused, recalling only men in gray coming from all directions.

As he stared from half a block away, the priest leader tapped him on the shoulder.

"I'sa sometin' wrong? Why we no go?"

"No," Tommy said. "Nothing is wrong."

He turned and looked back toward the courthouse. He spotted Father Bryce with two or three men walking toward the courthouse.

"Listen," Tommy told the head priest, as he tapped his watch. "Do you want to meet the Cardinal?"

"*Cardinale, di New York?*" the priest asked.

"*Sí, sí,*" Tommy said.

"*Oh, onore, grande onore. Certo! Certo!*"

"It's a-late, late, follow me," he said as he began to jog in place.

"*Ah, capisco,*" the priest said as he too began to jog in place, mimicking Tommy. Soon all the priests were jogging in place.

"Good," Tommy said. "Now follow me." He waved them on and began jogging up toward the courthouse steps. He kept one eye on the men atop the steps and the other on Father Bryce. When he was close enough he called to him. "Bryce, Bryce . . ."

Tommy and the jogging prelates got closer and closer. Tommy saw the hit team begin their descent as Father Bryce paused.

"Bryce, Bryce!" Tommy yelled again. This time Father Bryce turned his head. He stared at Tommy and the holy rollers closing in on him. Tommy kept his eyes on the gray team. In a moment Father Bryce was surrounded by twenty priests all dressed in the same black suits and white collars. Priests were coming and going. The hit team in gray stopped in their tracks. Bryce was no longer a viable target, short of a holy massacre on the courthouse steps. They dispersed into the crowd.

Father Bryce was visibly perplexed. "Tommy, Tommy, what are you doing here? What's this all about?"

Tommy was trying to catch his breath. He watched as the gray team split up and scattered into the bowels of lower Manhattan. "It's a long story, Cardinal."

"*Lui è il Cardinale?*" the priest asked.

"Yes, *sí,* yes," he said, breathing heavy.

"*Scusi, scusi,*" a visiting priest said. "You take picture, please, all together."

"Yes, good idea," Tommy said. "You can give it to the undertaker so he'll know what I used to look like."

Back in the apartment Tommy found Jake walking back and forth with Lucy at his side. "He's been practicing," she said.

Tommy did not answer. He sat at the table and put his head down and began to cry.

"What's wrong, Tommy boy? You want manicure?"

"Tommy, what's wrong?" Jake asked. "Did they do it? Did they get to Father Bryce?"

"No, no, they botched it."

"What then?"

"Do you really have to ask? Don't you know? We just screwed Fat Pauly Fazzula out of millions of dollars. Our mom's dead, and I need to sell her gold teeth to bury her. We ain't got a pot to piss in. We'll only fool Bile for a few more days, then we're out on our collective ass. And you ask what's wrong? Which is okay because there will be men in gray following us for the rest of our lives, it won't be long."

"Do you have any ideas?" Looney asked.

"I'm fresh out of ideas," Jake added.

Tommy sat at the table. "Maybe we're thinking all wrong. Maybe instead of hiding we should go public."

Jake picked up his head. "What do you mean?"

"Listen, we're as good as dead anyway. I say we walk right into the café. Walk right in, walk tall, and make ourselves known. If anything happens to us then, witnesses will point a finger at Pauly. He'd have to think twice about swatting us if our murder will point to him."

"When, my dear brother, has there ever been a witness to any murder that ever happened in this neighborhood over the last fifty years?" Jake said.

"Good point," Looney said. Tommy got up from the table.

"Where are you going?' Jake asked.

"As stupid as that plan is, it's the only card we have to play."

Tommy, Looney, and Jake walked arm in arm down Mulberry Street headed toward Fazzula's café. Jake was deliberate in his gait, mustering all he had to balance himself with Tommy lending support. "Let go," he said. "I want to walk in on my own." Pippy was perched on Looney's arm.

This Little Italy neighborhood had a life of its own, a pulse, a heartbeat. Its residents understood the unwritten laws. They understood the Fazzulas and Carozzas of the world and their places in it. They kept its secrets within the bricks and mortar, understanding that looking the other way meant living another day. Yet they sensed an uneasy feeling on the streets that all was not well in this tranquil mob haven. There were whispers, rumors, conjecture. They saw and noted the comings and goings and knew something was amiss and about to blow. The sight of the three brothers confirmed their suspicions. They gravitated toward the doorways of their shops, the ledges of their windows, nodding ever so slightly, a tip of the cap, a raised eyebrow to acknowledge the Rossini Brothers as they passed, for their courage or stupidity. Thanking God it was not them. This was high drama, *High Noon, Gunfight at the OK*

Corral, The Magnificent Three. Maria saw Tommy and started to run toward him. A brisk wave of his hand kept her at bay.

As they approached the café, the sound of sirens in the distance blared and got closer and closer. Inside they saw Fat Pauly Fazzula slumped in his barber chair. His arms dangled at his side, a newspaper and an espresso cup on the floor. His head was back, eyes open, mouth open. Tommy recognized death. He walked over tentatively to be sure. Instinctively he pulled the gun from his pocket, wiped it clean, and put it in Fazzula's pocket. He heard ambulance and police cars come to a screeching halt outside the café. Medics rushed in with a stretcher and continued back into the café. Patzo was behind the counter, cleaning, packing a cardboard box with detergents and cleansers. The EMS workers slid Fazzula's massive frame onto the floor and ripped open his shirt.

"Let's get a line in him," one said.

"No point," the other said.

They created a port in his arm and began an I.V. drip. Events moved quickly. "He's gone, he's gone. Cardiac arrest!" In moments electrical paddles were placed on his chest.

"Clear," one said.

As the electrical impulse went through Fazzula's torso, his body bounced off the floor and fell back with a thump.

"Increase . . . ," the medic said

The other complied, "Clear."

Again, the pulse sent the lifeless corpse up and down with a jolt. The medics felt for a pulse, the other banged on his chest.

Patzo stood behind the counter his head down, his fingers crossed.

"What happened?" Tommy asked him.

Patzo shrugged. "Don't know," he said. He walked into the room, oblivious to the lifesaving efforts before his eyes. Methodically, he picked up the *Daily News* pages scattered across the floor and the demitasse cup and saucer alongside the barber chair.

Tommy walked closer to the door. Fazzula's face was purple. "Christ," he said.

The medics stopped working to revive Fazzula. One sat at the table and began to write a report. "Massive coronary," he said.

"Ya think?" the other agreed.

"What else?" Santo Olivetti said. "Look at the size of this guy. He was an accident waiting to happen." He walked over to Patzo. "I'm Detective Olivetti. Have you noticed anything different about him lately?"

"Oh, not really," he said, "he was complaining of chest pains the last few days."

Olivetti noted it in his book. "Just as well. Grand jury just indicted him. I was coming to give him the news."

As paramedics disconnected intravenous tubes and packed their equipment, Patzo sprayed a spritz of Windex and wiped the surface of the table. He returned to the counter and placed the cup in the sink, giving it a rinse.

Pippy was quiet, watching every move Patzo made. The EMS slid Fazzula onto a stretcher, covered his body, and rolled him out of the café. Patzo, Tommy, Jake, Looney, and Pippy watched as Fat Pauly Fazzula was shoved, unceremoniously, into the city's meat wagon before it sped off.

"Holy Jesus," Jake said.

"I don't friggin' believe it," Looney added.

"Kill the asshole," Pippy chimed in as Patzo placed a few more items for disposal into a box.

"You guys want a cup of espresso?" he asked.

Tommy noticed he did not stutter. "I could use one for sure, with something stronger."

Patzo began to make the espressos as the implications of the last few minutes were kicking in.

Jake fiddled with the sugar dispenser. "Are you out of your mind? Put that sugar down." Tommy tapped his fingers on the box Patzo had left on the counter. He was speechless as he thought about the last few minutes. He stared at Patzo, who avoided his gaze, as, he was sure, did Pippy. He tapped his fingers, *tap, tap,* and stared at the boxes. An empty box of Brillo, an empty can of Ajax, and some old sponges. Then Patzo began pouring antifreeze into the sink. He looked at the counter. There were five or six bottles of antifreeze.

He picked up one of the bottles and stared at the skull and crossbones above the lettering. POISON, DO NOT INGEST. He stared in disbelief at Patzo again, then Pippy. The bird looked guilty as sin. It came to him in an instant. He had seen them the day the bird was in the walk-in box and wondered then why antifreeze was needed. He thought nothing of it at the time. He tapped Jake and Looney on the shoulder and showed them the bottle. The brothers stared at each other, each coming to the same conclusion verified only by Pippy.

"Kill the asshole," he said.

⧉

At Pawn Brokers on the Bowery the clerk took the loupe from his eye. "Seventeen hundred dollars," he said. "That's the best I can do."

Tommy was in no mood to negotiate. "Okay," he said.

Tommy knew he had to bring clothing to the funeral home. His mother made the decision easy. When he looked in her closet, it was there, a blue dress with a note. "Give this to Sotto. It's big, but they know how to tuck it. The shoebox on the floor has the shoes and personals." Carrying the dress and two shoeboxes, he made his way to the Sotto Funeral Home on Hester Street. As he waited in the office, his hand ached. He rubbed it and rubbed it but to no avail. He heard a noise, and in a moment a young man appeared in the doorway of the office.

"You look like your father," Tommy told him. "Unbelievable," he said, "just like him." He rubbed his hand. "It's uncanny."

"Thank you. Dad's been away now since ninety-one."

"Away? Your father's in jail?"

"No, no," the young man explained. "We try not to use the word 'dead.' We say 'gone' or 'away.'"

Tommy was embarrassed. Sotto came from a different land, with a different language and a different nuance. "Oh, I understand. Well, he wasn't bad. He took care of my father's funeral."

"I know," the young man said. "I took the liberty of pulling out your father's file."

Tommy saw the file in his hand clearly stamped with PAYMENT DUE.

"Perhaps you'd want to do the same for Mom as you did for Dad."

"Yeah, I think that takes a lot of the guesswork out of it. I mean, if it was good enough for Dad, and Mom made those decisions, well then why not."

The young undertaker opened the file. "It seems your dad had a three-day wake."

"Three days?"

"Yes," he said.

"Well, does that have any bearing on the cost of everything?"

The man nodded. "Of course, three days costs more than one day," he said.

Tommy thought for a moment. "Well, Dad was young and so well known, and had lots of friends. Probably took that many days for people to pay respects, if only to make sure he was dead. Mom's been out of commission for a while; and oh, yes, she didn't want people to look at her. She's so vain, and all."

"I understand," the man said. "Let's look at other items. Your dad had three limousines."

"We'll drive ourselves," Tommy said; but the thought of him and his brothers dressed in black in a yellow Prius following a hearse made him shudder.

"Dad had laminated prayer cards, two hundred fifty of them . . ."

"There's nobody left," Tommy said. "Get me twenty or so. I want her picture on it. That's important."

"Dad had the premier floral package . . ."

"Mom hated flowers. She was allergic."

"Dad had a mahogany casket," the young Sotto said.

"Solid mahogany?"

"Is there another kind?" the undertaker asked.

Tommy's head sank onto his chest. "I guess not . . ."

The undertaker nodded. "Perhaps we can also talk about a small balance that was due on your father's funeral," Sotto Jr. asked.

Thanks again, Jesus, Tommy thought.

"I was unaware of a balance," Tommy said.

Sotto Jr. continued, "There was a small balance of seven hundred dollars."

I should have guessed. "I see," Tommy said. "I'm sorry about that. Did you send a bill? I've been in Arizona for years, I had no idea."

"It's quite all right," the junior Sotto said. "We hate to press on these sensitive matters."

"I understand," Tommy said. *Time is on your side,* he thought.

"Well, here's what I think we should do."

After a few moments and final plans, Tommy reached into his pocket and pulled out a roll of hundred-dollar bills wrapped around an envelope. He knew the roll looked impressive. He counted out seven hundred-dollar bills, leaving the unmistakable impression that there was more where that came from. "Mom's expenses will be paid at the cemetery. Cash." He added, "Does that work for you?"

"That will be fine, Mr. Rossini."

"And we'll take the mahogany," he added. "This is her dress," he said as he handed it over the desk. "And her personals and shoes are in here." Then he handed him a second shoebox. "And please, I want you to put these in Mom's casket."

Sotto opened the shoebox and saw hundreds of plastic memorial cards. Tommy had taken them off the wall and the windowsill. "They need to be with her," he said. Sotto nodded and left the room. Tommy sank back into the chair and cried and cried.

❧

The funeral, in better days, would have been more elaborate. The high polished mahogany reflected the sun. Tommy and Looney assisted the cemetery pallbearers as they carried the casket down a path lined with headstones. They stopped at a conspicuous opening in the granite line, like a missing incisor tooth in an otherwise brilliant smile. There they placed her casket along with a modest bouquet of flowers upon the ground.

As mourners gathered, Tommy Rossini was in deep conversation with Mr. Sotto. His arms did the talking as they flailed, diagramming the eight-grave plot for the young undertaker.

"What is he doing?" Looney asked.

"You don't want to know," Jake assured him.

"Pretty chintzy," Looney said, "isn't it? I mean, the whole funeral."

"Hey, we did what we could. Mom would understand. Besides, knowing we're together was all she ever wanted."

"I guess," he said. "If she had her way she would have been buried in a cardboard box and given you the rest of the money," Looney said.

"And he would have taken it," Tommy said, as he joined the group.

The priest continued with a prayer, "Rid yourself of anger . . ."

As he finished the prayers, the last of a small group of friends passed the casket and placed a flower upon the grave. Maria Forzano was last. She came up to Tommy.

"Father told me what you did."

"You can't believe him," Tommy said. "He's a priest."

She smiled, and leaned in to kiss his cheek.

Tommy saw the junior Sotto standing patiently off to the side. He walked up to him with Looney and Jake not far behind. Tommy reached into his pocket, but it was Jake who pulled out a check, saying, "I got this, Tommy."

"Thank you, Mr. Rossini. As you requested we'll not deposit it till Monday."

As he walked away, Jake muttered, "Yes, Monday, 2020." He began to laugh, which spread to Tommy and then Looney and even Father Bryce.

The laughter subsided at the sight of a man in a dark suit and hat who appeared from behind the trees. He carried a small attaché.

"Feds?" Jake asked.

"No," Tommy said. "Unless they're scraping the bottom of the barrel."

"No, boys," said Dory. "That's the man; that's the man who came to see your mother . . ."

The man walked over to the Rossini brothers.

The three boys looked at him. "I'm sorry," the man said. "I'm sorry to intrude on your mother's funeral, but I have been trying to catch up with you for a few days now."

"Listen," Tommy said, "if you're a bill collector . . ."

"Wait," Jake said, "I'll write him a check."

"As long as he can hold it for a while," Looney added.

The laughing started again, uncontrollable laughter.

The little man seemed annoyed. "No, not at all. I'm not a bill collector. My name is Murray Kaufman. I'm an insurance agent. More specifically, I'm your mother's insurance agent."

He leaned his attaché case on a monument and removed papers from it. "I am going to need your signatures before I can process this claim."

The brothers exchanged glances. "What claim?" they said in unison.

Kaufman was surprised by the question. "Her life insurance policy."

"She had a life insurance policy?" Tommy asked.

"Why, of course. It was a fully paid policy, but she kept adding to it. Maddie was a smart woman. Anyway, she's had it for years, and it kept growing. Each month I'd come by the apartment, and she'd give me a jar with coins in it. I went the extra mile for her because when I started she was my first customer."

Jake reached for the policy in Kaufman's hand. "How much are we talking about here, Mr. Kaufman?"

"Oh, well, let's see . . ." he mumbled to himself, "compounded, adjusted . . . the face value being $500,000 . . ."

"Half a million dollars!" Tommy shouted.

"Oh, no, no," Kaufman said. "That's the face value, but there's also a cash value in the account. I started this forty years ago. We're looking at $756,932.27. There are three beneficiaries, all of you, all her sons."

"Holy Christ!"

"You're shittin' me," Tommy suggested.

"No, sir, not at all. Your mother made sure the premiums were paid. This is not a joke."

The Rossini brothers made their way back to the car. They stood for a moment and digested the news. Looney pulled out a brochure of his Vermont dream. "I'm gonna do it, he said. "With my share, I'm gonna do it."

Jake pulled the paper from him and looked at it. "A place like this needs promotion to separate it from every other bed-and-breakfast joint. Promotion is the key. I could probably help with that. A piano, music . . . I've got ideas."

Tommy looked at the brochure. "Forget a piano. This place is too small to make any money." He looked closer. "Is that a lake behind it? You could probably blast out the back and extend it along the lakefront. Then you'd be talking."

Looney was excited at the thought his dream might come through. "And Penny can do the cooking," Looney said.

There was quiet. "Do you think that's wise?" Tommy asked.

"Really," Jake chimed in.

"Don't start. Don't break my balls," Looney said.

On the very day the *Daily News* reported that three bodies had been identified, unearthed from the basement of a condemned building once owned by Paul Fazzula, Carmine Luca, otherwise known as Patzo, stood at the foot of his mother's grave watching two caskets lowered into the ground alongside hers. He placed a bouquet and bowed his head. After a silent prayer he turned and nodded in the direction of a late-model Chevy. After a flash of the high beams, the car pulled away. The same news reported that a gun found on Pauly Fazzula's body had been identified as the same weapon used to kill Monsignor Burns. In a private ceremony the third body, that of Enrico Forzano, was laid to rest at St. John Cemetery in Queens.

With Tommy at her side, Maria Forzano put final touches on fresh plantings around her father's grave.

A week later, at Patzo's insistence, Jake, Tommy, and Looney walked to the café on Mulberry Street. There were workmen on a scaffold out front. Patzo saw them as they approached. "Guys, wait there. I'm glad you came. Wait for me." He ran out the front door.

"What's going on?" Tommy asked.

"Look," Patzo said pointing to the facade above the doorway. "Do it, fellas!" he shouted. With that, the workmen removed a cover, revealing a neon sign: PATZO AND PIPPY'S PLACE. Welcome to my grand opening!"

"What the hell," Jake said.

"I have an uneasy feeling Johnny Pump is going to appear," Tommy said.

"I wouldn't worry about that. He was called to a meeting in Brooklyn a few days after Pauly went down."

It took four men to carry a floral arrangement into the café. A red ribbon read CONGRATULATIONS, CARMINE! Patzo looked at the card. It wasn't signed. "Look," he said. He showed it to Jake. "It's from Carozza."

"How do you know it's from him?"

"He calls me Carmine . . ."

"Come in, come in, it's a long story, a long story. You see, I knew, I knew Pauly killed my family. Carozza told me. I was a spy for him, kinda, sorta, and I told him who really set him up. I told him it wasn't you, Tommy. You see, I was working with Carozza. We were partners. I told him Pauly set him up with that arson job, and he told me who killed my family. Come in, let's have some espresso."

"That sounds good," Looney said.

"Under one condition," Tommy said. "Easy on the antifreeze."

"Kill the asshole," Pippy said.

"Quiet, Pippy, quiet." Patzo giggled like a schoolboy, as did Jake, Looney, and Tommy.

EPILOGUE

At the shelter on Twelfth Street, Father Bryce Gleason opened the mail. He separated bills from correspondence. One letter, bearing a return address from Stowe, Vermont, stood out. He opened it to find a cashier's check for fifty thousand dollars. There was also a note:

In Loving Memory of Maddie Rossini
Sometimes God winks.
P.S. Maria sends her regards.

CPSIA information can be obtained
at www.ICGtesting.com
Printed in the USA
FSHW010619170421
80475FS

9 780692 936832